SECOND CHANCE

Dylan S Hearn

To Sarah Brown & family
All the best
Dylan Hearn

Second Chance
Copyright © 2014: Dylan S Hearn
Published: 24th January 2014
Publisher: Wet Feet Publishing
ISBN-13: 978-1495330445
ISBN-10: 1495330443

The right of Dylan S Hearn to be identified as author of this Work has been asserted by him in accordance with sections 77 and 78 of the Copyright, Designs and Patents Act 1988.

All rights reserved. No part of this publication may be reproduced, stored in retrieval system, copied in any form or by any means, electronic, mechanical, photocopying, recording or otherwise transmitted without written permission from the publisher. You must not circulate this book in any format.

Find out more about the author and upcoming books online at www.authordylanhearn.wordpress.com or @hearndylan.

Cover Design by James, GoOnWrite.com

For Michelle.
I know you won't read this as you've already read the book.
For the rest of you reading this, let's keep it as our little secret.

Acknowledgements

This is my first novel and it wouldn't be here if it wasn't for the love and support of many people. I would like to thank my editor, Ben Way, for agreeing to edit my book pro bono, and for providing the bucket full of hyphens. I would like to thank Rebecca Hope, Daneel Boxwell and Emma Coombes for managing the tricky balance of being honest, insightful and critical while remaining encouraging throughout. I would like to thank my family and friends who have, to a person, been incredibly supportive, even if they privately thought I was having a mid-life crisis. For the regular visitors to my blog www.authordylanhearn.wordpress.com, I thank you for picking me up when I was feeling down with the odd kick up the backside when I became too self-absorbed. Finally I would like to thank Michelle - my love, my heart, my reason. Without your unstinting support in the face of all logic, this book would never have happened.

Did I say finally? Well, not quite, because my very final thanks goes to you, dear reader; who for whatever reason decided to take a punt and buy my book. You have made a middle-aged man inordinately happy.

Prologue

The Past

The life that they knew was gone. Nothing would be the same. Not now. Maria stared out into the storm, her window thrumming as wind flung rain hard against it. Part of her wondered why they were even bothering to carry on. It didn't look as if their work would ever be needed. There were bigger things to worry about.

"Maria, I think you should look at this."

The climate had finally delivered on its promise. Incremental changes had led to this point, but despite warnings of what was coming they hadn't been prepared. Even now, days after the storm's peak, the malevolent clouds remained, spitting misery over the country. She'd heard that the evacuation of London had finally started, far too late for the thousands already dead. And still parliament remained divided on how best to deal with the crisis. It would be laughable if it wasn't so tragic.

"Maria?"

She got up from her workstation. "What?"

Josh's screen was covered in blooms of pulsating light. She watched as he expertly manipulated the neural recording, diving into the three dimensional model, heading down towards the brain stem before spinning back. Neural activity ebbed and flowed across the twin hemispheres of the brain. From this viewpoint it was similar to ghost lights shimmering across the arctic sky.

Even though she had been studying neural recordings all her adult life, Maria had only a vague idea of what this subject had been thinking. By sight she could read core emotions— whether a person was happy, sad, fearful. What she couldn't do, looking cold like this, was understand what had caused those emotions. As she'd explained to Josh when he'd first arrived, the human brain wasn't a book with each word identical from copy to copy. When an individual thinks of an object, that object is intertwined with a thousand other factors. If a person had once owned a dog as a well-loved family pet, when they thought of the word dog the pleasure centres of their brain would activate; if they had been attacked by a dog as a child, fear and pain centres would fire. Maria had spent her life capturing thousands of neural recordings to see if she could identify a common brain language, but after many years of trying she had come to realise that each brain had its own vocabulary, related but separate from one another, as unique as a fingerprint.

"Have a look at this recording and tell me what you see."

Maria snapped back from her thoughts and studied the screen. The clarity was truly astounding; each individual synapse captured as it fired. Josh panned out to make the whole brain visible and a familiar pattern emerged. "The subject is thinking about something painful," she said. The pattern would have looked very different if the subject had been experiencing actual pain.

"Now look at this." Josh brought up a second recording. "I've run analytics and it's identical to the first."

The pattern appeared to be the same, although it was impossible for her to tell for sure just by looking. "OK, so they were thinking about the same event. Perhaps somebody repeated a question."

Josh turned to her, excitement lighting up his face. It was the first time she'd ever seen him smile. "You would think so, but the first is a recording and the second a simulation. I fed the set of recordings into the neural simulator and this is what it produced."

"I don't remember saying you could use the neural simulator." She regretted snapping at him as soon as she had spoken. He shouldn't have used it without asking—the neural simulator was her baby—but she also knew that Josh had no comprehension of why he would need to ask her permission. There were some things he just didn't understand.

"I wanted to know if the level of detail captured in these recordings could make a difference to what we've been able to produce so far." He brought up another set of recordings, oblivious to her annoyance.

The second set looked less distinct than the set they had just seen, not as clearly defined. "This information came from our old scanning technology. I fed the data into the simulator then ran both the recorded and simulated processes side by side. As you can see, the two veer away from each other over time." He brought up another set. "If you look at this recording and simulation using the new scanners, you can see that the patterns of the two feeds remain consistent. The synthetic brain matches the biological one."

Maria tried to contain her excitement. "How often have you run this test?"

"Five times so far, all from different points in the recording. I know I need to do further tests, but I'm confident they'll just confirm the results I've already seen."

Had they done it? Had they finally produced a fully functioning neural simulator? Her mind raced at the implications. They would no longer be reliant on human test subjects. They could run millions of simulations simultaneously, condense years of research into a few days.

"Run those tests. I'll need further confirmation before we can publish, but it looks like you're on to something. Well done."

Energised for the first time in months, Maria turned to

leave but Josh grabbed her arm, pulling her back. "Wait, I haven't finished."

He was pointing at the screen. "I've known for a while that the simulator works. All it needed was the right quality of information. That isn't why I called you over. This is what I wanted you to see." There were two new recordings running side by side. From a first look, they appeared the same, synaptic blooms ebbing and flowing as if synchronised. "These two sets are identical. The one on the left is the original, the right is a simulation. The analytics say they are the same down to the synaptic level. The point is, they were instigated from two different start points."

"So the simulator is able to reproduce a known pattern?"

"No, you don't understand. I started the simulation from a point two minutes before the original subject suffered a fatal stroke. As the simulation isn't affected by biological weaknesses, it kept running. It's been going like this for days, way past the point where the original subject died."

"I don't understand the excitement. It's great that the simulator can reproduce patterns that have already been seen, but it just means that the simulator is doing what it was designed to do."

"But it isn't just matching the odd pattern. The original recording was taken from months previous. The neural simulator is matching activity seen in the original but never sent through as part of the data transfer. And not just once or twice but hour after hour after hour." Josh looked at Maria, the smile back on his face. "I don't think it's a simulation any more. I think we've brought the subject back to life."

Part 1

CHAPTER ONE
The Politician

Stephanie slumped into the chair, the upholstery enveloping her in its womblike embrace. Her cheeks ached from smiling. What a day. What a crazy, unbelievable day. Still, now she could relax. And have a drink. She really needed a drink.

The air in the club was hazy, the tell-tale aroma of narcosmoke permeating everything. Flashing lights created a stuttering montage, each shot highlighting mating rituals unchanged in generations. The dance floor was a mix of the beautiful and the banal. Throbbing beats intermixed with pheromones to produce an aphrodisiac of industrial strength. The rhythmic pounding produced rhythmic thoughts and the dancers responded viscerally. Gasps erupted as imagery exploded onto the their datalenses. Stephanie watched the manufactured euphoria take effect and was surprised to realise that she had lost interest in the whole charade. It wasn't a physical thing, despite her aches and pains, but the realisation that what had once been attractive had lost its shine. She could see the manipulation and wasn't prepared to accept it. She had moved on.

A tingling at the back of her neck let her know that the psychoactive was kicking in. That warm feeling of being held in an embrace made its syrup-like progress down her spine. Now this was a manufactured euphoria of which she was very happy to succumb. She sunk further into her seat and let the sensation envelop her like a cocoon. On the dance floor a beautiful young woman caught her eye. Surrounded by men, the woman seemed lost in music, yet she toyed with her admirers, both desiring and rejecting their attention. Her actions triggered memories that made Stephanie smile.

"Come and have a dance. This is meant to be a celebration, you know." Addy reached across the table to grab her hand. The club had been her idea. Nobody had wanted to jinx the campaign by pre-arranging a victory celebration, so once the results had been announced they had been at the mercy of Addy and James. He had wanted to go for a meal but she, as usual, had been irrepressible.

"I'm happy sitting here." Stephanie replied. "Go enjoy yourself. You've earned it."

With one last imploring glance Addy was off, screaming and waving her hands in the air as the music changed up a gear. For a moment Stephanie lost her in the throbbing mass but then she reappeared, dragging James to the centre of the dance floor. Stephanie couldn't suppress a laugh as the admiring glances he initially gathered turned to amusement.

"I think we should buy James some dancing lessons."

Sian looked across into the throng. "Waste of money. He should stick to the Legislature. His moves there are much more effective."

A waiter appeared with four glasses and a bottle.

"Champagne? That's a little old fashioned isn't it?"

"Compliments of the management, Delegate Vaughn. I've been asked to tell you that a victory isn't complete until it is toasted with champagne."

"Then how could I refuse?"

He passed a glass to each of them in turn, then pressed a button on the bottle causing the sides to frost. Stephanie's gaze lingered on the waiter as he left, hoping for a backwards glance that never came.

"So this is it. This is what we've worked towards." Bubbles

tickled the roof of her mouth as she sipped her drink.

"It's just the beginning. Make the most of it; you're probably going to be the last delegate to win an election, unless somebody dies in the next few weeks that is. Still, we couldn't have picked a better day, what with the commemoration of Thomas Doleman. It's a sign; he stood up for the people against corruption and vested interests when he signed the Miracle. Now it's our turn to take a stand for the people against the government."

A note of exquisite beauty rode up Stephanie's spine and into the pleasure centres of her brain, overriding her irritation at hearing Doleman's name. They should use this narcosmoke in the Legislature, she thought. It would certainly make things less confrontational. She slipped off her shoes and pulled her feet up, the contact of skin on fabric generating further waves of pleasure. "We really did it."

"Yeah, we really did," Sian replied, a lazy smile on her face. "Your Grandparents would be proud."

Stephanie grunted. "I doubt it, they hated politicians like Doleman after what happened."

"Why? If it wasn't for him signing the Miracle, we would never have recovered from the Upheaval."

Stephanie held up her hands. "Let's leave it. Today's not the day for disagreement." She smiled at her friend. "So what happens now?"

"I'll consolidate your support in the district with Addy. You spend time at the Legislature doing what you do best. James will help identify which delegates are the priority. We'll need plenty of support if we want to deliver the next phase of the plan."

Sian's words washed over her. It had been fun, up to now. She'd never believed for a minute that Sian's plan would work, yet here she was, a fully fledged delegate. The possibilities were endless. Stephanie luxuriated in the sensation of featherlike strokes on her neck. This narcosmoke really is good, she thought. Then she saw Sian staring into the space above where she sat.

"What the hell…" The words died on her lips as she saw the tall, handsome man smiling down at her.

"Sorry for interrupting. I just wanted to offer you my congratulations. Not in an official capacity, of course; the Prime Delegate is still angry that you displaced one of our most loyal party members. Sadly, this is very much a personal one from me. I'm looking forward to seeing a lot more of you, Delegate Vaughn. At the very least, I think I'll enjoy our conversations much more than those I had with your predecessor."

"I'm sure we'll have plenty to talk about, Delegate Gant."

"As long as it's not all work."

Stephanie felt her heartbeat merge with the deep throb of the music's bassline. This was a game to which she was intimately acquainted. Her smile was measured, encouraging but not too forward. Let the man work for her attention.

"Well, you will have to excuse me. It would be just my luck if some Journo captures the two of us together. I'm in enough trouble with the PD as it is."

"I appreciate you stopping by."

He leant down and kissed her cheek. "My pleasure."

Sparks crackled over her skin from that simple touch. Stephanie realised she was completely under the narcosmoke's spell, but couldn't stop herself from following Delegate Gant with her eyes until he was swallowed by the crowd.

"You should be careful. He didn't become the Prime Delegate's enforcer through his charm. That's one person you don't want to get on the wrong side of."

Sian looked concerned, but in cases like this she'd always had a tendency to overreact. "Don't worry, I can look after myself." Plus if he wants to play a little rough, Stephanie thought, where's the harm in that?

CHAPTER TWO
The Information Cleanser

Randall emerged into consciousness at the sound of his alarm. He groped for the snooze button, refusing to open his eyes, but instead of reaching the control unit his hand collided with a water beaker, knocking it to the floor.

With a groan he forced his eyes open. Bright autumn sunlight streamed through his undrawn blinds, inflaming his already throbbing head. Randall's groping fingers located his datalenses and he placed them onto his eyes, their coolness acting like kisses. His clothes from the previous night lay strewn across the floor. In the middle of his now soaked top was the beaker. Good, he thought, saves me from having to get a cloth.

In the bathroom, memories of the previous night bubbled to the surface as Randall dabbed at his face with a cloth. A mixture of weariness and disappointment hit him with each recollection. Why had he gone to that club? What must the youngsters have thought, seeing him stagger around like that? He removed the tell tale blue stain of narcosmoke from around his nose. There were scratches on his forearms. Another set of random drunken injuries to add to the collection. He grabbed some gel and wiped it across his forehead, sighing as the throbbing in his head eased.

Downstairs a tub of half eaten pasta lay on the work top.

Randall turned the kettle on and checked his messages, mentally sifting through the detritus for the nuggets that needed his attention. Not too bad for overnight, he thought. Three messages from Seegers marked urgent, a further seventeen from the analytics system and a voice-call from Lise. Flicking to personal he noticed two urgent reminders from housekeeping, one for an overdue service of the rainwater filtration unit and a second to confirm placement of the grocery order.

Groaning, he opened the refrigerator door. It was nearly empty. The milk pouch was three-quarters full but the out of date label mocked him. A number of other packets blinked at him as well. Today would be a black tea day.

Randall called up some soothing music and scanned the news aggregators. As usual, celebrity and sports topped the ratings.

"Filter: Remove "celebrity", "sports", "gossip", "scandal". Date range: 24 hours. Sources: Political neutral. Scope: National, International."

Fifteen people killed at a political rally in Milwaukee. Concern from the markets as there is no sign of political assassinations by either side abating...

The Shijie Heping corporation officially opened their latest Saharan solar plant, boosting the transcontinental grid by 15%. Despite this, energy costs are expected to remain high for the foreseeable future...

At the unveiling of a statue celebrating the life of Thomas Doleman, Prime Delegate Asquith commented on the latest UN report critical of the UK's planned implementation of the Global Electoral Standard. Countering charges of incompetence, Asquith said that once implemented, the new standard would bring greater accountability to the Legislature. The project has been criticised in the past by the opposition, with Delegate Maddison calling it "a return to government for the wealthy rather than the majority."

Same shit, different day. "Change Scope: Local."

Delegate Ramsey was left stunned by last night's shock defeat to the independent candidate, Stephanie Vaughn. Vaughn proclaimed her victory as a wake-up call from the electorate, stating they were fed up with the status quo and wanted politicians who would deliver on their promises.

The slap of recognition hadn't lessened since yesterday. He remained shocked by the profound effect reading her name had on him. Why now? Why after so long? He flicked to the next article, scared of what may happen if he lingered.

Unemployment rate in the region still rising, as major government funding moves to other regions...

Local businesses struggling as demand drops...

City plans to turn off lights as Aurora Borealis predicted to be visible across most of the country this Autumn.

Friends call on missing student to get in touch...

Rumours of an economic boost to the region as unnamed sources state the Re-Life Corporation planning major launch...

Shit. Where did that come from?

"Call: Thijs Seegers. Cleanser System: Check for echoes of any quarantined information from the past ten days."

"Morning, Randall. Nice of you to finally check in."

"Morning. Have you scanned today's Aggres?"

"Not yet. The board wanted an update on the datacleanse."

"You could always tell them we need more resource."

"We have the resource, you just need to use it more effectively."

You might have enough resources, Randall thought, but you'd rather make the rest of us struggle and come in under budget than give us what we need to do the job properly. The kettle clicked and he poured the water into the transfuser.

"So what have you found?" Seegers asked.

"Someone's got a whiff of the launch. The Journo must have spoken to somebody on the inside because all datasphere scans have come back clean until now."

"Check it out, but it's probably come from the marketing group. They mentioned the other day that they were considering a little teaser to help bump the share price prior to go-live."

Now you tell me. "Brilliant. This will make our job twice as difficult. We'll have Journos sniffing all over the datasphere."

"Then make sure everyone in your group does their job," Seegers replied. "If that happens we still control the agenda."

Randall swallowed hard. He refused to give the bastard the satisfaction of a reaction. "OK. I'll talk to Lise and make sure she's up to speed." As he spoke, the cleanser scan results came through.

Search results negative. 483 new items in quarantine awaiting decision.

"I've just sent you a file," Randall continued. "I ran a scan as soon as I read the headline and we're clean." He took a quick glance at the report. "However, looking at some of the quarantine files, a number of Journos have already started the hunt."

"Then you had better get on with things. Let me know if anything else comes up."

Seegers' icon winked out. "Tosser." Guess who'll be picking up the pieces again. Randall poured himself some tea and took a sip, wincing at the bitter taste. "System: Sort quarantine items by risk. Prioritise highest to lowest."

Even hungover, Randall was the best Information Cleanser he knew. For as long as he could remember, he'd had the gift of identifying patterns where others couldn't. It was as if he'd been born with an extra sense. He could detect patterns within seemingly random information. When immersed in data, anomalies prickled at him, a physical irritation that allowed him to see both the pattern and the likely cause. Actually reading the data never seemed to work. He had to see through it, allow the information to wash over him, unfiltered, and let his inborn senses do the rest.

The quarantine list formed in front of his eyes. Randall released the positive comments about Re-Life. He reviewed the sources of those remaining, ensuring anything from too big an organisation were left alone. Those from competitors he forwarded to the marketing group to counteract; all news aggregator enquiries were ignored.

The final group of items were comments from individuals. As Randall hunted around the kitchen for something to eat, he allowed the data to flow over his eyes, analysing the data with his subconscious while he looked for something to settle his stomach. He had hoped to find a pattern in the data suggesting industrial disruption or sabotage, but nothing tickled his senses. Disappointed, he spoke a command and an algorithm reviewed the list, ranking each commenter for perceived influence. If their influence was negligible, any data relating to them was quarantined, never to hit the datasphere.

Finding nothing fresh in the cupboards, he walked to the dispenser and selected a cereal. He'd have to eat it dry, but given the state of his stomach, dry seemed the best option.

"System: Play Lise Stenberg message."

"Hi Randall, it's Lise. Call me back you miserable bastard."

Randall smiled despite himself. He'd have to have words with her one day, remind her that he was her boss. Not today, though. He made the call. "Where was the 'please'?"

"It didn't seem appropriate at the time."

He barked out a laugh. "What did you want?"

"It's the wedding."

Randall's heart sank. For the last six months all he'd heard about was the bloody wedding. Why had he said that she could call him at any time? "What's up, finally getting cold feet?"

"Stop kidding around Rand, I'm serious. It's becoming a right mess."

"Uhuh."

"It's Erik's mother. She won't stop interfering. You know how we wanted a small ceremony, just friends and immediate family? Since she stuck her oar in we've gone from 50 to 450 guests and even now she's not happy."

"Hmmm. What does Erik say?"

"I don't understand him. You remember how he handled our landlord; straight in and no backing down. With his mother he's a different person. He just seems to roll over." Lise let out a sigh. "I know it's difficult for him. He's really close to his parents, especially his mother, and they are paying for the bloody thing. Still, the way things are going, I'd rather be poor and have the wedding I want than all this interference."

It was a young girl's argument that had nothing to do with the wedding and everything to do with control. Randall's sympathies lay with Lise's fiancé. He knew what it was like to be manipulated like this, although he'd loved it at the time. He thought back to the picture of Stephanie Vaughn celebrating her victory. The blow was softer this time, without the additional impact of the unexpected, but he was still shocked at how raw the wound felt. How long had it been? Fifteen, no twenty years. She'd hardly changed, unlike him. Quiet on the other end of the line brought him into the present. "Is a few more guests really an issue?"

"That's not the point! Everything is being questioned: what colour the flowers are, what we plan to eat, the music during the ceremony. She never directly says no, she just has this way of saying 'are you sure?' and 'do you really think that is a good idea?' It drives me up the bloody wall."

"I'm sure it will settle down."

"If I'd have wanted platitudes, I'd have called my mother."

"If you want my advice—and I don't have the best track record in this area—I think you and Erik should take some time out and try to remember why you decided to get married in the first place. All of this nonsense is temporary. What really matters is what you have together." He couldn't help but think of Stephanie as he spoke. "Whatever you do, don't throw that away."

There was a silence before Lise replied, her voice unusually soft. "Thanks Rand, I knew I could count on you."

"You're welcome. Look, before you go, I was speaking to Mr Seegers earlier. He wants to make sure everything is clean for the Re-Life 2 launch."

"Tell him everything's fine."

"Lise, this is important. Doing well on this is the sort of thing that gets remembered. Cocking it up will be remembered too. I know it's a tough time for you at the moment but don't lose sight of your job. You've told me you want to get on in the company; this could be your big chance."

"OK Rand, I hear ya. Thanks again and take care."

The call icon blinked out.

Right, thought Randall, I'd better get dressed.

CHAPTER THREE

The Investigator

"Dadda. Up."

Nico looked down to see Gino standing beside him, arms raised. Smiling, he bent to pick the toddler up. "Cuddle," Gino said, and threw his arms around Nico's neck, gripping him tightly. Thanks Gino, he thought, I needed that.

Fran slipped her arms around his waist from behind. "Good luck today and don't worry, I'm sure it will be fine."

"I wish I had your confidence."

"They'd be fools to ignore everything you've done because of one case. They know how good you are."

"I'm not sure they'll see it that way."

Fran gave him another squeeze before shouting through to the lounge. "Maria. Come and say goodbye to Daddy."

"Bye Dad." Maria's muffled voice drifted through to the hallway.

"Don't worry about her," Fran said, "she's working on her school project with her friends. She's really happy with the datalenses you got her, though."

"I know." Nico handed the squirming Gino to Fran and opened the door. "Look, I'll see you tonight. Love you."

"Let me know what happens. Love you too."

Nico's feeling of dread increased the closer the pod got to his office. He had travelled this route most days yet today felt different. In the outside world, everything appeared to be normal. There were people jogging barefoot through the park, mud sliding off their micro-coated sole sheaths. A group of young mothers talked as they watched their children in the play area, misted breath giving form to their words. The benches were full, people gazing blankly into space, their inner eye focussed elsewhere. Nico thought back to when the trend for outdoor working had started. He had been a young investigator, just learning the ropes. Park robberies had formed the bulk of his early cases. Distraction is the easiest way to rob someone, and nobody is more distracted than when they access the datasphere. Of course, all that changed once increased surveillance was brought in; the risks became too great and the thieves went to the Scrambles, but by then Nico had made his name by how quickly and cost-effectively he had delivered convictions.

His pod took a left turn, zipping across the oncoming traffic without a pause. Nico flinched. No matter how many times it happened, he still couldn't get rid of the fear of crossing the oncoming stream. Buildings passed by in a brown-green blur, their vertical gardens showing signs of the autumn shut down. His hands felt clammy and his shoulders and neck were tense. This is ridiculous, he thought, you're a grown man, but he couldn't stop the shiver of fear as the pod slowed to a halt and the doors peeled back. Nico stepped outside, ignoring the clipped tones of the automated message. "Thank you for using the Municipal Pod Corporation, we look forward to your custom again soon."

He walked across the pavement, glanced at the retina check and stepped inside the building. All through his career he'd walked this same path, one step after another, the occasional hello to a colleague or nod to one of the seniors. It was a daily occurrence, something he'd never really thought about. Now, though, he felt every step.

Head down he walked through the reception area and into the openplan office behind. He caught the occasional glance as he went, each look cutting into him. The disappointed looks were bad enough; people he respected having judged him and found him wanting. Worse were the looks of sympathy. Don't give me your pity, he thought, I don't deserve it. The seniors had rightly gone ballistic. Crime Agencies make money through their reputations. People needed to trust that you could help them, that they could get justice. Even worse, the Legislature wouldn't pay for an unsolved crime and his last case had been well and truly solvable.

"Nico, hold up a minute."

He looked up to see one of the assistants waving at him. Nearly made it, he thought. He put on a smile.

"Hey. How are you?" Nico asked.

"Good thanks. More to the point, how are you?"

"Is that a new haircut?"

"No, and nice try but you won't change the subject that easily."

"I think you'll find I just did." Nico started towards his workspace.

"Chowdhury's after you. He asked me to tell you to see him as soon as you walked in."

For a moment, Nico thought his legs were going to give way. He turned back, trying his best to appear natural. "OK, you've let me know. Do you think I should go now or do I have time for a coffee?"

"Have you ever known him to be patient?"

Nico shook his head. So this is it, he thought, making his way to the elevator. At least they aren't keeping me waiting. His hands shook as he called to the elevator.

Chowdhury's office was on the top floor. Nico stepped out of the elevator, feet sinking into the deep-piled carpet. Sitting behind a large black desk was Chowdhury's gatekeeper. Nico nodded a greeting, he'd known the man for years. The gatekeeper stared blankly in his direction, but the large double doors opened.

He stood at the far end of the office. A large, stocky man, Deepak Chowdhury was an imposing presence even in a room this size. Giant datascreens took up two walls, their surface filled by key business data: crime clearance rates by type, speed of clearance, profit margins by case type; a myriad of statistics displaying the health of his business. In the centre of the room was a large conference table with space for 20 people. At the far corner was Chowdhury's desk, an enormous slab of dark wood that looked like a child's toy within the massive room. Closer to where Nico was standing was an informal sitting area, two small sofas facing either side of a low table.

Nico cleared his throat. "You asked to see me Mr Chowdhury."

Chowdhury continued to stare out of the window. "Have you ever been on an airship, Nico?"

The question took him by surprise. "No, though I've always wanted to."

"When I was a child, my parents took me to our ancestral home. The journey lasted a week and I was mesmerised the whole time. I couldn't get enough of looking at the towns and cities far below. The ability to catch glimpses of people living their lives, lives that I would never have known about except for this illicit glimpse from above. I must have observed the lives of millions as we travelled and that fascination has never left me. It's funny, really. It doesn't matter what you achieve, in the context of our planet's size and complexity, it's insignificant." He turned to face Nico. "I keep saying I'll go again but I never seem to find the time. This is the best I can do."

"I'm sure you'll go again someday, sir."

"Maybe." He gestured to the couches. "Please, sit."

Nico perched on the edge of the sofa, his heart racing. There was fruit on the table, immaculately presented on a tray surrounded by flowers. Nico caught himself staring at the fruit's perfection, trying to work out if it was real or not.

"We've a new case for you." Nico looked up with a start, all thought of fruit forgotten. "Have you seen the story about the missing research student, Jennica Fabian? Yes? Well her university contracted us to investigate and it looks like the case might not be as straightforward as we originally thought."

Nico only half heard what was being said. He wasn't being fired. Not only that, they were giving him a new case. He was startled from his thoughts as information flashed onto his datalenses.

"The assessment team have carried out their initial analysis and it's a mystery. The girl to all intents and purpose disappears. We have footage of her going out for a drink with friends and later moving on to a nightclub. She then takes a pod which drops her a few hundred metres from her apartment. She gets out, walks under some trees and vanishes. I've sent you a file with everything we have."

"Are these the only visual feeds available?" Nico asked. "What about her data connection? Do we still have a trace?"

"As I said, you have the information sent as part of the case bid. Everything else is up to you." Chowdhury leaned forward. "I'm not going to lie to you, Nico. After your last case, well, people were calling for your head. Your record in recent months has been mediocre. You've let things slip and I've lost money because of it. However, I'm not in the habit of throwing away many good year's service - plus a fortune in training investment - just because a person has a poor run."

"Thank you, Mr Chowdhury. I won't let you down." Nico meant every word. He'd been given a life and he wasn't going to throw that away.

Chowdhury waved his hand, dismissively. "In normal

circumstances, this case would have been passed to a junior investigator, but given its peculiarities we need someone with a bit more experience." His eyes locked onto Nico's. "It's the ideal route back for you. The case is well within your capabilities, and if you clear it up quickly we should make a nice profit, plus it will be good PR for the agency." He leaned forward. "I don't need to tell you what will happen if you don't."

Chowdhury got up and held out his hand. "You'll report to Corey Ackerman but you'll have a free hand to do what you think is best. Any issues, go to Corey. If you're still not getting anywhere, you can come to me." There was something in Chowdhury's tone that let Nico know that his problems were the last thing he wanted to know about.

Nico shook Chowdhury's hand. "Thank you Mr Chowdhury. I'll start right away."

"Use whatever resources you see fit but I don't want you burning the profit margins on this. Where possible, do the bulk of the data work yourself."

"I will."

"Good, then you'd better get on with it." Chowdhury walked back towards his desk.

Nico couldn't believe it. He hadn't been sacked. He wanted to jump up and scream, unburdened of the pressure of the past week. He should call Fran and let her know. No, he should talk to Corey first, get the lowdown of the case from him. He needed to find his feet, and fast.

His mind raced as he entered the elevator. Where to start? He needed to know the girl's movements for that day. Who had she been with? Did anything happen out of the ordinary in the weeks leading up to her disappearance? Who were her friends, her family? Where had she been on the night she disappeared? A rough plan started to form.

The elevator doors started to close and Nico caught one last glimpse past the gatekeeper and into the vast office space behind. Chowdhury was sat behind his desk, staring out of the window once more. There was a sadness to what he was seeing, this large, successful man, surrounded by objects but totally alone in such a vast expanse of space. To Nico it seemed that the more money, wealth and power you had, the lonelier you became. There were millions of people whose dream was to be like Chowdhury, yet what they never seemed to think about was: what then? As the elevator doors sealed shut, Nico realised that despite years of trying, Mr Chowdhury still hadn't answered that question.

CHAPTER FOUR
The Re-Life Technician

The scuffing of the Technician's quick-paced shuffle reverberated through the tunnel. He was excited. It had been a while since he had been this closely involved in the process, in fact it had been a while since he seen the outside of his lab. He had thought that he'd been forgotten, a relic from another time sent off to pasture, but it appeared not. A small part of him was irritated at being hauled away from his work, but they had been very persuasive and the thrill of recreating a life had never left him.

A buzz from overhead caught his attention. One of the lights was flickering. In a production area of this importance, somebody should have dealt with that, he thought. It was sloppy. The Technician looked down the corridor, seeing other areas of shade. I would never have allowed such shoddiness in my day, he thought.

The sound of footsteps made the Technician jump. He instinctually dropped his eyes to the floor as a member of staff passed by. Once, when he was younger, he'd fought hard to adapt his behaviour, but that uncomfortable feeling around strangers had never gone away and he had regressed during his years of working alone. The man took no notice of him and was gone in seconds. The Technician had a furtive look behind to be sure before taking a side corridor, leaving the main thoroughfare behind.

Ahead the 'Restricted Area' sign glowered at him. This had better work, he thought, as he held the alloy sheet to the retina scan. For a moment, nothing happened. The Technician started to sweat. Had he been misled? If he couldn't get in his task would be over before he had even started. The light changed from red to green and with a mechanical groan the heavy door slowly opened. Swirls of mist danced with an ethereal beauty as the two atmospheres intertwined. His mind started to ponder the fluid mechanics behind such an effect. It was an area he had never studied but had always interested him. Then he shook his head. He had a task to do, there was no time for distractions.

Behind the security door was a vast, circular room. It had been many years since his last visit but he still felt the excitement of being part of something truly spectacular. He walked past rows of lozenge-shaped machinery radiating out from the central control section, his feet clanking on the metal walkway. A fine mist sprayed down on each module, giving them a slick, slug-like appearance; the overspray cooling his skin as he walked past. The Technician wrinkled his nose at the fetid atmosphere. Despite six large extraction fans in the room's ceiling, the organic odour was overpowering. It was repulsive. Why did biology have to be so disgusting? This was why he preferred theory. Let others deal with reality. In his world, gelatinous secretions were to be avoided.

The room was empty, just as he had been told it would be. He looked up at the surrounding datascreens, each one displaying what was required to control the most important change in human development since the capture of fire. This chamber was the start point, the genesis. He was momentarily overcome with a sense of satisfaction. Without his work, none of this would be here.

Standing at the centre of it all, the Technician couldn't help but become intoxicated by the power at his command. He surveyed the surrounding conception vessels. From this angle they looked like worshipers supplicating before him. That's right, he thought, know me as your god. Worship me as I create the miracle of life. Eyes closed, he raised his arms, bathing in the adulation of his imaginary flock. He could hear them praising him, giving thanks for what he had achieved. His head swam with the concept of science as religion, society worshipping at the altar of progress. If only the real world worked this way, he thought. It would be a much better place, both for him and for society as a whole.

A large clang broke his reverie. The Technician dropped his hands. The feeling of shock took him back to his childhood and being caught stealing supplies from the lab stores. He glanced up but nobody was there. Blood rushed to his cheeks. Idiot. What if somebody had seen him? He felt ashamed at his actions and his subsequent reaction. It was ridiculous that he should be haunted by such feelings after so long, an unwanted emotional response programmed into his DNA. He sat in a chair next to a console, eager to be finished and away. He had been too long out of his comfort zone. His head touched the headrest and a neural connector slid out to touch his temple. Immediately he was at one with the command systems.

System: Access data file D792-664fgyrr-77

It was frustrating that he couldn't do this from his own lab, but his instructions were clear. All actions had to be completed hardwired. The process was far too sensitive to be trusted to take place over the datasphere. A small icon appeared in front of him, the acorn from which the tree of human life would grow.

System: Analyse file for imperfections

He waited for the results of the scan. There hadn't been a failure in over 15 years but given the importance of this task, he refused to take any chances.

Second Chance

Zero imperfections found
System: Begin host generation process for subject D792-664fgyrr-77

Now for the final step. He spoke the security code he'd been asked to memorise, then watched as all traces of his access disappeared from the system. The neural connector slid back into the chair. He'd done as he had been asked; the process was started. Normally the process would continue through without any need for further intervention. However this was a special case. He had been told to monitor the process closely and ensure the modifications took place when required. The Technician felt a shiver of excitement. To experiment with a life; since the law change he'd never thought he'd have the chance again. They had trusted him to do this task, and he would deliver. He wouldn't let them down. He would prove to them that he was as valuable as he had ever been.

CHAPTER FIVE
The Politician

As she gazed around her office, Stephanie wondered again why she'd agreed to try to become a delegate. It was disgusting. The walls were a faded green, the paper slightly peeling due to damp. Large dark squares marked where pictures used to hang. The carpet, once a neutral beige colour, had turned grey, and the furniture looked as if it had been handed down through the generations. And people talk of the glamour of politics, she thought.

There was a brisk knock and Stephanie caught the smell of coffee before Sian had even entered the room. She had missed her friend while attending the Legislature. They had been working together so long that it felt strange now to be apart. Sian looked immaculate, her dark grey tailored jacket and skirt enhanced by a bright yellow top, her blond hair pulled back into an offset knot, not quite on trend but then she had never followed fashion that closely. She placed the coffee on the desk and pulled up a chair.

"We've got a full day today so I'll be quick. The team are on standby waiting for the strategy meeting to start. Key agenda points are: trending issues in the district, a review of the national policy points and how we believe they will play, followed by the influencing action. After the meeting you have calls lined up with each city council, a meeting with the

Mothers Alliance—they want to know your plans for increasing recreational facilities for children in the district, and another with our donors to check on what progress we've made on lowering local taxation. There are also 15 people waiting to see you for the drop in surgery. I've sent through briefing notes for the calls and I'll interview each of the drop-ins so that you're fully briefed when you start."

"Good morning to you too, Sian"

Her friend turned scarlet as Stephanie knew she would. "Sorry. Good morning. How was your evening?"

"As good as can be expected. It's a pleasure being invited to premieres, but opera? You'd have enjoyed it more."

"You know how useless I am at that sort of thing."

"You'd have been fine, plus it would have been nice for someone else to be berated about the lack of arts funding. They're convinced we have a secret stash of money somewhere." Stephanie yawned before picking up her coffee. "One of the tenors looked quite nice though."

"Opera is the last thing you should be funding. It's seen as elitist and you would take quite a hit in the polls."

"Thank you Sian, I had worked that one out for myself." Stephanie took a sip from her cup, warming her hands. The cold of the room had already insinuated its way into her bones.

"Anything else happen of interest?"

"No."

"Good. I'll start the meeting then." Without waiting for Stephanie's go ahead, Sian said, "System: contact 9:30am meeting group. Send info docs to all attendees."

The meeting icon flashed onto Stephanie's datalenses.

"System: accept invite."

Key data visuals sprang up, with the agenda and briefing documents filed onto the left-hand side for easy access. Further icons blinked into life as each team member joined.

Stephanie muted her vocal channel. "I take it that you're

driving the meeting?"

Sian gave a quick nod. "Thank you all for being available so promptly. I'd like to start with our keynote policy. It's been five weeks since the election but we've made little progress on tax cuts. We're still in our honeymoon period but won't be for much longer before our poll ratings start to drop." Charts and projections demonstrating Sian's points appeared as she spoke. "Stephanie's maiden speech to the Legislature has helped—the electorate can see that we're trying to get things moving—but if we don't make any progress soon we'll be viewed as incompetent. I don't need to remind you that the Global Electoral Standard is about to become law, and once in place we become hostage to the polls. I'm sure none of you want to be associated with what would be the shortest delegate term on record.

"Addy, I need to know how much time we've got based on your latest polling estimates. Are there any easy fix issues that could give us some breathing space? James, you're the expert on the Legislature. What are we missing? Who's on our side, who we can persuade and who are our main blockers?"

Both Addy and James were straight out of University, raw, energetic and with a strong belief that things needed to change. Their passion and commitment had been key on breaking Stephanie into the big time.

Addy replied first. "Polling trends suggest that with no major positive or negative influences, we only have a few month's grace. After that we'll be in the danger zone."

"Wonderful," Stephanie said. "So you're saying that if I don't deliver anything quickly, I'll be a three month delegate."

"I don't think it will come to that," Addy continued. "I've already identified several issues that we can tap into to improve your ratings. Since the trunk road was transferred to grid, levels of unemployment in construction have reached nearly 30 percent. Any investment in infrastructure would give a significant ratings boost."

"We don't have the funds available," Sian said, "and we can't raise local taxation for infrastructure projects when our main pledge was to *reduce* local taxes and create growth through increased individual prosperity. Next?"

"Do we have any examples on how wasteful the last regime were?" said James. "That's always good for a few percentage points."

"Good idea James," said Sian. "Pull up the data once we're finished. If you find anything that looks extravagant, let me know. If it's still happening, even better, as we can put a stop to it and take the credit."

"If my office is anything to go by, I don't think my predecessor was particularly profligate."

"I'll get onto it anyway," James said. "You never know."

"Stephanie needs to make a public statement on the electoral reforms" Addy said. "It's the biggest story of the moment and while public opinion seems to be broadly in support, there have been some murmurings about how the reforms are being implemented."

Stephanie opened her mouth but Sian jumped in. "We should keep quiet for the moment. I can see why the public want greater accountability, I just think it will be a distraction from our core message."

"I agree with Addy." Sian glared at Stephanie as she spoke but she ignored the look. "Everything points to the legislation being popular with the electorate. Our support would be an easy win."

"Those 'murmurings' are getting louder," James said. "A number of delegates don't like the fact that you have to have continuous datasphere access to take part. Some of those representing the poorer districts are angry that their core support will be excluded from the democratic process. There have also been localised protests in some areas."

"What's the level of support in our district for that viewpoint?" Sian asked.

"We haven't asked the question," Addy replied.

"Then go ahead and run a poll. For the time being, our stance is that public servants should always be accountable to the public." Stephanie watched closely as her friend sought to regain control of the agenda. She knew what her role was meant to be, but she couldn't help reminding Sian on occasion that she had an opinion too. "What else have we got?"

"There's the case of the missing student," Addy said. "She's been gone since the day of your election. Nobody noticed as she was due to go travelling the day after she disappeared. It was only when she didn't return home that her housemate raised the alarm."

"Are you sure she didn't just extend her break?" Sian asked. "She wouldn't be the first student to miss a few lectures."

Addy flashed up reports from the local News-aggre. "She never left. They found her luggage in her room and her tickets were never used."

"Pollscan: Analyse article," Stephanie mumbled the command under her breath.

The conversation continued as Stephanie's secret program came to life. It produced a series of projections on the political impact of the research student. She hadn't needed the program for a while—Sian's political instincts were usually strong—but when it came to areas outside of politics Sian sometimes struggled. Two trend lines materialised out of the mass of data. The program projected that being publicly involved with a successful investigation would cause her poll rating to jump 12 percentage points. If the girl was found dead, her numbers would remain static.

"Sian, could you organise a newscon for this afternoon. If it's possible to talk to the girl's parents beforehand, even better," Stephanie said.

Sian turned to face Stephanie. "I'm not sure this is a good idea. If people think you're playing politics with this case, it could lead to trouble."

Stephanie held Sian's gaze. "If I can do anything to help find this girl, I will. We agreed to run for the Legislature so we could truly represent the people. If I can't help with a case like this, what's the point?"

Sian's eyes flashed, hating having her words thrown back at her. "OK, I'll arrange the meeting."

"Thank you."

"Now we have a plan to keep our heads above the electoral water for the next few weeks," Sian continued, "let's move on to what can we do to get our keynote policy moving in the Legislature."

It was James' turn to flash up data. "You can see those delegates likely to support a tax break highlighted in blue. The second group, in pale blue, are those who—based on their voting records—may be persuaded to support a motion on lowering taxation. Those in red and orange are the groups predicted to vote against. The greys are unknown."

The numbers didn't look good. The blue blocks accounted for just 23 percent of delegates, with the red and orange at just over 40. To achieve their goal, they would need the majority of undecideds to back them.

"I've also had a chat with an old school mate," James continued. "He works as an analyst for the government and says that they are looking to implement further tax increases during the next budget. Most of this new revenue is to be allocated on a new set of tidal barriers around Orkney and Shetland."

"That's ridiculous," Addy said. "We are already a net exporter of energy."

"How sure are you that this information is correct?" Sian asked.

"Quite sure. I've known him for years."

"See if you can get another source. If your information's confirmed, this could be the opening we've been looking for."

"I'll dig around."

James immediately went into the detailed plans on how to persuade each delegate to support their motion and Stephanie's mind started to wander. Sian had convinced her that the country was ready for change, yet the raw data showed just how big their challenge was. All this back-room dealing was a world away from the adrenaline rush of the election campaign. That was the part she had loved. Now it came to the politics, she could take it or leave it. The blur of infographics slowly merged, becoming an impressionistic collage. Could she really keep this up? She had to have a successful run to prove the value of Pollscan. After that, well, she could sell it to the highest bidder and retire. Her mind drifted to how she would spend her riches when Sian touched her arm.

"Stephanie. Your speech in the Legislature seems to have borne fruit. We've been contacted by a number of delegates who are interested in doing business with us. One of them, Delegate Maddison, said that he and a group of like-minded delegates want to talk further about your ideas."

A series of datasphere articles appeared as Sian spoke.

"Delegate Maddison might be popular in his own district but are you sure you want to be seen allying with him?" James said, highlighting headlines about "Mad Maddison" from some of the more extreme News-aggres. "Shouldn't we wait for someone more moderate to come out against the budget?"

"There's no harm in meeting the group to hear what they say," Sian said. "If we make it part of a series of meetings with all political groups, including the government, it will remain poll neutral."

James' silence was telling. He wasn't buying it, but he wasn't prepared to push things further.

"Is there anything else urgent I need to be made aware of?" Sian asked. "No? OK, I think we're done. Come back to me with your ideas, and James, I need to know quickly just how accurate your budget information is."

Stephanie watched the icons disappeared as each member of the team dropped out of the conference. The office coalesced as she came back to reality, along with a frowning face.

"OK, out with it Sian."

"Linking ourselves to the missing student is a mistake. I didn't say so in front of the others but it's bad politics and I don't think we should go there. You should have spoken to me before the meeting."

How dare she. Stephanie banged her cup onto the table. "I am not a child, Sian. I have opinions too. And a brain. I made just two contributions during the meeting and both were challenged. It's not on. I know that I wouldn't be here if it wasn't for you, but I'm not going to keep quiet if I think something is right. If you had wanted to have total control, you should have stood as a candidate yourself."

"You know that's impossible."

The hurt look pulled Stephanie up. "I know, and I'm sorry. But I'm not a puppet, Sian. We're meant to be a team."

Sian stared at her cup for a moment. "You're right. I'm sorry too. I'll arrange the meeting as agreed." She stood up. "I just want to make sure we don't make any stupid mistakes. We have a great chance to make a difference, *you* have a great chance to make a difference." She paused for a moment. "Shall I send through the first of the walk-ins?"

With a groan, Stephanie placed her head in her hands. She may have won that battle but Sian always knew how to hit back where it hurt.

CHAPTER SIX
The Information Cleanser

The conference room was small, with an oversized oval table in the middle and a refreshment bank to one side. A stunning view of the surrounding cityscape took up two sides, angular skyscrapers rising up from suburban greens and browns. Randall watched a flock of birds flying in the distance, their wavelike movements ebbing and flowing in the morning sky. What he would give to have their freedom. Instead he was here, an offering to the gods of management control. Of course, the cityscape was a mirage; the meeting room was in the centre of the conference building. Even so, Randall felt his feet tingling as he walked by the image, his vertigo not believing that what he was seeing was a just a datascreen.

His team stood in a huddle by the dispensing unit. Looking across to them, Randall felt a brief moment of paternal pride. They were a good group. Not perfect, but damned effective at what they did. Lise especially was turning into an excellent information cleanser. Standing next to her was Sylvianne, the graduate trainee who was almost as good as she thought she was; although her straight-out-of-university 'I know everything' cockiness didn't do her any favours.

Lise was the first to spot him approach and held her arms wide to give him a hug. Randall deftly stepped to one side.

"You're looking smart today," she said, a look of amusement on her face.

"I always do."

The others turned as they heard his voice. Robert, the final member of the group, had along with Lise worked on the Re-Life 2 campaign since its inception. He was smiling as usual, but the mischievous look in his eyes told Randall to be on his guard. Sylvianne looked flushed. It seemed that he had arrived just in time.

He punched a button on the dispenser. "So how is everybody?"

"We're having a bit of a debate, as it happens." Robert said, grinning. "Maybe you could help. Have you seen the latest Aggres?"

"Leave it Robert," Lise said.

A document flashed up on Randall's datalenses. What was he up to now? He paused briefly, weighing up whether to open the file, but decided in the end that knowing what was going on was better than not.

Exclusive - first photo of missing student.

Under the headline was of a picture of a group of young people surrounding a table stacked with drinks. Just looking at all the alcohol made Randall sweat. He dragged his eyes away from the table to study the group. They looked to be in their late teens, some seated, drinks in hand; others standing, arms around each other's shoulders.

We can exclusively reveal the first confirmed image of the missing student, Jennica Fabian, the article continued.

Randall was at a loss. "I'm sorry, Robert. I don't understand."

"Have you not spotted it yet? Keep looking." The smug grin never left his face.

Randall spent a few moments reading the rest of the report but was still none the wiser. "No, you've stumped me."

"The girl," Robert insisted. "Look at the girl."

Randall looked at the photo once more. There was the missing student, circled, near the front of the group. Suddenly it was clear why Sylvianne looked bothered and decided that he needed to put a stop to whatever was going on. "Look, I don't have time for this. Why don't we just take our seats?"

"Come on Randall, you can't tell me that's not Sylvianne."

Randall sighed. It was true, Sylvianne did have a passing resemblance to the missing girl. They both had long brown hair, parted on top and tied back into a pony tail. Their faces had a similar shape, although Sylvianne's nose was slightly narrower. Robert must have seen the photo on the way in. He was a good analyst, conscientious despite his reputation for messing around, but when he saw the opportunity to make fun he had the tendency to keep going long after the amusement had stopped. Randall smiled reassuringly towards Sylvianne.

"OK, there is a similarity, but let's leave it, eh?"

"It's not just a little *similarity*," Robert mimicked. "It *is* her. My guess is that Sylvianne has been playing student every night, obviously missing her old lifestyle. Unfortunately she's been caught out. She doesn't have time to work on the launch and enjoy the student parties, so her 'Uni' friends have reported her missing by mistake." He laughed at his own joke. "It's no coincidence that our work ramped up around the time she 'disappeared'." Sylvianne looked as if she wanted to punch Robert as he spoke. He turned to look at her, his face all innocence. "So which one was your boyfriend?"

"Oh fuck off!" Sylvianne stormed out of the room, glaring at Randall and Robert as she went.

Great, thought Randall. I've been in the room two minutes and I've already got a mutiny on my hands. He looked towards Lise who raced out after Sylvianne.

Randall turned to the grinning Robert. "You and I are

going to have words."

"Whatever you say boss," he replied, bowing mockingly.

Before he had a chance to go and check on Sylvianne, Seegers walked into the conference room, striding to the head of the table. Some of the attendees jumped out of their seats in their rush to say hello. That's right, Randall thought, lick up to the boss. Torn between leaving the room and doing his duty, Randall ended up taking a seat near the door. It didn't take long before the girls returned. Lise took the seat next to him but Sylvianne took a seat next to the front, as far from Randall as was possible.

"How is she?" he asked.

"I'll tell you later."

Seegers cleared his throat and the cityscape darkened. A welcome message appeared on the screen. He scanned the room until everybody was quiet, his motion reminding Randall of the first time he had seen a shark. He had the same dead eyed look that had given Randall nightmares for weeks afterwards.

"As you know, we are very close to the launch of Re-Life 2. Today's meeting will run through our progress to date, identify the excellent work done so far plus any areas we could improve upon." Seegers looked over the rims of his dataglasses. We all know which part you'll be focussing on, Randall thought. "I hope you have all prepared the pre-work as requested. Please make sure when presenting that you send your information to the datascreen and that all attendees have their datalenses turned off."

Randall stared at his boss, once again wondering why he had been the one chosen. The two of them were polar opposites. The tall, slim Mr Seegers was immaculately dressed. His face was all angles, sharp cheekbones and a jutting chin. Randall was a little more relaxed about what he wore, preferring comfort to the latest trends. Seegers was known to smile, especially if he was hitting his targets, but to

Randall his lipless grimace always brought a chill into the room.

The first presenter stood and Seegers took the spare seat next to Sylvianne. Randall watched as the graduate flushed. Careful what you say Sylvianne, Randall thought, the bastard doesn't forget anything. A few minutes into the presentation, Seegers started a side conversation with Sylvianne. Randall felt his heckles rise. You should be paying attention, he thought, annoyed at the lack of respect. The presenter continued to direct his presentation towards Seegers but his eyes had a panicked air. The poor guy must be dying inside, Randall thought. Sylvianne, on the other hand, was loving the attention; taking full advantage of her opportunity to speak to the big boss. Across the table, Robert mimicked her hand movements, only stopping whenever Seegers turned his head. Sylvianne, though, could see exactly what he was doing. Randall looked on helpless from the other end of the table.

Finally, something the presenter said peaked Seegers' interest. His gaze locked on the poor man and the questions started.

"What made you think this was a one-off?"

"Where do you believe the information came from?"

"Are you sure those numbers are correct?"

The more questions he answered, the more questions Seegers asked. Randall thought it completely unfair. By anyone's standards the cleansing work around the launch of Re-Life 2 had been a success. Given the scale of the project it was a stunning achievement that nothing had leaked. Even the Journos had lost interest. Yet Seegers kept going, looking to highlight even the smallest inconsistency. By the end, the presenter looked shattered, despite a token 'well done' from the boss. The only good news from that session, as far as Randall was concerned, was that he was left with just half his original allotted time to fill.

* * *

Second Chance

The group dispersed during coffee break, leaving Randall alone at the table. He thought back to the report on the missing student. Something about the girl's name kept nagging at him.

"System: Search name Jennica Fabian."

A list of headlines appeared, most from the past couple of days. One of the titles caught his eye. "Delegate Stephanie Vaughn meets with parents of missing student." He felt the familiar stab as he read her name. He should have moved to the next item, but he couldn't stop himself from reading more.

Recently elected Delegate Vaughn made a surprise visit to the parents of missing student Jennica Fabian today. In a speech from the steps of their house, Delegate Vaughn asked for anybody who had any information as to the whereabouts of the missing student to come forward. She said, "I call on the Chowdhury Crime Agency to ensure all available resources are mobilised to ensure Jennica's safe return. At the same time, if any member of the public has information that can help clarify what happened on the night of the 17th October, no matter how small, please contact either myself or the Chowdhury Crime Agency."

Randall stared at Stephanie's image, unable to stop despite how it made him feel. How could a person still exert this grip after a gap of 20 years? He felt annoyed with himself that he had to look at the article in the same way as he used to prod at a sore tooth with his tongue, just to make sure it was still hurting. He shut the file down. "System: Remove sources: aggregator, gossip. Sort: by type."

The old hurt lingered as a new list of data sources appeared. Most categories were of little interest: biographical, educational, financial; all except one. So that's where I've seen your name before, he thought.

"Open category: quarantine."

"Here's your coffee Rand, black and strong as you like it."

Randall was still focussed on the datasphere but sensed the cup Lise placed in front of him. He quickly closed down his connection. "So what happened with Sylvianne?"

"Her best friend disappeared when she was ten. They never found a body."

"Shit. I'll speak to Robert."

"Sure you will."

He meant it, he would have a word. "So are you enjoying the meeting so far?"

"It's OK."

"You didn't think Seegers was a bit rough? You'd have thought the poor presenter had shagged his sister the way he was interrogated."

Lise shrugged her shoulders. "He's just doing his job."

"Really? You didn't think he was being too tough?"

"No more than I would be in his position. The buck stops with Seegers at the end of the day."

It was a different pain this time, but one much more familiar. Yes, he thought, Seegers, not me, the backstabbing bastard.

"Tell me again why these echoes appeared?"

Randall grimaced. His presentation had been going well up to this point. "We tracked the leak to a personal diary of one of our employees. Once the echo appeared, we followed the data trail to a conversation between two of our employees who had read the diary entry before we were able to quarantine it. This second conversation was only picked up during a deeper scan."

"So why wasn't it picked up originally? Was it a system error?"

"What's important is that it was identified and quarantined before any damage was done."

"What's important is that we understand what happened and learn from it," Seegers replied. "Bring up the logs. I'd like to know more."

Randall swallowed. He knew what was going on. Seegers wanted to rub his nose in it. "Maybe this should be parked. We can review it outside the meeting."

"Nonsense. We need to learn from our mistakes as a team. I don't have a problem if mistakes are made, but if we don't review those mistakes, other members of the team can end up repeating them, and that is something I *do* have a problem with."

There was an eagerness in his eyes. Seegers was loving this. It was a chance to assert his authority and remind Randall, and his team, who called the shots. Randall took a slow breath and unclenched his fingers. "Please. It's not necessary to go through this now. I'll take you through it later."

"I would like to know why this happened."

"Why did this happen? Well, I can tell you what would have prevented it from happening. Having enough resource to do the job properly would be a good start point. We've all been working 16 hour days solidly for months. It's a credit to the team that this type of thing hasn't happened more often. If you want us to learn from our mistakes, by all means go ahead, but why don't we look at the root causes as well."

The room went quiet. Everybody was staring at him.

"Thank you for your thoughts, Randall. I don't see the others complaining. Still, let's park that idea and we can review it outside of the meeting."

Randall walked back to his seat. He didn't know what was worse, the smirk hidden behind Robert's hand, Lise's look of sympathy or the cold blank stare from Sylvianne.

Through the afternoon Randall kept quiet, not wanting to give Seegers another opportunity to put him down. The air had became stale and with a certain inevitability energy leached out of the room.

While the meeting drifted, Randall reviewed the missing girl's document they had quarantined. It had been taken from a thought board used by students and data researchers. The content was fairly mundane. She had been analysing the collection and transfer of a vast amount of data as part of her studies and was concerned about some form of discrepancy. According to the text, data had either disappeared or was not captured during a transfer process, only to reappear once the final destination was reinitiated. The document was a call for help, asking other specialists to review her findings and identify whether the results were true or, if necessary, where the fault may lie.

There was a datacube attached to the document. Randall opened it, hoping that a few minutes immersed in the mass of data might take his mind off his day so far. Instead, he read the header and took a sharp intake of breath.

Transiessence data, Subject: 177xy43-at98964.
Property of Aristeas plc.

Shit, he thought, this could be a major problem.

Once Seegers brought the meeting to a close, Randall got up. He needed to speak to his boss, but Seegers was talking animatedly via datasphere in the corner. He waited nervously while the others filed out of the room. The team came over to say goodbye but it felt more like duty than desire, despite Lise squeezing his hand. The wait started to become uncomfortable. Whoever was on the other end of the call was clearly giving Seegers a hard time. Randall was about to leave when Seegers turned to face him.

"Randall. I don't have time to talk about resource now. Can we do it tomorrow?"

"It's not about that. I've found something you need to know about."

"Are you sure it can't wait?"

Randall shook his head.

"OK. Go on."

"There's a case flying high in the local aggre ratings about a student who went missing a few weeks back. I was shown the report today and her name looked familiar. I dug around a bit and found that we had quarantined something the girl had written, just before she disappeared."

The dead eyes stared at Randall. "Go on."

"The quarantined blog identifies her as a researcher working on Re-Life."

Seegers didn't say anything but his eyes spoke volumes.

"I've run a deep scan, and as far as I can tell there are no other documents linking her to us. This appears to be the only one."

"We're this close to launch and now our name is linked to a major crime."

"There's another thing. Delegate Vaughn has thrown her weight behind the investigation. This isn't going to go away any time soon."

Seegers looked lost in thought, his fingers drumming on the table in front of him. "OK, let's start with what we know. Which agency is investigating this? Do we have we any idea how the case is progressing?"

"It's been taken on by Chowdhury's. I don't know for certain but the fact they've held a press conference probably means they're struggling."

"Hmm, Chowdhury's is one of ours."

"Really?" Bloody hell, thought Randall, is there anything Aristeas don't own? "Perhaps you could have a word higher up, find out what's going on?"

"Don't be ridiculous." Seegers snapped. "It's bad enough that the girl is linked to Re-Life. If a Journo found out that we were asking questions about the investigation, or being seen to interfere, it would be a disaster. Does anybody else know about this?"

"No, just us."

"Keep it that way."

"Shouldn't you at least brief the board?" Randall asked.

"The board won't be interested in this, not unless it blows up. Anyway, the last thing either of us wants is their full attention."

If I was you, Randall thought, I'd get this out in the open

as quickly as possible. Still, he wouldn't be unhappy if it blew up in Seegers' face.

"The investigation is key," Seegers continued. "We need to know how close they are to solving the case. Can you do this?"

"I can't infiltrate their systems if that's what you're asking. Their security is much stronger than what we're used to tackling."

"Do you have any idea how sensitive things are right now? We don't have the luxury of 'can't'. I want to know what you *can* do."

Randall paused for a moment. This could be it, he thought. If I play this right I can prove myself more useful to the company than him. "There could be a way to find out what's going on."

"Go on."

"I know Delegate Vaughn. I could talk to her, ask her what's happening." Providing she'll ever agree to see me, he thought.

"How do *you* know Delegate Vaughn?"

Randall ignored the jibe. "We were at university together, classmates." More than a classmate, he thought, much more. "She's just been elected as Delegate for my district. I could use that as an excuse to get in touch."

"It seems a bit flimsy."

"Do you have a better idea?"

Seegers walked over to the view of the cityscape. "OK. Find out what you can but whatever you do, don't say anything about Re-Life."

"I won't," Randall said. Given what I said to her the last time we spoke, I may not get a chance to say anything at all, he thought.

CHAPTER SEVEN
The Investigator

"I think I've found something. Can you link in?"

"Sure, give me a moment."

Nico waited as Corey accepted his invitation. He'd been working all hours trying to find any kind of breakthrough. The evidence sent through as part of the bid was as Chowdhury had said. Jennica Fabian had left her apartment at around 7:30pm with a female friend and taken a pod to the city centre. They were at the Tranquil Bar from 8:03pm to 9:17pm, then went to the Tsunami Bar, where they stayed late as part of a larger group until 11:00pm. Their final port of call was Eternals, a well-known nightclub, where they remained until 11:45pm, at which point Jennica left, taking a pod that eventually dropped her at the bottom of her street. Cameras captured her walking towards her apartment but she never arrived. She walked under the thick tree canopy and disappeared. Nico had reviewed the footage repeatedly, looking for anything out of the ordinary, but nothing had materialised.

Having exhausted all avenues with the existing material, Nico had looked to fill the gaps. Using Jennica's journey as a start point, he collected footage from those businesses she had visited, as well as other premises on her route. Most footage was available directly from the datasphere. Nico knew from experience that this was the most efficient method to gather evidence. As an investigator, solving the crime was everything; as part of a business, profitability was king. It was a fine balance, and Chowdhury had stressed the importance of profit, but given the nature of the case his primary goal was simple: to find the truth of what happened that night.

There were so many questions to answer: Who was the female friend with whom Jennica had left the apartment? What happened in each of the bars they'd visited? Was footage available from each of those venues? The same for the nightclub. Did they interact with anyone in the bars or nightclub? If so, who were they and what were their movements for the rest of the night? The list seemed endless but Nico had been here before.

From the footage available, the analysis team eventually identified 681 people who were in the vicinity of Jennica that night, of which 37 were identified as potential suspects. Finally Nico had something to work with.

"OK, I'm on. Show me what you've found."

Nico rewound the footage from the Tsunami bar and played it again, the cocktail of Denolodryl and Represtomol running through his system giving everything a sharpness that enabled him to memorise every detail of every frame.

"I spotted this group here." Nico highlighted a group of youths. "If you watch, they scan the bar for a few minutes before spotting Jennica and her friend." He forwarded the footage. "They don't make a move at first but there's hardly a minute where they aren't looking in the girl's direction. "If you look here, you can see them encouraging one of their number to go over to where the girls are."

Some of the bigger youths were laughing, pushing a youth in a red top in Jennica's direction.

"At this point Jennica's friends arrive and they leave to go to the nightclub."

"It all looks pretty innocuous."

"That's what I thought, until I managed to get my hands on the footage from Eternals."

It had been the last footage to arrive. The owners had taken a lot of persuading, agreeing to hand it over after receiving written confirmation that they would not be prosecuted for any illegal activity made by their patrons on their premises. The quality wasn't great, despite Nico's best efforts, because of the amount of Narcosmoke the club used.

"You watch what happens here." Jennica and her friends had taken a table towards the rear of the club. Shortly afterwards the group of youths arrived. "I'll play you the tape from here so you can see for yourself."

Nico forwarded the clip to 11:35pm, 25 minutes after Jennica's arrival. The youth in the red top approached Jennica's group. He looked unsteady on his feet, probably a combination of the alcohol and Narcosmoke. Nico zoomed in so Corey could focus on the pair. Red said something. Jennica turned her back to him. From his expression, you could see that Red was annoyed. He pulled at Jennica's shoulder, causing a number of Jennica's friends to intervene. There was an altercation, a lot of pushing and shoving but nothing more serious. Then Red's companions appeared.

"Uh, oh. Here we go."

"That's what I thought," said Nico, "but watch." The male youths pulled Red away from Jennica's group and back towards the bar.

"They clearly didn't want a confrontation, but as you see here and here, Red has to be stopped going back to Jennica and her friends.

"Why would they pull him away if you think they were after Jennica?"

"I don't think they were. Let me show you the footage as Jennica left. It's ten minutes after the confrontation."

The camera was focussed on the club's entrance. You could clearly see Jennica standing next to one of the club's doormen. A pod appeared and Jennica climbed in. As the pod left, Red arrived. He talked to the doorman, handed something over, and ran down the hill.

"He's chased after her."

"That's what I think. I've sent the footage off for lip reading analysis, but my guess is that Red's paid the doorman to find out where Jennica lives." Nico called up a city map. "We know that it took Jennica 15 minutes to reach the end of her road, but the pod would have had to have taken a circular route to get there. Red, meanwhile ran directly towards where she lived. He could easily have made it there before her."

"Do you have footage of his route?"

"No. He went through the Scrambles so we've no chance of finding out."

"Do you have any idea what this 'Red' said to her?"

"No, but I'll get the footage analysed as well. If he made some form of threat, I'd like to bring him in."

The evidence was flimsy and normally he would have waited to find something less circumstantial, but Corey had been on his back ever since Delegate Vaughn's press conference. Nico hoped the additional pressure would work in his favour.

"Track down Jennica's friends first. If you find out the youth did say anything threatening, you can bring him in. I also want you to track down the doorman. There's a potential conviction there and it isn't on Eternal's premises."

Nico smiled to himself. Corey was never one to miss a trick. "Will do. Thanks for your help."

Finally he was getting somewhere.

CHAPTER EIGHT
The Politician

It was not an imposing building. If structure and design represented a building's function, the Legislature, home to the governing assembly, looked like a monument to obduracy. It was a squat, steel-clad featureless box similar to countless others. The Legislature was no symbol of political might, but a symbol of political folly. Folly not in its design, but that it was needed at all.

Stephanie walked through the rain towards the building's entrance, avoiding a small, sodden group of demonstrators standing under the newly erected statue of Thomas Doleman, their hand-drawn placards about voter rights slowly losing coherence as the rain took its toll. She glanced at her reflection in the glass door. Just as she had thought, her hair was starting to frizz up. While Sian shook the umbrella, Stephanie looked up at the words embossed into the steel cladding above the doors, a reminder to those who served within as to why the building was needed at all.

NEVER AGAIN

Once through the double doors they entered a vaulted lobby teeming with people. The Journos stood in uncomfortable packs, preferring the safety of numbers but each trying to spot the latest political casualty or rising star before the others. Personal assistants moved across the lobby as if they belonged, hands gesticulating as they conducted their internal conversations. Small tour groups clustered around points of interest, drinking in the atmosphere as their smartly dressed guides spun tales of political intrigue.

Stephanie guided Sian through this Brownian dance to the elevators, nerves increasing with every step. The outcome of their meetings would decide their political futures. If they left empty handed, the long-term impact to her ratings could be fatal.

She didn't know whether it was instinct or luck, but while they waited for the elevator to arrive, her eyes picked out Delegate Gant on the other side of the lobby.

"Can you give me a minute?"

Without waiting for Sian's reply, Stephanie walked towards the Prime Delegate's enforcer. He was in conversation with a group of men, his face like thunder.

"I've had it with that shit. Send him the pictures we have of him in bed with that little whore of his. Let him know that if he doesn't toe the line, the next person to see them will be his wife."

As soon as he finished speaking the group dispersed. Stephanie paused, part of her wishing she hadn't heard the conversation but another part excited by what she had heard, wondering who the 'little shit' could be. Delegate Gant looked up and caught her staring in his direction. Before she could turn away a large smile transformed his features.

"Now here's a sight for sore eyes. Delegate Vaughn, how lovely to see you again. How are you settling in? This place can be quite intimidating at first."

"Everybody's been more than welcoming."

"Glad to hear it." His gaze seemed to bore deep inside her and despite the smile it wasn't an entirely comfortable experience. "It was an interesting maiden speech you made the other day. If I was a more sensitive soul, I would say you were unhappy with some of the things we are doing in government. I'd really like to have a chat with you about it some time."

"I'd be delighted. I'll talk to James and ask him to set up a meeting."

"Wonderful. Maybe we could go for a bite afterwards?"

Stephanie could feel herself flush. "That sounds like fun. Now if you'll excuse me, I'm running late for a meeting. It was nice seeing you again."

Gant took hold of her hand and raised it to his lips. "And you."

Stephanie found Sian waiting by the elevators.

"Is everything OK?"

"Fine. Gant wants to meet with us to talk over my maiden speech."

"That's the last thing we want. Hold him off for now as we don't want to give anything away. Once we have a clearer picture of our support we can find out what they have to say."

"Fine." Looks like I'll have to wait a bit longer to find out just what a bite with Gant entailed, Stephanie thought.

James met them on the fourth floor. This part of the building was a rabbit warren of meeting rooms and offices, but James led them expertly through the maze. Stephanie checked her polling data as they walked. Over the past few days her numbers had started to drift, not at a concerning rate but at a rate that would become problematic if not addressed. Her Pollscan projections showed that she needed a quick resolution to the missing girl case. What the program hadn't foreseen was how any lack of progress reflected back on her. It was her fault, she had only asked for the impact of a positive or negative resolution.

"We're nearly there," James said, turning to his right.

"Remember what we went through," Sian said. "I've sent through a list of the group's major policies from the past two years, with a yes or no against which we would be prepared to support in exchange for their help. If they spring anything new on you, park it for today to make sure we can fully assess it before giving an answer."

James stopped by a door halfway down the corridor. "Is everyone ready?"

"As much as we'll ever be."

The Maddison group were up first, 20 in all but Delegate Maddison was the key. If she could persuade him, the rest would follow.

James knocked gently on the door and entered. The conference room was smaller than she had expected. On all four walls were pictures of great delegate orators from the past, working their magic in the debating chamber. Sitting opposite the door, elbows resting on the table, was Delegate Maddison, his grey hair immaculately styled as always. He was the only person in the room.

"Stephanie. So we finally meet." He stood up, offering her his hand. "You look startled. I don't bite, you know, despite what some aggre's would have you believe?"

Stephanie took his hand. "Delegate Maddison, a pleasure to meet you too. May I call you Bobby?"

"My friends call me Bobby."

She gestured to Sian and James. "This is Sian Tunstall and James Connell, my political advisors. I believe you've already talked."

"Good to meet you both." Turning back to Stephanie he said, "Shall we get started?"

He took a small, metal cylinder from his pocket and threw it into the air. Once it had reached its zenith, the cylinder mutated, small silvery wings peeled from its surface before it spun on its axis, hovering above their heads. Seeing her confused expression, Maddison said, "There are people who would love to know what we talk about today. This lets me know if you have any listening devices secreted upon you." He smiled as he saw the questioning looks on their faces. "Also, would you mind disconnecting yourselves from the datasphere for the duration of our meeting? They have ways of listening over that too."

The detector made a deep thrumming sound before dropping back into Maddison's hand. "You're all clear. Now, if you don't mind, you're datasphere connections?"

Stephanie looked across to James. His face was a mask but she knew what he was thinking. She mumbled the command and her link to the datasphere disappeared. The others did the same. It felt akin to losing a limb. Ignoring the loss, Stephanie composed herself. It was showtime. "I'm sorry if I looked a little surprised when I walked in, Bobby, we were expecting to meet up with both you and your partners today."

"We don't like being in the same room at the same time. We'd be too big a target to resist. The more we're spread out, the more resources they need to keep tabs on us." He chuckled to himself. "Thanks for agreeing to meet with me, though. Most new delegates wouldn't dare. I think they believe I have political rabies."

Stephanie refused to look in James' direction.

"I really enjoyed your maiden speech to the Legislature," Maddison continued. "You came across as both forthright and honest, qualities lacking in most delegates. You made a point of saying you had been elected on the promise of voting for what you believe is right, as opposed to what is politically expedient. Have you any idea how many enemies you made with that sentence?"

"I think the electorate are fed up with platitudes and are looking for people with conviction. My election proves that. If I've put a few noses out of joint, that's more down to their conscience than anything I said."

Maddison laughed. "You may be right, though I would keep that opinion to yourself, at least until you're more established. Still, the reason I asked to meet is to find out whether you actually meant what you said, or if you are just another puppet."

The question felt a little too close to the truth for Stephanie's liking. "It's nice to know that trust still plays a role in modern politics."

Maddison leaned forward, all signs of joviality gone. "My automatic trust of people died years ago. I've been lied to my face far too many times. Don't take it personally. If I was convinced you were play acting, we wouldn't be having this conversation."

Stephanie felt her anger rise. She didn't have to listen to this. Sian looked across, subtly gesturing for her to calm down. She leant forward, matching Maddison in both pose and demeanour. "I have not lied to you or my electorate. I believe passionately that we need to change, that all candidates should communicate clearly what they believe in, and—if elected—deliver what they promise. If not, if we succumb to external pressure, we'll end up repeating the mistakes of the past."

Maddison started a slow clap. "Bravo! What a performance. The problem is that it's just words. My granddaughter could have learnt that answer off pat and she's seven years old. What I want to know is: why? What brought on this epiphany?"

Stephanie felt as if she'd been slapped. Was she really so transparent? "Sian, why don't you explain to Delegate Maddison how we came into politics."

Sian gave Stephanie a panicked glance, a flush of embarrassment spreading from neck to face. Stephanie nodded to her. Just tell him the truth, she thought, your truth.

Sian cleared her throat. "It started while we were at university. We'd become friends in the first year as our rooms were opposite each other in the halls."

"You didn't study politics." Maddison was looking at Stephanie.

"No, data analysis."

"During a contemporary politics lesson," Sian continued, "the lecturer introduced Andy Hawthorne to us. He was young, not much older than us, charismatic and clearly an idealist. He talked about the rot at the heart of modern politics, how rudderless the government had become, reacting to one short-term issue after another while the overall direction remained unchanged. I was impressed. He seemed to touch on certain fundamentals that were never talked about, never even raised on the datasphere. I volunteered to help his campaign. It didn't take long for Stephanie to see how excited I was so she decided to volunteer too."

Stephanie remembered clearly how infatuated they'd both been by Andy Hawthorne, though for different reasons.

"We worked all through summer, drumming up support. Andy often spoke at the campaign office, expanding on his plans. He wanted to expose the hypocrisy and deceit that lay at the heart of government. Most evenings, Stephanie and I were often the last to leave. Andy would stay behind, thanking us for all the hard work and sharing a joke or two. I would have done anything for him at that point."

Yes, Stephanie thought, he knew how to get what he wanted.

"We were elated when Andy was elected, celebrating long and hard into the night. The next day he went to the Legislature and made his maiden speech. It was one of the blandest speeches you've ever heard. No mention of hypocrisy. No mention of a broken political system. No mention of long-term vision or questioning the direction in which the country was headed. We were stunned, but still wanted to give him the benefit of the doubt. The next day, two of his campaign staff came in and closed the office. We were let go with their thanks. Given the effort we had put in, we both naively thought that we would get a job on his team, but it didn't happen. We never saw him again."

Stephanie looked across at her friend. You were let down

intellectually, she thought, I was let down emotionally. We should have seen it coming but were both so innocent.

"In the months afterwards I kept an eye on his voting record," Sian continued, "hoping to see him make the changes he'd talked about, to influence the direction of discourse. Nothing happened. We were so angry. Stephanie walked away from politics completely while I worked with other candidates, hoping to find someone with a spark of integrity."

It was a long time since Stephanie had seen her friend so animated.

"I remember Delegate Hawthorne," Maddison said. "He was very much as you describe. In fact I'm surprised he didn't try it on with you, given his reputation. Perhaps that only started once he arrived here." Stephanie almost shrank under Maddison's gaze as he spoke. "He spent most of his career rubber-stamping government policy, only changing towards the end, although I'm sure you were both past caring by that point. He died in a boating accident. Sad, really."

Maddison got up and walked to the dispenser. With his back turned, Stephanie glanced across to Sian and James. Sian shrugged her shoulders. James looked unimpressed.

The clink of crockery caused them all to turn. "OK, so I buy your motive," Maddison said. "What I don't understand is what took you so long? It's, what, at least 20 years since Delegate Hawthorne was part of the Legislature?"

"I wanted nothing to do with politics after what had happened," Stephanie said. "I went back to data analysis." And developed the Pollscan prototype.

"As I said. I worked for a number of prospective candidates. I hoped to find somebody—I don't know— somebody worthy." Sian laughed to herself. "I know it sounds naive, but I was looking for somebody who would deliver on Andy Hawthorne's promises."

"So what changed."

"We bumped into each other four years ago," Stephanie replied. "Sian was about to quit politics for good, while I was at a bit of a loose end. We talked about our time with the Hawthorne campaign and I mentioned that most people I knew were disenchanted with politics."

"It was then that it hit me," Sian interrupted. "If we both felt this way, and we knew that most of our friends did, perhaps now *was* the right time for a change. I knew I didn't have the charisma to run for office myself, but Stephanie was the ideal candidate. I asked if I could campaign on her behalf and to my surprise she said yes."

"I'd never thought to run myself but when Sian asked I realised that instead of moaning I could actually do something about it. The rest, I think, is public record." Stephanie looked squarely at Maddison. "So, is that good enough for you? Because if it's not, then tough. We don't have another story."

He smiled and nodded. "Good enough."

"We want to change the system but we need time," Sian continued. "Unlike yourself, we don't have the luxury of a stable electorate. Stephanie needs to be seen to be delivering on her campaign promises and quickly. If not, we will be in real danger once the Global Electoral System comes in."

"Don't get me started on that sham of a system," Maddison growled.

"Our key policy pledge was to reduce personal taxation. When I announced the policy it gave me the biggest poll boost of the campaign, winning us a lot of financial backing from local businesses."

"The only way to reduce personal taxation is to cut the number of infrastructure projects planned for delivery," Sian said. "This would generate enough surplus to fund a significant tax break across the board. Our problem is that the government is planning to announce yet another new infrastructure project, this time in the Shetlands—"

"I'd heard the same thing," Maddison interjected.

"—and Orkneys as part of the new budget proposal, which is frankly crazy. We are an energy exporter, the last thing we need is more energy production."

"My plan is to push for a no vote during the budget debate. I know you've been against these infrastructure projects in the past and I need support to push the no vote through." As she spoke, Stephanie felt the moment approach. She leaned forward and looked Maddison straight in the eye. "So, Bobby, are you with me?"

Maddison sat, chin resting on his hands, fingers forming a point by the bridge of his nose. If he backs out now, Stephanie thought, at least I can't be accused of not giving it my best shot. Sian gave her what appeared to be a supportive smile.

"You've been open with me so I'll be open with you. I think your ideology stinks. I'd much rather the money was used for government-funded social schemes to lift the poor out of financial and educational poverty. We live in a country where only 45 percent of the population search the datasphere for anything other than entertainment, gossip or to shop. People are intellectually impoverished, not having the skills to interrogate the datasphere intelligently enough to identify truth from fiction, not even knowing what questions they should ask. If you really want to make a change, we need education programs so the electorate can challenge the status quo, like you are, rather than be spoon-fed whatever the major corporations would have us believe. If you really want change, we need to kick the population out of its apathy."

Stephanie's heart sank. The team would never agree to this and her backers would be furious. It was the complete opposite to what she had promised during her campaign.

"What you are offering," Maddison continued, "however well intended, will give further funds to the same corporations that are driving government policy."

"Come on, surely you don't really believe that." James slumped back in his chair in exasperation.

Maddison ignored the comment. "I'm prepared to concede that what you are suggesting is slightly better than where we as a nation are currently, but other than that you won't be changing a thing."

Stephanie desperately wanted to use Pollscan, but it was impossible without datasphere access. Sian and James appeared disengaged from the conversation. She realised that if she was to get anything from this meeting, she needed to act. "You said that education is key. What if we compromise, use some of the funds to improve education for the poor, the rest on tax breaks? Is that something you could support?"

"Why should I compromise?"

"Because without us, you'll never get this type of opportunity again. We need each other. I'm not saying you compromise on your beliefs, just the level of what you can initially deliver. If we get a tax break and you deliver investment in education, we both win. If the education funding proves popular, you'll find even more support for it during the next budgetary round."

"That might work. It depends on the details."

Stephanie stood up, holding out her hand. "Then let's agree to it in principle and work out the details over the next few days."

Maddison held up his hands. "Before I agree to anything, I want you to know what you are getting into. Are you sure you're ready to face down the government? Because they can get pretty nasty when threatened."

Stephanie nodded. "We discussed this at the very start. We're committed."

"OK," he said, shaking her hand."If we can find a meeting point I'll support your blocking motion and make sure the group are with us."

"Thank you Bobby, you won't regret this."

"I hope not." He picked up his jacket and walked towards the door. As he reached for the handle he stopped and turned, looking at James.

"I know you think I'm crazy, but then again you're too young to remember the Upheaval. It's one thing reading about it in the history books, quite another to live through it. I grew up near to a refugee camp. I was lucky, things were beginning to return to normal when I was young. My family had enough land to raise crops and guns to protect us from the last remaining scavengers. In the camp, the poor Dutch lived on next to nothing, but at least they finally had somewhere to stay, unlike most of their countrymen.

"If you ask school children today what caused the Upheaval, they will say the polar icecaps melting, rising sea levels, extreme weather patterns. People are already forgetting that it was politicians under the sway of big business that blocked any real progress against climate change until it was too late. The words "Never Again" on the front of this building are there for a reason, yet today's politicians are forgetting why the words were put there. Well I haven't forgotten. It was only because of brave men and women like Thomas Doleman that we managed to turn things around. Even then it was too late to prevent the hardship that followed. I don't want us to go through that again. And if you think I'm being paranoid, check the voting records. There's a pattern if you look hard enough. I know you think I'm an old fool but check the voting records and then tell me there's no external influence on the Legislature." With that, he went out of the door.

Stephanie's thoughts were racing. She had managed to broker a deal, without relying on the team. Not only that, she had enjoyed it. Perhaps there was more to this than she had initially thought.

"My god, he really is as crazy as people say. Surely he's

been tested for the standard psychological defects?" James was shaking his head in disbelief.

"He's passed psych profiling, neural profiling, the lot. Most people just write him off as a little eccentric," Sian said. "Still, eccentric or not, we need to be careful being associated with him. If word gets out that we've made some sort of pact, it could finish your political career."

"If I hadn't just made that deal, my political career would have been over before it had started. I know you think he's crazy, but we need his support. With his voting block in place, our numbers are large enough to leverage some of the other fence-sitters."

James looked at Stephanie with a curious expression on his face. "You're right. It's just, I hear this sort of thing all the time. People want to believe that there is some form of conspiracy, when most things happen by coincidence. People like Maddison don't help.

"A lot of what Maddison said is true, though even he forgets to mention that Doleman was happy to do nothing for years before making his stand."

"But he made a stand when it mattered."

"Too late for my parents."

James stared at Stephanie, openmouthed. "I'm sorry. I forgot."

"Don't be. It's history. Very old history."

"Why don't you quietly sound out some of the unknowns who haven't responded as yet," said Sian. James nodded.

Stephanie had not been much more than a baby when her parents had disappeared, and while she tried to summon anger at the the ghost of Doleman for what had happened, she failed. It was a reflex action, a second hand emotion she had inherited from her Grandparents. She'd never known her parents and so couldn't miss them. The people who did grieve for them were her Grandparents, and that oppressive undercurrent of loss was one of the reasons she had been so keen to leave home as soon as she could.

In an effort to change the subject, Stephanie thought back to the polling data. "It's been some time since I had the press conference with the Fabian family and I've not seen any progress. My poll rating is slipping and I think that's why. Can you chase things up for me, Sian?"

"Sure," she replied, although she frowned as she said it.

"Is there a problem?"

"No, no problem. I'd be surprised if Addy isn't already on it but I'll double check." She opened her mouth to say something else before closing it again.

"Come on Sian, you obviously want to say something."

"You had a message from Randall Jones, offering to help find the missing girl. I wasn't going to say anything but—"

"What? Randall Jones? University Randall Jones?"

"Yes, University Randall Jones."

"Christ, I haven't thought about him in ages." Stephanie let out a little laugh. "Randall bloody Jones. Now there was an error of judgement. Do you think he still has the ponytail?"

Sian grinned. "I doubt it. My guess is that he's fat and bald."

Stephanie gave Sian a mock appraising look. "Not all of us can retain our good looks and youthful charm you know. So why does he think he can help? Is he an investigator or something?"

"No, he's some kind of data wonk. He said he'd wanted to get in contact ever since your election victory and was reminded again after seeing your press conference. He says he has access to cutting-edge analysis tools that may help with the search. He wanted to meet up to tell you more."

"It sounds a bit odd," Stephanie said. How strange, she thought. Randall Jones. And they had just been talking about Andy Hawthorne too. "Still, if he can give us information that will help find the girl…"

"Think of the poll boost."

Stephanie did her best to feign shock. "Don't you mean

'think of how happy the girl's family will be'?"

"That's not what I meant."

Stephanie smiled at her friend's discomfort. "Get back to Randall, sound him out to make sure he's genuine and not looking to rekindle something that never was," Sian had started grinning again, "and if it all checks out, book him a slot early next week."

As the three of them walked out of the meeting room, Stephanie smiled to herself. Randall Jones. Bloody hell.

CHAPTER NINE
The Investigator

Nico settled back into his chair, allowing the darkness of the soundproofed room to envelop him. He nervously checked through the list of witness statements, video and audio evidence, lip reading analysis and many other items that he'd collated over the past few days. He was striving for an inner calm, a stability that would allow him to do his best work, striving for the peace that eluded him. Those pills he had taken had better kick in soon, he thought.

At the signal, he closed down all extraneous information and focussed on the live link. He moved his head from side to side, stretching his neck until he heard a crack. He then twisted his torso, first left and then right, using the seat back to leverage his spine until that too cracked. He could hear his heartbeat thumping loudly in the quiet of the room. This was the most important interview of his career. Right now, Corey Akkerman was sending out a statement to inform the world that a suspect was being held in connection with the missing student. Nico had asked Corey not to say anything until they had hard evidence linking the suspect with the crime, but had been overruled. It was just one more slab of pressure to be piled onto the rest.

He took a sip of water. Over the feed he saw a door opening and a blindfolded young man was led into the brightly lit room, clearly disoriented. The door closed, merging into the wall so no traces of it's existence remained. The suspect was alone.

Nico reclined his chair to its full extent, then waited; the sound of the suspect's breathing mixing with his own. The youth stood still, arms slightly raised as if waiting for a blow.

"Good afternoon. Could you please confirm that you can hear me."

The suspect flinched from the unexpected sound. "Yes." His voice was higher pitched than Nico had expected.

"Good. You may take your blindfold off."

The suspect raised his hands to his face and removed the covering from his eyes. Squinting against the light, he looked around the room. There was nothing to see, no distinguishing features, nothing to focus on. Through the video feed, the suspect looked as if he was floating in a void.

"My name is Investigator Tandelli. Listening to this interview is your court-appointed solicitor. If you prefer your own, speak up now." Nico waited for a reply that never came. "Good, then let us begin. Could you confirm that your name is Charles Adrian Willby and that you reside at Flat 136B, The Cornucopia, Westland."

The youth mumbled something.

"You'll need to speak up."

"My name's Chad," he said, his voice cracking slightly, "only Gran calls me Charles."

"OK Chad, can you confirm that you live at the stated address."

"Yes."

"How long have you lived at that address?"

"About eight months." Chad looked around as if trying to get a fix on where the voice was coming from. "Is this something to do with the rent? I told Mr Florence that he'd get it by the end of the week."

"No Chad, this isn't to do with the rent. If you look in front of you, you'll see some footage taken from the evening of 17th October. Could you confirm that the person circled wearing a red top is you."

A previously white wall sprang to life, displaying the carefully prepared footage from the night Jennica Fabian disappeared.

"Yeah, that's me."

"Could you please tell me where you were and who you were with."

Silence.

"Chad, answer the question. Where were you and who were you with?" Nico repeated.

Again, silence. Chad looked towards his bare feet, arms folded.

"Chad, this will go much easier on you if you just answer the questions." Nico kept his voice smooth, showing no emotion. "If you don't answer the questions freely, I will be forced to administer a drug to make you talk. Before I do, I am obliged to warn you that it has a number of side effects including hair loss, nose bleeds, painful joints, headaches and nausea." A legal challenge flashed at the edge of Nico's datalenses, quickly quashed by the Chowdhury legal team.

"Now, I'll ask you one final time, could you please confirm where you were and who you were with in the footage?"

"The Tsunami Bar. I was with the boys."

"Thank you Chad. You'll be pleased to know that this has been confirmed by your friends."

Chad's head shot up. "You're lying."

"I'm sure your friends are very loyal, Chad, but you would be surprised how cooperative people become when facing charges of accessory to kidnap and suspected murder."

Chad stared at the screen. "What?"

"Where is Jennica Fabian, Chad?"

Chad shook his head, a look of incomprehension on his face. "Murder? What do you mean murder?"

"Where is Jennica Fabian?"

"Who's Jennica Fabian?"

"You know who Jennica Fabian is, Chad. She's the girl you were seen staring at in the Tsunami Bar. If you watch the footage, you can see your friends pointing her out to you." Nico highlighted Jennica. "Does this bring back any memories? You and your friends had been talking about her for long enough. Now, where is she, Chad? What have you done with her?" The legal warnings flashed up at an increasing rate.

Chad stared at the screen, frowning. "How should I know where she is?"

"Let's move on. If you could look at the screen again, we can see footage from Eternals nightclub. For the record, could you please confirm that the group you see is you and your friends from earlier."

"Yes, that's us."

"And could you confirm that you and your friends are looking in the direction of a group of people, including Jennica Fabian."

"If that's who you say it is."

"Good. Can you tell me why your friends are pushing you towards Jennica's group?"

"I don't know."

"Surely you must know, after all, you and your friends had been stalking her all night."

"I can't remember."

"I suggest it's because you'd picked her out as your next victim. Is that right?"

"No."

"Then tell me what's happening."

It was hard for Nico to see the youth's expression, but his body language spoke volumes. "They thought I should snag her."

"Snag her?"

"You know, invite her home."

"And that's why you approached her."

"Yeah," he looked up, an insolent sneer on his face, "They wanted to see the master charmer work his magic on her."

Nico smiled to himself. "Your friends gave a different story. They said that you have trouble talking to the opposite sex; that you stumble on your words, make a fool of yourself. They said it was always 'a great laugh' watching you attempt to 'snag' girls. Is this true? Do you have problems talking to people you find attractive?"

Chad's shook his head. "Nah, that's not true. They're just having a laugh."

"So they're telling lies."

"Yeah."

"You aren't a failure with the opposite sex?"

"Nah. I'm the man. They love me."

"Then would you mind giving me the names and addresses of women you've previous 'snagged'? I'm sure they wouldn't mind. If what you say is true, they'd be honoured to say they had spent the night with you."

Silence.

"Let's go back to the beginning," Nico said.

The interrogation had been in progress for three hours, replaying the opening sequence, Nico asking the same question in different ways in the hope of finding inconsistencies in Chad's answers. Slowly, Chad's bravado was chipped away until finally Nico felt he was ready.

"Can you talk me through what is happening now, as you approach Jennica."

Chad straightened a little, his sullen expression returning. "Nothing. Just talk, that's all."

"That's not true, is it Chad? If you look at the screen, a little more than talking happened."

Chad looked up, slowly pacing the room as he watched the recording unfold.

"According to independent testimony, you approached Jennica and said, 'Hello gorgeous, what's your name?' Is this correct?"

Chad didn't answer. On screen, Chad spoke to Jennica, who turned her back on him.

"That's quite some opening line from the master charmer. However, your charms appear not to have worked. When Jennica turned away, you are reported to have said, 'What's up with you? I only asked you a fucking question.' Is this correct?"

Still no answer. Chad's eyes remained on the screen, his mouth a thin line.

"According to witnesses, you then said, 'Who the fuck do you think you are? How dare you turn your back on me, you fucking slag.' Is this correct?" Nico spoke the words without emotion, but combined with the raw images from that night you could feel the menace with which they had been said. Chad watched the footage, occasionally closing his eyes and turning away, always to be drawn back.

"After you said those words, some of Jennica's friends intervened. You put up a struggle and were reported to have said, 'You haven't seen the last of me, you fucking bitch. I could have you any time I want. You just see, any time I want.' Do you deny saying these words?"

Still nothing. Chad's pacing had increased, although his eyes never left the screen.

"It seems a strong reaction to me. After all, she only turned her back on you. Are you a violent person Chad? Do you get angry often? Are you frustrated with your lack of success with women? Does this make you hate them?" With each question, legal fireworks blurred at the edge of Nico's vision. "Do you hate women, Chad? Is that why you get angry? Did you hate Jennica too? Is that why you wanted to hurt her, for rejecting you?"

"No." Chad answered, his voice almost a whisper.

"You did though, Chad. You did want to hurt her."

"No, I didn't."

"I think you did Chad, I think you hated her and that's

why you got angry."

"That's not true."

"Yes, it is. You hated her because you thought she was looking down on you."

"No, I didn't."

"I think you did."

"It's not true."

"Then why did you get angry that night?"

"Because the bastards were laughing at me." Chad's cheeks glistened in the light.

"Who? Jennica's friends?"

"No, the boys. They're always laughing at me."

"So you got angry because your friends saw her reject you and you knew they would be laughing at you."

"Yes."

The legal battle stopped. Nico relaxed. He hadn't realised how tense he had been until that point. He rubbed his fingers around his temples. The stimulants were reaching their peak. His whole body tingled, his mind as sharp as cut glass.

"Let's move on. This next footage is of Jennica leaving the club. Shortly after getting into her pod, you appear. Why did you follow Jennica out of the nightclub?" The legal warnings started again.

"I didn't follow her."

"So, it was just a coincidence that you arrived just as her pod was leaving."

By this point Chad had slumped to the floor, tears streaming down his face.

"Why did you leave, Chad?"

"I'd had enough of the others, I just wanted to get out of there."

"It was nothing to do with Jennica?"

"No, nothing to do with her."

"So why did you ask the doorman where she was going?"

Chad looked at the screen in horror. "It's not what you

think."

Nico smiled to himself. "What do I think?"

"You think I went after her."

"Did you?"

"No."

"You've already said you were angry with her. Is that why you chased after her, because you were angry?"

"No."

"So, I'll ask again, why did you ask where she was going?" Nico's fingers were drumming on his arm rests. He tried to relax, to remain patient, but it was difficult when he knew he was close. Come on, come on.

"I wanted to apologise. I wanted to say I was sorry for being an idiot." Chad looked abject, all signs of the master charmer having disappeared.

"So you left the club and ran across town to meet her. She refused your apology and in your anger at being rejected once more, you attacked her. You 'had' her, as you'd so clearly threatened earlier."

"No, that's not right."

"So what is right? Tell us what happened."

"I wanted to catch her up, to say sorry, but I realised I'd only end up making it worse, so I went home."

"You went home."

"Yes."

"And then what did you do?"

"I went to bed."

"Are you sure that's what happened?"

"Yes."

"Then how do you explain the fact that her student ID bracelet was found at your home?"

Chad had his head in his hands. You're mine, Nico thought. Now all he needed was his confession.

Corey's icon appeared. Nico muted his sound feed and answered the call.

"How's it going?"

"Not bad. I've just hit him with the ID bracelet. I don't think it'll be too long before he cracks."

"Good. I've had a few Journos on who want to know more. I'll let them know that we're close to a confession."

"Please don't. At least wait until he's confessed before saying anything. All we have at the moment is the bracelet."

"You're being too cautious. We have a suspect, a motive, evidence linking the suspect to the girl. The only thing missing is the body. Leave this to me. Just make sure you nail the bastard."

Nico's focus returned to the interrogation room. Chad remained on the floor, his body wracked with sobs. He looked beaten.

"OK Chad," said Nico, "You were about to tell me why the ID bracelet belonging to Jennica Fabian was found at your home."

"Because I stole it." Yes! Nico's heart was racing. He had him.

"Why did you steal it?"

"I wasn't thinking, I just saw it lying there and took it."

That's right, thought Nico, you just saw it lying next to her body and took it as a trophy. "Did you bring Jennica back to your apartment?"

"No, well, not really."

"What do you mean, not really? Either she was there or she wasn't."

Chad looked down, swallowing hard. "She was there, but only in my head."

"Come on, Chad, we've come this far. Just admit it. That's where you stole her bracelet, at your apartment."

Chad shook his head. "No, you've got it wrong. She never came back to mine."

"You said she was there."

"She wasn't, not really."

"You're not making any sense. Where did you get Jennica's bracelet?"

"It was in front of her, in Eternals. I saw it there as they pushed me onto the table. That's why I said I could have her whenever I wanted. I took the bracelet home, loaded her details onto a jack site and took some dreamshaper."

A dribble of sweat trickled down Nico's neck. He brought the footage of the scuffle up onto his datalenses. Chad was approached from the side by one of Jennica's friends, who pushed into him causing Chad to grab hold of the table where Jennica was sitting. Chad looked down, his hand resting on the table edge. Nico zoomed in until the edge of the table took up his whole vision. Chad seemed to grab something off the table as he pushed himself upright. Nico reviewed the footage again. It was difficult to see, the narcosmoke and poor resolution frustrating his efforts. Chad's hand went down flat, but came up clenched before going into his pocket. There was a glint from the bracelet one moment, then it was gone. Nico felt sick. It was happening again. What had been an open and shut case was falling apart in front of his eyes. He'd missed it. He'd missed a vital piece of information and now no matter whether Chad was telling the truth about what had happened in his house or not, the only physical evidence they had linking Chad to the missing girl had been stolen from her before she had disappeared. His case had collapsed. It was happening all over again.

CHAPTER TEN

The Information Cleanser

"Hi Randall."

Stephanie's breath sparkled as she spoke. Her face was framed perfectly by a matching hat and scarf. Randall spotted a few strands of hair peeking out from under her hat, maybe a slightly different shade than he remembered. Then again, they had all changed in the last 20 years. One thing that hadn't changed was her smile. Broad and honest, it transformed her face into the Stephanie he remembered. Her eyes, scrunched up by her raised cheeks, creases slightly deeper than before, were the same beautiful green eyes, indicators of mischief and more.

She reached forward and gave him a hug. "It's really good to see you, you've hardly changed."

Randall shivered. He could feel the shape of her body through her thick, winter coat. There was none of the awkwardness he had expected. Even after all these years they fit together seamlessly. Holding her felt like the most natural act in the world.

His reverie broke as Stephanie gently pulled herself away. Oh god, I didn't hold on for too long, did I? He looked up but her smile hadn't slipped.

"Er... It's, um, really good to see you too."

"Can you still do that trick?"

"What trick?"

"Two thousand, six hundred and twenty times four hundred and sixty-nine."

"One million, two hundred and twenty-eight thousand, seven hundred and eighty." Randall felt himself go red as Stephanie grinned.

"Sorry, I couldn't resist. It was the first thing I remember you saying to me." She sat on a bench, indicating for him to sit next to her. Her colleague sat the other side of her. Randall looked at her colleague again. Was that Sian? "I'm sorry we had to meet in the park," Stephanie said. "There's been a water leak at my office and the repair men are driving me crazy."

"No problem, I love the park, especially this time of year." Except my feet are freezing, he thought, because I'm wearing the wrong type of shoe and there's an icicle of snot forming on the end of my nose; all because I've been waiting for at least an hour in case you were early. Other than that, it was a great idea.

"So tell me everything?" she continued, placing her hand on his. "What are you up to? Are you in a relationship? Married? Do you have any children? I have to admit that I had a sneak peak on the datasphere but for some reason I couldn't find anything about you." She grinned, looking every inch the naughty child.

"I'm not in a relationship. I was married but we split up a few years ago. No kids."

"I'm sorry. You never know, these things often turn out for the best." She smiled and with that smile Randall's worries about the meeting dissipated. Perhaps time could heal all wounds. Perhaps more than heal.

"Now you will have to excuse me but my day is rather full. You mentioned to Sian that you might be able to help us find Jennica."

"I don't know about *find*, but I thought that maybe I could help."

"I didn't know you were an investigator? Are you freelance or do you work for an agency?"

Randall laughed. "No. No such thing. I work in data analysis." He could feel his flush returning. "You remember my speciality was deep data analysis and retrieval? Well that's what I do."

"You'll have to forgive me but I don't understand. If you're not an investigator, how do you propose to help?"

For a brief second her look of irritation brought back some uncomfortable memories. "My job gives me access to cutting-edge data analysis tools. They might help find things you can't access any other way. When I saw you asking for help, I thought that maybe I could find something the investigators had missed."

"So, you are some kind of researcher?"

"Um, sort of."

"What do you mean, sort of?"

"Well, research is part of what I do."

"Look, Randall. I don't have time for this. What is it that you do?"

Terrified she was about to leave, Randall said. "I'm an Information Cleanser." One look at Stephanie's face told him he had made a mistake.

"I thought information cleansing was a myth. I'd heard rumours but... How can you do that? How can you censor people? I mean, what happened to you?"

Perhaps time wasn't a healer after all. The partially healed wound in his soul ripped open at her accusation. The hurt he'd learnt to ignore surged through him, made worse by the fact he had thought he had seen a flicker, a possibility of something between them. "It's not like that, really it's not. I just make sure that no lies or misinformation are spread about the company I work for—"

"It's the UN's role to police the datasphere."

"Yeah, and we all know how effective *they* are," Randall's anger latched onto this familiar target. "Too slow, too expensive; if they did their job properly I would agree with you, but they don't. I do the job they should be doing, only quicker and more efficiently." He looked at Stephanie, hoping she would see past his job title to the person behind the role. "My morals haven't changed. I'd never do anything unethical. If it came to that, I'd leave. My job is to shield the company from people who want to smear them, people who don't have the same morals that we do."

Stephanie turned to Sian, who looked back, eyebrows raised. This is it, he thought, but instead of leaving she asked, "So who do you work for?"

"I can't answer that."

Sian got up. "OK, I've heard enough."

Stephanie pushed herself to the edge of the bench. "Look at it from our perspective, Randall. It's been over 20 years since we last spoke and suddenly from out of the blue you're back in contact. You say your motives are pure but in our line of work *nobody* does anything without wanting something in return." She placed her hand in his once more and her eyes softened. "It's been genuinely lovely to see you but I need to know if I can trust you. It's up to you, Randall. Either you tell us something we can use or…"

No. He couldn't let her leave, not again. Randall felt dizzy, struggling against the sense of deja vu. He tried to concentrate on what she was saying. Her mouth was moving but all he saw was the plumpness of her lips, remembering back to when they'd kissed and how she used to trap his bottom lip between them.

"OK, I'll tell you, but only you."

Stephanie smiled and colour flooded back into the world. "Why don't we go for a walk, stretch our legs for a bit. Sian, there's a lovely little coffee shop over there. Could you pick me up a latte for when we return?"

Once Sian left, Stephanie stood, holding her arm out. "OK, I'm all yours," she said. "Are you coming?"

Randall jumped up, his feet almost slipping from under him on the frosty path. Laughing, Stephanie grabbed his arm. "Careful now, you're on thin enough ice as it is."

Randall felt his cheeks glow. He wouldn't have been surprised if they were steaming. He wrapped his arm in Stephanie's and started off down the path, luxuriating in the close contact.

"What I'm about to tell you is totally confidential. Only three people know about this including you, and the other one would quite happily hang me if he ever learnt I'd told you."

"I have confidential meetings every day. If I couldn't keep a secret, I wouldn't be able to do my job."

Randall took a deep breath. "I work for Re-Life."

"The cloning people?"

"Not cloning, life extension." It was an automatic response, something he'd used many times whenever anybody asked him what he did, not that he'd needed it for a while.

"I considered taking a policy out myself once, but the thought of someone opening up my skull was a bit too much. Why can't you just clone and be done with it?"

"Because it wouldn't be you, it would be a copy of you. That's what makes Re-Life special. With Re-Life, if you die, your personality and memories live on within a synthetic brain and then get transferred to the clone. To the person involved it's just like falling asleep and then waking up. The continuous link means it is you, not a copy, that is created."

Stephanie wrinkled her nose. "I still don't want anyone cutting my head open."

"That's one of the reasons we're launching a new version. Unlike the old system, with the new one you just swallow a pill and nanomachinary builds the implant in your brain. It's cheaper too, because you don't need surgery." Randall raised his hand to his hairline, pulling it back to show the scar. "Unlike us early adopters.

"That's why this launch is so important. Lots of people were put off because they couldn't afford it or because they're a little squeamish. Now they don't have to worry. It's going to be huge. My team have been working overtime to make sure nothing leaks before launch. Anything that puts doubts in the public's mind could be really damaging. We've spent weeks cleansing the datasphere, taking out anything that could potentially erode our message. Negative comments, complaints, customer service issues, fabricated conspiracies; you name it, we've been blocking or deleting it."

He could feel Stephanie stiffen. "I still don't like it. Messing with the datasphere is illegal."

"That depends on two things, how good your legal team are and, more importantly, if you get caught. This is big business. Somebody like Aristeas plc trade on the reputation of their brands. They've learnt from the mistakes of the first Re-Life launch, how long it took to gain people's trust. They will do anything, use any resources necessary in order to control the launch." Well, almost enough resources because of that bastard Seegers, he thought.

"It's making money by suppressing information."

"And how is that different from what happens in the Legislature?"

Stephanie stopped, pulling her arm from his. "How dare you."

"Do you really believe the public gets told everything that happens there? Look, we're no different from each other. I told you, my morals haven't changed and nor have yours. All I do is make sure that the truth isn't lost in the mass of uneducated or malicious opinion."

"Your company's truth."

"*The* truth. I wouldn't do it otherwise." Randall held Stephanie's gaze, hoping that she saw he was being genuine.

"I don't see what this has to do with the missing girl."

"One of the documents we cleansed was an entry by

Jennica Fabian. It was part of a general trawl for negative comments. What she had written was pretty innocuous, but it contained a document that linked her to Re-Life. She'd been looking at part of the Re-Life process as part of her doctorate."

"I wasn't aware of that."

"You wouldn't have been. There is nothing on the datasphere that links Jennica with Re-Life. Trust me, I ran a very thorough search."

"So what was in the document? Why was it quarantined?"

"It was nothing really, just a query on some data. It got caught because she was casting doubt on part of the processes, although she herself was unsure as to whether she had made a miscalculation. Our problem is that any link between a criminal investigation and Re-Life has the potential to screw up the launch. If the conspiracy theorists have their way, everything will be blamed on us. My boss saw the danger as soon as I told him. He wants me to find out how quickly the case will be resolved. The longer it goes on, the more chance that somebody will link us to the girl. If the case is over quickly, nobody will be interested."

"And so you came to me."

Randall nodded. "I know it's been a long time since we were last in contact but it was the only thing I could think of. I thought that if I offered to help you, I could also find out what was going on. You would be happy and my boss would be happy." He felt dejected. *And now you see the full extent of how pathetic my life has become.*

"Look, I'm sorry. I never meant to waste your time. I really thought that I'd be able to help but I can see how this looks." Randall turned to go. "Good luck with the investigation and your political career. It was a bit of a shock to see you in the Aggres after all these years but I'm glad you're doing all right. You're one of life's good guys. If anyone deserves success, it's you."

"Wait Rand, just wait a minute." Stephanie stepped

forward, grabbing his arm. The cold weather really did suit her. Her pale complexion looked flawless, just a slight pinkness around her nose the only blemish. "Can you really help?"

"If there is something on the datasphere, I'll have a better chance of unearthing it than the agency will."

"Then do it. I need to find the girl and quickly. The investigation is a mess. First they told us that that they were close to getting a confession, only to call us back an hour later to tell us they were letting the suspect go. I need a quick result as much as you do. If you can do your digging, I'll keep you informed of what's going on."

Randall smiled. He could have floated. "Thank you Steph. I really do appreciate it."

Stephanie squeezed his arm. "I wasn't joking when I said it's been good seeing you again. It's a shame that it's taken something like this for us to meet, but I'm really glad that we have. You look after yourself."

Randall thought about giving Stephanie a hug, but by the time he'd decided she was too far gone to try.

Sian handed the steaming mug of coffee to Stephanie. "So, how did it go?"

"He hasn't changed, well his personality hasn't. Still, he could be useful."

"Anything to give us leverage over those fools at Chowdhury's."

The coffee scalded Stephanie's lips as she took a sip. "Mmm. I asked him to do some digging for us. He wants to know how the case is progressing and I don't see any harm in that."

Sian nodded. "It's about time we spoke to the agency. I'll call them up and arrange a meeting. If we find out anything useful, we can let Randall know."

"OK, but any contact with Randall must go through you.

I'm happy to flirt with him today, but I don't want to deal with any fallout. Last time around was bad enough."

CHAPTER ELEVEN
The Re-Life Technician

Its official name was 363A Gestation and Manipulation Chamber, but to everyone else it was known as the vat room. The Technician looked across the vast cavern. Rows of transparent vessels curved into the distance. If he stared hard enough, he could make out vague shadows floating within those vessels closest to him, their shapes and sizes corresponding to the degree of development of each duplicate. What was staggering was the sheer scale of the operation, and it was about to get many times larger once the new process was launched.

The Technician stepped away from the portal and relaxed into the control chair. There was a familiar sensation as the neural sensor engaged. Pre-agreed commands flowed into the system and a gigantic insect-like machine climbed the racking in front of him. He smiled to himself. They had thought him mad when he had suggested taking the picker design from the insect world, but it had been proven a masterstroke. Yet they had soon forgotten who had come up with the idea.

Someone had remembered him, though. When the man had first approached, he said that he needed somebody both experienced and trustworthy, somebody who understood the big picture. He had told him that his task would not just secure Re-Life's future, but the future of humanity. Why the man had felt the need to bring up the future of humanity he had no idea, but Re-Life was different. It was human nature to protect one's children.

That had been weeks ago. Since then, he had heard nothing. Nobody had contacted him to ask on progress. Nobody had thanked him for implementing the plan without detection. For all intents and purposes he had been forgotten again. He wasn't sure why it bothered him so much. Rejection wasn't a new feeling. It had been many years since the board had come to listen to him speak, so long in fact that he didn't even know who was in charge of R&D any more. Over time he had become happy to be left to work on his pet projects. Still, he had enjoyed those early years being at the centre of things. At the time the world had been recovering from the chaos caused by the shortsightedness of previous generations. While that danger had waned, another grew, but everybody had been so focussed on the cure they hadn't stopped to think about what came next. Luckily for humanity, and for him, one of the few companies that did was Aristeas plc.

The picker transferred the vessel from its back to the conveyer, where it would be transported to the monitoring station. The high powered MRI and ultrasound scanners delivered detailed analytics indicating that the duplicate was progressing well. There were no signs of abnormality and its development perfectly matched the biotemplate projections. The Technician reviewed the feed plan for the coming weeks and adjusted two specific feeds that would subtly alter the duplicate's brain chemistry. Once the adjustments took effect, he would need to monitor the brain development closely. If the duplicate veered too sharply away from the original biotemplate, alarms would be triggered. He would need to adjust the biotemplate daily to match the growth in the globus pallidus and lateral ventricles that his changes would cause. This was why he was needed; nobody else had the expertise to manage this process without tripping the alarms.

He shut down the control systems, ensuring all evidence of his activity was eradicated, then shuffled off to breakfast.

CHAPTER TWELVE
The Information cleanser

"Hi, can I speak to Delegate Vaughn, please."

"I'm sorry, Delegate Vaughn is busy right now. May I help?"

Randall felt his shoulders tighten. It was obvious that she was avoiding him. He'd not spoken to her once since their meeting despite numerous attempts. He'd tried calling her openly, he'd tried using anonymous filters, but every time he was shunted through to one of her team.

"Can you let her know that Randall Jones would like to speak to her. I'm sure she'll take my call."

"Oh, hi Mr Jones. This is Addy. We spoke earlier. Look, she knows that you called but she's really busy right now."

"Can you tell her it's urgent."

"I'll do that but as I say, she's really tied up. Maybe you could call back later this afternoon. She may be able to talk to you then."

Randall felt his temper bubbling away at the fringes. He took a deep breath. "It is very important I speak to her now."

"I know, Mr Jones, but it's just not possible. Would you like to talk to Sian?"

"No. I'd like to talk to—"

"Then I'll make sure Delegate Vaughn knows you called."

The icon blinked out. Randall sat for a moment, his hand

shaking. It was happening all over again. How had he been so stupid, letting himself fall for her like that? Since their meeting he couldn't stop thinking of her; the shape of her mouth, the look of mischief in her eyes. That one moment when she'd hugged him had felt so right, yet he should have known. Idiot. IDIOT!

His cup flew across the room, smashing against the wall opposite. What had made him think she'd be interested in him again? Why had he thought things would be any different from before? Memories long suppressed rose to the surface. He had loved her so much. She'd been his first love and was still the strongest. The pain of her leaving had torn him apart and now it was happening again. He thought back to the meeting. It would have been obvious if he'd not been blinded by stupidity. He had seen it in her eyes when he'd told her he was an information cleanser. That look of contempt when she'd heard what he'd done with his life, seen the pathetic person he had become.

Randall looked to where his cup had smashed but saw nothing through the tears. His soul ached with remembered pain. No matter how hard he tried to forget, the echoes of his past still shaped his life. For the last couple of weeks she had avoided his calls, refused to speak or meet. He recognised what was happening because it had happened before. She was nothing if not consistent. Back then he'd had no idea of what was about to happen. He was happy, deliriously so at how their relationship was going. He'd even ordered a ring. Then, out of the blue, it had stopped. She wouldn't answer his calls, wouldn't see him. After classes she would race off before he had time to talk. And she had never given a word of explanation, not even after he finally managed to pin her down.

He'd spent years trying to work out what he had done wrong, what was so wrong with him that she had ended it in that way. The question had tortured him, like it tortured him now. His thoughts circled, reinforcing and strengthening the anger and self pity like the folds in worked steel. He was sure that his meeting with Stephanie would have been different if he'd been in charge. It was like before. After months of soul searching he had realised that he'd been weak, meekly going along with whatever she had wanted. He must have been so boring for someone with her strength of character. That was why she had had enough. She was looking for someone stronger, more dynamic, more successful. And yet instead of being able to show her his success, he had come to her as some lackey for that bastard Seegers. The thought of Seegers swelled his anger, amplifying his pain. The bastard had stolen his job when he was at his lowest, taking away everything he'd been working towards, ruining his life. Now he was seen as a nobody, a no-hoper. Not even his team gave him the respect he deserved. He couldn't go on like this. Enough was enough. He'd show her that he was different, that he was strong. He'd show her how worthy he was of her affection. From now on he wasn't putting up with shit from anyone.

CHAPTER THIRTEEN
The Investigator

Nico's eyes felt drained. He had been living on a cocktail of drugs for weeks and was now paying the price. He felt so tired that he had to raise his eyebrows to open his eyes, his eyelids failing to respond to his brain's commands. The case was all falling apart. For three days he'd looked for anything to support their case against Chad Willby. He'd reviewed the footage, step by step, microsecond by microsecond. Remnants of the dreamshaper drug had been found at Chad's home; the digital transformation process morphing Jennica's features onto the porn mannequin were found within Chad's personal files, including the transaction used to purchase the footage. Despite Nico's best efforts, Chad's story held.

It appeared that Chad was a typical teen, his bravado hiding a core of insecurity as he struggled to understand who he really was. By the time Nico had finished interrogating him, reviewing his statement, pressing his answers and challenging his assertions, the boy was broken. He had curled into a ball as his fabricated porn played out on every wall of the interrogation room, horrified and humiliated by what he saw. Each caress, each touch, each grunt and thrust and grind and rut, actions that the dreamshaper drug had converted from image to full sensory experience now added to his humiliation. Nico had used the footage in an attempt to show how sexually obsessed Chad had become with Jennica, saying that it was a visual keepsake, a reminder of what had really happened that night. Chad's protestations only provoked Nico to go harder, pushing Chad over the edge to that all important confession.

It never happened.

Everything they found only served to confirm Chad's story. All evidence pointed to the fact that Chad was innocent. The purchase of the porn footage and digital manipulation were time-stamped at the time that Jennica disappeared. Nico had followed the evidence and it had come up short. He now believed that Chad's true persona was the young man who had chased after Jennica to apologise for his actions. Given a few more years he would have become a model citizen. Sadly, Chad's fate had been sealed the moment he had confronted Jennica. Corey was on the warpath. He wasn't interested in truth, he was interested in statistics. Chad wasn't responsible for Jennica's disappearance, but theft and the possession of dreamshaper were still crimes. It was rule number one at the agency: regardless of whatever you were investigating, if through the course of the investigation you discover other criminal activity, you had to prosecute. Adjacencies was the term the agency used. Corey may not get his confession, but Chad would become yet another profitable transaction for the Chowdhury Crime Agency

Nico jerked upright, woken by a noisy group being guided to the exit.

"You can tell her she's making a big mistake if she supports this change. You're taking away people's vote. The public won't stand for it. There'll be trouble, you mark my words."

A blonde-haired lady was politely, but firmly, ensuring the group left. "You made your opinions very clear. I am sure she will consider what you said."

Sitting next to Nico, Corey seemed oblivious to what was happening across the room, his gaze locked on a poster commemorating the Miracle. Nico thought back to his school days where the importance of the Miracle had been drummed into them. It was the moment in time where world's leaders finally threw off the shackles of self interest and corporate influence. That miracle of a UN resolution provided the template by which humanity recovered from the environmental disasters caused by previous generations. He could still reel off a list of their names, even now.

"See anything interesting?" Nico needed to stimulate his brain otherwise he was in danger of falling asleep again.

"Just a reminder of when politicians had balls," Corey replied. "Are you clear about the meeting?"

"Yes, you'll handle the questions. I only answer those questions directed specifically to me."

"And the overall message?"

"We are progressing well and expect to get a conviction shortly."

"Good. Hopefully if we stick to that we can be out of here without too much damage."

Some chance, thought Nico. Journos had been all over them since their last statement, most likely encouraged by Delegate Vaughn's office. Corey was made out as a figure of fun, fuelling his bad mood. If nothing else, the Aggre's liked a simple narrative.

The blonde woman from earlier walked across to where they sat. "Delegate Vaughn will see you now. If you would like to follow me, please."

Delegate Vaughn's office spoke of power. Her large, antique desk dominated the room, surrounded by books—actual paper books—on law, legislation and the history of the district. Nico's feet sank into the carpet as he stepped into the room. Everything smelt new, fresh, as if the change in representation had brought in more than just a new tenant.

From the doorway, Delegate Vaughn was half hidden by a vase of freshly cut flowers, their colours complementing the decor. She glanced up and indicated for them to take a seat.

"As I've said to you before, Bobby, we are fully aligned. I've been working hard to keep my side of the bargain, I just need to know that you are still on board." She paused a moment, concentrating on what was being said. "Yes, I know your stance on that but I think instant polls are a good thing. At least they'll hold delegates to their promises. Now you'll have to excuse me, I have a couple of visitors. We'll speak soon. Bye."

Delegate Vaughn reached across the desk to shake first Corey's and then Nico's hand. "Thank you for taking some time out of your busy schedules. Things must be difficult right now, what with all the speculation surrounding the case." Nico saw Corey stiffen. "I believe you have already met Sian Tunstall," she pointed to the blonde lady. "Given the amount of public concern, we'd like it very much if you could give us a first-hand account of where you are. I don't think any of us are happy with the way the Aggregators appear to be twisting our statements. We thought it would be better to hear things directly from you, giving you the chance to correct some of what I am sure are misrepresentations."

Nico laughed inwardly to himself. Here's your rope, Corey. Who are you going to hang with it?

"It's always a pleasure to meet with our public representatives," Corey replied, "and may I offer you some belated congratulations on your election. It's good to see new people willing to *serve* the electorate."

Delegate Vaughn nodded, a slight raise of the eyebrows the only indication she had registered the inference.

"Good," Tunstall said. "Then in that spirit of openness, you won't mind telling us how you managed to have a suspect on the verge of a confession, only to release him six hours later."

Corey cleared his throat. "This investigation has not been

straightforward given the time elapsed between the girl going missing and us taking up the case. Despite this, Charles Willby was quickly identified as the prime suspect and, after a short period of time to gather evidence, was taken in for questioning."

"But you now believe he's innocent?" asked Delegate Vaughn.

"No, not at all. However while under questioning, despite admitting to a series of other crimes, the suspect was able to produce an alibi for the time of Jennica Fabian's disappearance."

"So the evidence wasn't there." It was Tunstall again.

"The evidence was there," Corey answered, "however the suspect was able to provide explanations that are in the process of being investigated. We had no choice but to release him as the legal detention limit was up. We will continue further investigations with a view to bringing a prosecution."

"If what you say is true, your incompetence has left him free to attack again?"

Nico could see the whites of Corey's knuckles as he gripped his seat. "We have him under 24 hour surveillance, Ms Tunstall. He won't commit another crime."

"Forgive me if I don't have the same confidence in that prediction as you."

Careful Corey, Nico thought. They're trying to get you angry.

"Do you have any other suspects, Chief Investigator?"

"To date we have tracked down over 1127 different lines of enquiry, leading to 15 suspects who were in a position to abduct Jennica that night." All of which have been shown to have alibis, Nico thought.

"And do you have any evidence to link these people to her disappearance?"

"The evidence-gathering exercise is ongoing."

"And what about Jennica?" asked Delegate Vaughn.

"Have you any idea what has happened to the poor girl?"

"We have been able to fully trace her movements, right up to the point she disappeared."

"Yes, I have seen the footage. So what you are saying is that you have no idea what happened to Jennica, or where she is."

"No, that's not what I said. What I said was—"

"We heard what you said, Chief Investigator," Tunstall interrupted. "What's clear is that you don't have a suspect, you don't have any idea where Jennica is, you don't have any motive, in fact you don't even know whether a crime has been committed at all. What I suggest, Chief Investigator, is that you don't really have a clue."

Corey glared at Tunstall and Vaughn in turn, Adam's apple bobbing as he swallowed his indignation.

"What about you, Mr Tandelli? What do you believe happened that night?"

While Nico had been waiting for his supervisor to explode, all attention had turned to him. He glanced across to Corey but his eyes were fixed on Tunstall, clearly struggling to hold his temper. Nico took a deep breath.

"I don't know."

"At last, an honest answer." Tunstall said, ignoring the man at Nico's side.

"And why don't you know investigator?" asked Delegate Vaughn.

"Because she disappears. She leaves her pod, walks down the road, goes under some trees and disappears. There is a blind spot in surveillance coverage because of the tree canopy, but what's clear is that she goes in but doesn't come out. We've checked everyone who was within a kilometre radius of where she disappeared, from five hours before to five hours afterwards. Nothing goes into that blind spot that can't be traced out again. Nothing, that is, except Jennica."

"How is that possible?"

"It isn't. There's no missing evidence, we have all the

footage available. She just disappears."

Delegate Vaughn leaned forward. "Could anybody have tampered with the footage?"

"No. For a start it's highly encrypted. Secondly, we have footage from a number of different surveillance systems, some public, some private. I don't believe anybody would have the means, or the ability, to change them all."

"What about this suspect then, this Charles Willby?" Tunstall asked.

"It's Chad Willby, everybody calls him Chad."

"This Chad Willby then, why was he a suspect?"

Nico leaned back on his chair. "He'd had an argument with Jennica directly before she went missing, he had a motive, he fit the timeline, and we also had what we believed to be hard evidence linking him to her at his house."

"So why did you let him go?"

"He has an alibi."

"So, unlike Mr Akkerman, you believe him to be innocent."

"We're still continuing our enquiries."

"That's not what I asked, Mr Tandelli. Do you believe he is responsible for the disappearance of Jennica Fabian?"

"No, I don't." Corey shot him a look of pure venom.

Delegate Vaughn looked directly at Corey. "Thank you, Mr Tandelli. We appreciate your candidness." She turned to Tunstall who gave her a barely perceptible nod. "So what now, investigator? How are you planning to proceed with the investigation from here?"

"We will continue to analyse the footage, try to find some detail that we may have missed. We have a number of leads to track…" Nico felt his tiredness wash over him as he spoke. He was facing a hopeless task, his reputation was in tatters, and now had a boss who wanted to kill him.

"So you have in effect hit a brick wall."

He sighed. "It's looking that way, although I've been working as an investigator for many years and I have seen worse situations than this suddenly spring to life as a new piece of evidence is found." He hoped he sounded more confident than he felt.

Delegate Vaughn went to get up.

"I'd just like to add one more thing though, if I may," Nico continued. The Delegate paused, half standing, before sitting down again. "In my opinion we shouldn't be talking about a 'missing girl,' but an abduction. Jennica Fabian hasn't gone anywhere of her own accord. She's been taken, and whoever has taken her has done a bloody good job of covering their tracks."

"Why do you say that, Mr Tandelli?" Vaughn asked.

Corey was looking at him, his mouth a thin line as if he was having to bite his lip to prevent himself from speaking. "Both Chief Investigator Akkerman and myself agree that there is no way Jennica Fabian would choose to disappear in this way. She didn't have the ability to do so, and more importantly, if she had wanted to get away, it would have been much easier if she'd just not returned from her travels. The other point is that the surveillance where she was taken is excellent, except for that small blind spot. Whoever took her must have identified that weakness beforehand. Whoever they were, they knew what they were doing."

"So what do you suggest we do, Mr Tandelli?"

"I suggest we pray Delegate Vaughn, pray that whoever is responsible makes a mistake."

CHAPTER FOURTEEN
The Information Cleanser

He looked across the city from the 17th floor. It was late evening and soon the city lights would go out. Today the Aurora Borealis was predicted to arrive and everybody was excited. Randall, though, couldn't care less.

This past week had been hell. He was meant to be leading his team as they finalised the Re-Life 2 launch, the group of them forced to work together in an office so Seegers could keep an eye on them. It should have been the perfect chance to forget, but his task of tracking the investigation meant that all he did was think about Stephanie. She was there, at every pause, at every unguarded moment with that contemptuous look on her face as she'd realised how pathetic he was.

It didn't help that there was nothing to do. Their initial policy of hitting everything hard had been effective so the team were mostly twiddling their thumbs; sniping at each other and laughing at him behind his back. They must think he was stupid. No, they did think he was stupid. Part of him, the Randall of the past, wanted to walk away. But he refused to succumb. He'd had enough of all that bullshit, enough of absorbing all the crap that they threw at him. He would show them how he had changed.

The team were planning to meet up on the hotel roof terrace to watch the show. They had invited him, but he knew they were hoping he wouldn't come. They had avoided him where possible most of the week, aware that his mood had darkened. Even Lise. Well at least he didn't have to listen to her moaning about the wedding.

The last few rays of sun highlighted some gulls on the apartment block opposite. Two birds were fighting over a scrap of food, pulling at each end, wings flapping in their battle for control. A third bird swooped down, startling one of the pair, allowing the other to wrestle the food away and launch itself from the roof. Randall followed the gull as it flew towards the park, hoping the bird choked on its unfairly won meal.

Randall caught a shadow out of the corner of his eye. Turning around he saw Sylvianne standing beside him. "Mr Seegers would like to see you, he's in his office." She didn't look happy. Randall wasn't surprised; it was demeaning being used as a messenger.

Seegers sat staring at a wall, his attention elsewhere. Randall knocked. "You wanted to see me." There were no other chairs, so Randall was forced to stand awkwardly while he waited for Seegers to finish. His boss appeared agitated.

"Yes, yes, the cost is justifiable given the increase in productivity and the importance of the launch. We will still be under budget at the end, I can assure you." He paused for a moment, "Yes, I said that already, everything will be OK." He turned, noticing Randall for the first time. "Look, he's here now. I have to go. We'll catch up later."

Randall didn't know what was said on the other end of the line, but a flash of irritation crossed Seegers' face. Then those dead eyes focussed on Randall. "What's happening with the missing girl case?"

"There's nothing to tell. The last time I spoke to Stephanie's office they said that enquiries were ongoing." The same answer every day, he thought. Not from Stephanie, though. He fought to suppress the anger trickling up from his gut.

"When was the last time you spoke?" Seegers asked.

"Yesterday morning. They promised that if anything new cropped up, I would be the first to know."

"I'm surprised you haven't called them today. If it was me, I'd be onto them every few hours."

"I thought I'd wait until midmorning before trying again."

"You do know how important it is that this case is resolved, don't you?"

Randall could feel bile burning the back of his throat. "That's why I've been chasing them every day since the meeting."

"As I said, I would be talking to them every hour, pushing to find anything new."

But it isn't you, Randall thought. It's me doing the chasing. I'm the menial. He swallowed down the anger threatening to erupt. "With respect, I think that would be counterproductive. You can be sure that once they make a breakthrough, I'll be onto them hourly asking for updates."

"Well, I disagree. I want you to call them hourly from now on until you get somewhere."

"I don't think that is a good idea."

"This isn't a debate, Randall. Just do it." Mr Seegers looked down at his desk, waving his hand to dismiss him.

"Didn't you hear me? I don't think it's the right thing to do. I've given you my opinion, I know the people involved, and yet you ignore me. Do you think I'm stupid?" Randall could hear the pitch and volume of his voice rise with each question, but he didn't care. He'd had enough of being treated like shit.

Seegers let out a deep breath and stood. "I'm not sure how we got to this place, Randall, but you need to calm down. Why don't you go back to your desk, and we talk about this once you've had a chance to think."

"I don't want to go back to my desk, I want you to bloody well listen for once."

"OK, if that's how you want it, but I need a drink first." Seegers walked past Randall and into the main office.

Randall raced up to Seegers, grabbing his arm and pulling him around. "Where the bloody hell do you thing you're going? We haven't finished talking."

All activity in the office stopped. Seegers's eyes were wide in shock. He tried to shrug out of Randall's grip, but Randall refused to budge.

"Randall, let go."

"Not until you tell me why you're treating me this way."

Seegers glanced to his left. The office had come to a standstill, their argument flicking a switch, pausing all activity. Randall realised he was on a precipice. If he successfully stood up to Seegers, the team were his. If not, he had lost them forever.

"Let's go back into my office."

"What is it with you? Why do you always ignore anything I have to say? Do you have any idea what it's like, having your expertise treated like shit?"

"I'm not prepared to discuss this with you here, Randall."

"Why not? It's not as if I'm the only one who feels this way." Randall looked across to his team, expecting nods of agreement, but they stood motionless; some staring, others unable or unwilling to make eye contact.

Seegers gently placed his hand on Randall's shoulder, a false look of concern on his face. "Randall, we just had a disagreement, that's all. I gave you a free hand to deal with this but for whatever reason it hasn't worked. It's important that we get a resolution to the issue, which is why I asked you to increase the pressure."

"Don't try to make out you're being reasonable. This has nothing to do with finding a resolution and you know it. You're just shoving it in my face that you got the job and I didn't."

A strange expression crossed Seegers' features. "I think you'd better stop before you end up somewhere you really don't want to go."

"Why should we stop? I'm not worried. I've done nothing to be ashamed of."

"Randall, please."

"What are you worried about? It's not like it's a secret. Everyone here knows what happened."

"This isn't the place—"

"They know what you did."

"Randall—"

"I mean, what sort of man takes advantage of the break up of his best friend's marriage to get a promotion?"

"That's not true—"

"What does it tell you about a person, that when their best friend is at their lowest they stab them in the back?" Betrayal upon betrayal. Randall's memory of that time was hazy—he'd not coped well with what had happened—but he remembered the bitterness he'd felt to learn that Thijs would be his new boss, and the anger from that memory pushed him harder. "You took advantage of me. When I needed help the most, you helped yourself instead." His vision blurred as he spoke. "You were my friend."

"Stop Rand, please." Lise had run forward from her desk to take his arm, tears in her eyes. Why was she interrupting?

"Stay out of this."

"You've got it wrong, Rand. Please, just stop," she said.

Randall didn't understand. Why was Lise taking Seegers' side?

"You were exhausted," Seegers said. "It was a very hard time for you. We were all worried."

"Worried enough to take advantage when Jane left."

"Jane left before this happened. You were working all hours to get the promotion but what with the stress and your addiction… she couldn't deal with it."

"You broke down when you didn't get the promotion." There were tears flowing down Lise's face. Why was she so upset? "The doctors said it was best if you forgot, that you would heal quicker that way." She turned to Seegers. "They said he wouldn't remember any of this."

Randall tried to think but his mind just wouldn't work. Nothing they said made sense. Why were they lying? He looked at Seegers, then Lise, then around the room. Everybody had the same condescending looks on their faces. Why wasn't anybody supporting him?

Because they weren't his anymore.

A moment of clarity broke through. They had never been his. They knew who was the alpha male and it wasn't him. The humiliation was too much. Randall pushed past Seegers and walked out of the office.

Betrayal, after betrayal, after betrayal. Stephanie, then Seegers, then Jane. Now he could add Lise to the list. What they said made no sense. Jane had left him *after* his breakdown, after he'd failed to get the promotion. Their relationship had never been easy, she had always felt insecure, jealous even; a part of her sensing that he'd never stopped loving Stephanie. That was the irony, that *she* had left *him*. Randall tried to think back to the day she left but he felt like he was grasping at smoke. He knew it had happened, but his memory of it was insubstantial.

He heard footsteps from behind. "Mr Jones, are you OK?" It was Sylvianne.

Randall stopped. Sylvianne approached, holding out her arms as if to comfort him. He flinched. "Did you enjoy that? Are you happy, now that you've got what you want?"

"Happy? Why would I be happy?"

"Come on, you've never liked me. I've leant over backwards to welcome you and you've only ever been cold in return."

"That's not true."

"Yes it is. All you're interested in is your career. I bet you loved that little performance, real corporate power in action eh? Well if that's the sort of thing that turns you on, good luck to you. Now go snuggle up to Mr Seegers."

Her expression hardened. "I only wanted to see if you were OK."

"Well, now you know. I hope you're happy."

Randall watched her leave, then made his way to the elevators. There was a bar back at the hotel. He could get pissed on the company's expense. At least they were good for something. He tapped repeatedly on the elevator call button.

"Rand? We need to talk."

Why did you do it, Lise? Why did it have to be you? "Go away Lise, I want to be alone."

"You shouldn't be alone; trust me, it's the last thing you need."

He turned. "I don't want to be with you."

"Tough. I care too much about you to see you go and do something stupid."

"You care too much? I didn't see you care earlier. You didn't back me up. You didn't tell that bastard to stop lying. Not a lot of caring going on then, was there?"

"Come on Rand, that's not fair."

"Not fair, I'll tell you what's not fair. Having to listen to you whining about your bloody wedding and how you can't get your way, day in, day out. How about that for not fair?" Tears fell down Lise's face as he spoke. Typical woman, he thought, expecting tears to get her out of trouble. "Well here is what I really think. Don't get married. Call it off. You're both behaving like kids, fighting about who's attending and what colour the flowers are. It's pathetic. You aren't ready and I don't think you ever will be. All relationships end up in pain and yours has pain written all over it."

The slap knocked him sideways, the sting acting like a cold bucket of water to the heat of his rage. Why had he said that? As his anger cleared Randall realised he was looking at his last true friend. "Look, I'm sorry, I—" He went to take her hand but she pulled away.

"Go fuck yourself."

The final look of disdain before she left stabbed into him. Was this how it was going to be? Would he end up pushing away those he liked for the rest of his life? The bell for the elevator rang and Randall stepped inside, his body moving on instinct. Why had she backed up Seegers? Could it be true what she had said?

Outside the street was pitch black, and it took a moment for his vision to adjust. He saw an empty pod approach and flagged it down.

"The White Hart Hotel."

Randall tried to think, to remember what had happened at the time of his break up, but it was if he faced a closed door. In his core he believed his memories to be true, but what Lise had said had really shaken him. Could she be right? Had he really been at fault? He pushed the thought away, the implications too huge to think about, questioning the foundation of who he was.

Rather than take the thought further, Randall stared out into the street. All was dark. The pod headlights picked out people standing on the pavements in groups. Why were they huddled in groups in the dark?

The slight whisper of light bathed the street giving everything a phosphorescent hue. The glow intensified until it became almost dazzling. Randall looked up, speaking the command to see through the roof. There were pulsing waves of billowing light overhead, like ghostly sails fluttering on the astral breeze. It was the most beautiful thing he had ever seen. The streets were full of people, many open mouthed as the Aurora Borealis weaved it's magic. As he travelled through the city centre, the shimmering light seemed to make the buildings dance, performing a jig to the ghostly display. Randall sat mesmerised, all thoughts of what had just happened banished as he succumbed to the immensity of the display. He tried to predict where the lights would appear next, but it was as hopeless as trying to pin down memories of his breakup. Instead, Randall let the show wash over him.

A change in direction brought Randall back to himself. They were on the clearway on the outskirts of the city. His pod swerved to the right, the seat swelling to catch his momentum. His breath caught as it always did as the pod crossed the stream of vehicles coming the other way.

Randall's instincts screamed at him that something was wrong. His subconscious reacted quickest, seeing that the nearest pod was much too close. He managed a half inhaled breath, looking to shout a warning, when darkness took him.

CHAPTER FIFTEEN
The Politician

"I am pleased to confirm that the Global Electoral Standard implementation is moving ahead smoothly."

The Legislature erupted with cheers from the government side of the chamber. The Prime Delegate's smile never wavered as he waited for the noise to subside.

"The operating systems are in place and nearly 90 percent of the population are now linked," he continued.

"What about those without datasphere access?" The shout brought a rumble of derision from the government seats.

The Placater raised her hands. "Quiet please! There will be time for questions once the Prime Delegate finishes his statement."

There was a low murmur of discontent throughout the chamber. Public anger at the way the system was being implemented had grown in recent weeks and many delegates were worried about their positions.

"Thank you Madam Placater, but I am happy to answer the point. As previously reported, we have established a network of public terminals to allow those without datasphere access to register their views. This has come at considerable cost to the taxpayer. What this means is that everybody will have access to the most transparent electoral system this country has ever seen, bringing to completion the move from five year voting cycles to ongoing monitoring and accountability."

The roar of approval shook the bench she was sitting on. Stephanie found it hard not to be swept up in the moment. This was pure political theatre, and Richard Asquith, the Prime Delegate, was giving a master class.

Asquith pointed to the opposition. "When we announced our plan to implement the Global Electoral System, this lot said it couldn't be done." Mocking laughter erupted from the government benches. "Once the technology was developed, they then said we couldn't hit the agreed timescales." More laughter. "Now the technology is in place ahead of schedule, they say the process is flawed. The very same process that is being implemented in over 70 percent of countries around the world, including all major democracies. A process that has an approval rating in this country of over 75 percent. Yet they expect us to believe that they are right and the electorate—not just in this country, but the rest of the world—is wrong!"

Asquith waited serenely as the cheering erupted once more, then raised his arms in imitation of the Placater. The noise subsided as the chamber looked at him expectantly. Stephanie found herself edging forward in her seat. Asquith clicked his fingers.

"My fellow Delegates, with that click, the Global Electoral System is in operation." A few delegates cheered but Asquith signalled for quiet. He looked across to the other side of the hall. "I would like to offer some advice to my colleagues opposite. I suggest you re-think your opposition to this system, otherwise your only future involvement in politics will be to answer polling questions!"

The roar was deafening. The Prime Delegate sat down and the Placater approached the dais, holding her hands in the air in an attempt to bring order back to the chamber. Sitting next to the Prime Delegate, Delegate Gant leaned across and shook his hand.

The hubbub subsided and the slight figure of the opposition leader rose from her seat. She looked pale and out of her depth in the face of such grandstanding.

"The Prime Delegate may be keen to congratulate himself on the speed in which this system has been implemented, yet he failed to mention how much the whole thing cost and whether it was delivered within budget. The latest figures from the Statistical Office show that the project cost 30 percent more than publicised; the equivalent of 25 new schools. What does the Prime Delegate have to say about that?"

A murmur of support came from behind, although muted in comparison to before.

"I'd like to thank Delegate Hayes for pointing out the cost of the project," Asquith replied. "What she fails to mention is that the agreed budget projections she's talking about were published before the additional network of terminals was added to the project; an addition requested by the opposition."

Hayes rose to reply. There was movement from the seats in front of Stephanie and voices were raised as a familiar figure stood to speak, turning to laughter in some areas, particularly where the government sat.

"Please retain your seat," the Placater said. "If you have a point to make, you will have your chance."

"I will not sit down. The excluded deserve a voice in this debate." Bobby Maddison's voice rose above the noise. A look of irritation crossed the face of the opposition leader but it was clear that attention was now on the maverick delegate. With some resignation, she signalled that he could speak.

"All this talk of budgets and cost is just a sideshow," Maddison said. "You talk about this process being adopted in other countries, but you don't talk about how. Nearly every country to adopt this system first implemented a programme to ensure datasphere access for all. Without it, you end up with a political system that excludes the poor."

Second Chance

There were pockets of support from around the chamber to what he had said. Another delegate stood, her face red with anger. "How this has been implemented is criminal. My district is not wealthy. Over 40 percent of the electorate there do not have continuous datasphere access. How can you say that excluding these people from the political process improves democracy?"

"Exactly," Maddison answered. "What this government has done is roll back hundreds of years of political emancipation in the name of progress. We haven't had a system so skewed to the wealthy since the 1700s. It is a disgraceful piece of legislation implemented in a disgraceful way by a disgraceful government"

There were angry shouts, not just from where the government sat, but around where Delegate Maddison was standing. Stephanie looked back to where Gant and the Prime Delegate were sitting, expecting to see anger. Instead, Gant looked amused and whispered something in the Prime Delegate's ear, making him laugh.

The Placater rose once more. "I would like to remind the Delegate to keep all discourse civil in this chamber."

"Civil? Why should I be civil? Is it civil to create a political underclass? Is it civil to ignore the poor? There is anger on the streets of our major cities and in the countryside, real anger. Just because people are poor, it does not mean they're stupid. They know when they are being shafted, and they know who is responsible. What I'd like to know is who designed the implementation plan, the government or their political paymasters?"

A groan arose from the chamber, including many that had previously agreed with Maddison. Stephanie tried to see how many delegates remained unmoved. Anybody who could listen to Bobby's arguments and ignore the conspiracy theories could be open enough to vote against the government's budget proposal. She mumbled a quick memo containing the names of those delegates to report back to

James.

"You may mock, but why has the government gone in such a different direction to everyone else?"

Shouts of 'sit down' and 'boring' attempted to interrupt his flow. Face red with anger, Maddison didn't miss a beat.

"This has nothing to do with cost and everything to do with fear. Fear that the people will realise they are being duped. Fear that the electorate will see through the sham."

More laughter followed. Bobby Maddison glared at his colleagues. "Don't be mistaken. The people are angry and their memories are long. They remember what happened the last time the political classes were more interested in the will of big business than the will of the people. If this system is implemented, there will be blood on the streets. You can't suppress the will of the people. There will be blood on the streets and don't be surprised if some of that blood belongs to you."

The roar that erupted from the chamber had a palpable presence. Delegates from all areas jumped up to shout their disgust at what had been said. Some around Maddison tried to manhandle him back into his seat. The Placater was on her feet, calling for calm, but the anger ran unabated. Stephanie had never seen anything like it. She spotted a number of colleagues, people she would never have believed could get so emotional, screaming at Maddison as if he had threatened to kill them personally. One delegate spat at him from behind. There was one group of delegates, though, smiling at the uproar. What was Gant up to? she wondered.

A loud blast reverberated around the chamber, the shock so violent that delegates shrank away from the sound, covering their ears. Like a ship's horn, the noise continued to blare until the chamber was still. In the following silence, the Placater rose, her face pale but angry. "In over 25 years of serving our country I have never had to resort to such measures to retain order, yet your conduct leaves me no other choice.

"This session is closed. I will launch an investigation as to whether any Legislative rules have been broken, and if so, I will ensure that those involved will face the full force of any sanctions. That will be all."

The lobby was a crush by the time Stephanie exited the chamber. Some delegates appeared shocked at the way the debate had been halted, others bemused. Fighting through the crush came the Journos, scenting a story like salmon scenting their spawning ground. Stephanie veered away from the central lobby and headed towards a small access corridor. It was meant for serving staff, but today Stephanie wasn't bothered about protocol. She knew from experience that the wait for an elevator would be excruciating.

"Delegate Vaughn. I wonder if I could have a word."

Stephanie looked up, smiling at the handsome figure of Delegate Gant. As usual he was trailed by his security staff. "Delegate Gant. I'd be delighted. Shall we go to my office?"

"No need for that. I think here will do." He smoothly took her arm and guided her through a side door, the guards waiting outside. So, this is to be a private meeting, she thought, her pulse racing.

They were in an old storage room, half filled floor to ceiling with chairs, the odd table scattered here and there. The air smelt dry and dusty. It was clear nobody had used the room for some time.

"If you'd wanted to be alone, you only had to ask." Stephanie raised her eyebrows in mock anger.

"Funny, I've been asking your office for a meeting for a number of days now but you're always busy."

The smile remained but for once it didn't reach those pale, blue eyes. Bloody Sian, Stephanie thought. "I'm so sorry. My staff are a little overprotective. I'll make sure they know to put you through in future."

"Thank you."

"So is this business or pleasure?"

"A bit of both, actually."

Gant was standing close enough for Stephanie to smell the sweetness of his breath. Reaching up, she gently brushed some dust that had fallen on his lapel. "Why don't we talk business first, then…" She had been looking forward to this moment. A little flirt, a look, a knowing smile…

"I understand that you're planning to vote against the budget proposals next month, and that you're actively persuading others to take your side. The Prime Delegate would very much prefer for this not to happen."

Stephanie froze. This was the last thing she wanted to talk about. She tried to think back to Sian's briefings. "I'm not sure what you mean."

Gant pressed closer, his smile gone. "Please, Stephanie. Don't treat me like I'm an idiot."

"Come on, Zachary." She gave him her best impish smile. "You don't mind if I call you Zachary? I've no argument with the government. I'd be more happy to support the Prime Delegate's cause if it was in the best interests of my district. As far as I am aware, the details of the budget proposal haven't been made public, so I can't form an opinion until they have."

Gant's face hardened. "This isn't a game. You've somehow found out that the proposal includes a number of capital projects, so you've decided to try and overturn the bill. Isn't that right?"

The warmth from earlier had evaporated. Stephanie took a step backwards, looking for space in which to think, but Gant followed. Was he was bluffing or did he really know this? And if he did know what they were planning, where the hell he got his information from?

"Look, if what you say is true I may have a few issues, but I'm sure we can work them out. Why don't we go back to my office and talk this through." She looked up at him, smiling. "Then, once we've reached a compromise, we can move onto the other reason you wanted to speak to me."

"No."

Stephanie found herself pushed hard against the wall. She tried to move away but Gant's grip was solid.

"This is the last time I'm going to ask nicely. If you support the proposed budget you have nothing to worry about. If not, well things can get tough, especially for a new delegate who has a number of issues in their district."

"Get off, Zachary. You're hurting me."

"I mean, you're in a bit of a mess at the moment. Take that missing girl, the Re-Life researcher. Imagine what would happen if some Journos pointed out how little progress has been made since you threw your weight behind the case. It wouldn't look good, would it?"

Stephanie looked up at Gant. "You think threatening me with bad headlines is going to make me change my mind?"

Gant sighed, his look almost disappointed as he smashed her head back against the wall, sending a shockwave of pain through her body. Stephanie's scream was cut short as Gant's hand covered her mouth. She tried to shake him off but his bulk pushed against her. Slowly, Gant leant forward and whispered in her ear.

"I did warn you."

Stephanie felt a jolt as he wrenched her arm behind her back. This couldn't be happening. Not here. Her body, until now frozen by shock, reacted. She kicked out, causing a stack of chairs to come crashing down. The door, she had to get to the door. But it remained shut. They must have heard the noise, she thought. Why aren't they coming?

The world lurched and Stephanie found herself face down onto a table, Gant's bulk crushing the air from her lungs. Panic took hold as the reality of what was happening crashed in on her. Stephanie tried to shout but Gant's crushing weight plus his hand across her mouth made it impossible. Her head started to swim. She felt dizzy. The world started to fade and the pain in her arm dropped to a dull ache.

The pressure on her face disappeared and Stephanie sucked in a breath. As the air hit her lungs, sensation bludgeoned into her brain. She felt Gant's fingers claw at her thigh. In desperation she tried once more to kick out but she felt so weak, his weight sapping her strength.

"Don't tell me you haven't wanted this. It's not like you've made a secret of it, you dirty fucking slut."

Stephanie felt him yank her knickers down, then gasped in pain as he forced his fingers inside. Her mind baulked at what was happening, refusing to collaborate. She felt a savage thrusting, attacking her body and despoiling her soul. The attack on her body was nothing compared to the rape of her psyche. Her mind pulled away from what was happening, becoming an observer to her own assault. She relinquished control, laying numb until the only things moving were the tears running down her face.

It stopped as quickly as it began. Gant's grip on her arm relaxed but Stephanie remained where she was. There was a shift in his weight and for a moment Stephanie prepared herself for another attack. Instead, she felt him gently tuck a lock of hair behind her ear, almost as a caress.

"I suggest you think about who you want as your friends around here," Gant whispered. He tilted her head gently with both hands and smiled, almost tenderly, before slowly licking her from chin to cheek.

He got up and Stephanie sagged to the floor. She watched him adjust his jacket, smiling down at her as if nothing had happened. Behind him the door remained shut. It felt a million miles away.

"I think you get the message. It can be a little confusing when you are starting out; so many different people, so many interests that are intertwined. It's hard to know who you are dealing with. New delegates can get themselves into all sorts of trouble." He turned and walked to the door. "Please pass on my regards to Delegate Maddison."

The door shut behind him leaving Stephanie alone in the

room, her body shaking. Tears of anger and frustration flowed down her face, and it took some time before she was able to move.

"Hello Stephanie. That session looked pretty serious from the footage. Were you close to—" James looked up from his desk, then jumped to his feet. "Christ, you look terrible. Are you OK?"

She tried to smile, walking slowly to her desk before sitting down, her legs still shaky. She'd tried to scrub his scent from her body, yet no matter how much soap she had used she still couldn't get Gant's smell from her nostrils. "Can you get me a drink please."

"Coffee?"

"Do we have anything stronger?"

James walked to a cabinet and pulled out a bottle. He spoke but Stephanie couldn't focus, her mind back in the storage room, going over what had happened, wondering how she had let herself get into that situation.

"Stephanie? Are you sure everything is OK?"

"What? Yes, fine."

James held the bottle in front of her. "I've no idea what this is, it was a left over from by the last delegate who had the office. It smells strong though."

He poured the liquid into a cup and passed it to Stephanie. The burning sensation as it went down brought on a fit of coughing. The drink was foul but it had the effect she wanted, jolting her thoughts out of their cycle of shame. She wondered for a moment whether to call Sian, but then put the thought out of her mind. It was her word against three, plus saying anything would put Sian at risk and she couldn't do that to her friend. No, this was something she would have to deal with herself.

"Gant knows about our plan to oppose the budget proposal. He told me not to do it."

James' eyes widened. "How did he find out?"

"No idea. I didn't ask and I don't think he would have told me if I had." She could feel the slug-like sensation of his tongue on her cheek and came close to vomiting. No, not now, not here. She dug her nails into the palm of her hand to help her concentrate.

"What did you say to him?"

"Nothing. He asked me to pass on my regards to Bobby Maddison, though."

James shrugged. "Well we knew it was likely to happen at some point. I wouldn't worry about it. Now that we've got their attention we should use this opportunity to negotiate."

The urge to tell James almost overcame her: her fear, her anger, the feeling of helplessness she had felt as Gant had pressed himself against her. Walking out of that storeroom was the bravest thing she had ever done. The corridor had been empty, but there were still a few familiar faces around as she walked into the lobby. One or two had held their hands up in greeting, but she'd ignored them; desperate to get away from the store room, desperate to clean off his stink. She couldn't stop reliving the attack in her mind, trying to see if she could have done anything differently. Why had she allowed herself to get into that situation? Had there been an opportunity to stop it from happening? She went through the conversation they'd had before the attack once more, then stopped.

"James, could you give me a minute?"

James nodded, leaving the room.

Stephanie made a call. "Sian, it's Steph. Have you told anyone about Re-Life?"

"Re-Life?"

"The missing girl. Did you tell anyone about what Randall said?"

"No, no-one. I haven't even thought of it since Randall stopped calling. Why do you ask?"

"The government know what we're up to."

Second Chance

"It was always a risk."

Stephanie turned the cup in her hands. It had a picture of the old Houses of Parliament, Big Ben tower jutting out over the swollen Thames. It was part of a commemorative set sent to all new delegates, a reminder of their obligations. Stephanie looked at the picture and made up her mind.

"I'm going to ask James to go through the budget rounds for the last ten years. He's to look at what was said before, who was openly against it and how they voted plus anything of interest afterwards."

"Why would you want him to do that? If the government are worried, which they clearly are, now would be the perfect time to negotiate. If we get some form of movement out of them, it would play really well with the electorate."

"Keep an eye on James for me. Make sure he doesn't speak to anyone but us two."

"What? Surely you don't believe Maddison's conspiracy theories? Now's the time to negotiate."

Stephanie dropped her voice to a near whisper, but she couldn't remove the anger. "You got me into this place to change the system, yet the first chance we get you want to give in? Well I don't like being pushed around and I won't bow down to threats. If we give in now they'll just do it again and again, and I won't let that happen. Do I have your backing?"

There was silence for a moment. "OK, talk to James. I'll take it from there."

It was late by the time Stephanie arrived home. She closed and locked the front door, shouting to the house central command unit to blank out all windows. She then went from room to room to check that her command had been properly acted upon before checking both doors once again to make sure they were locked. Once in her bedroom, she took off her clothes and threw them in the waste disposal. She then showered, scrubbing her body to ensure that every last trace of Gant was removed. When she closed her eyes to rinse her hair it hit her again. Her arm wrenched behind her back, the feeling of helplessness as he pushed himself upon her. His breath filled her nostrils once more. Why hadn't she screamed, bitten him, stamped on his foot? Again and again she thought of all the things she could have done, disgusted with her submission. She started shaking, her body rebelling against the memory of what had happened. Then her shaking turned to sobs, and she slumped to the floor, hot water streaming down her face and mingling with her tears.

Stephanie sat on her sofa; each sip of brandy burning a trail to her core. The tears had been necessary, but never again. She refused to be a victim. If she went down that route her life would be over. If she submitted to the impulse to curl up and cry then he had won. She couldn't do that. She couldn't submit. She had to take control.

She thought about approaching an agency, making it official, but it was her word against his. Nobody had seen the two of them enter the room, nobody except his security and they wouldn't say a thing. If she lodged a complaint with no proof, the only person who would lose would be her. She wasn't stupid. She needed to find another way, something that he wouldn't expect. She made a call.

"Hello?"

"Investigator Tandelli, it's Stephanie Vaughn, do you have a minute?"

'Er, sure. Can you give me a moment." In the background, Stephanie heard the sound of a child crying. Gradually the sound receded. "That's better. What can I do for you, Delegate?"

"Please, call me Stephanie."

"OK, Stephanie. You'll have to excuse me but I'm a bit surprised by your call. Are you sure you wouldn't prefer to talk to Chief Investigator Akkerman?"

"Quite sure."

"This is a little awkward for me..."

"Investigator Tandelli, I understand how you feel but I promise that your boss won't find out about this conversation. I want to talk to you because I believe I can trust you. Can I?"

There was a pause. For a moment Stephanie thought he was going to stop the call. "You can."

"Thank you. I have some information that might be of use. It may be nothing but... Were you aware that Jennica Fabian was doing research on Re-Life?"

"No. Are you sure?"

"I've had it confirmed from two very different sources. One, an old friend of mine, told me that all records linking Jennica to Re-Life have been wiped from the datasphere because Re-Life were worried about the damage to their brand if they were connected to a crime."

"That's one hell of a confession."

"I know. He came to me because he said that he had the ability to look deeper into the data, to see if it is whole or if it's been corrupted in some way."

"We would know if that had been the case." There was annoyance in the investigator's voice.

"Like you knew that she worked for Re-Life?" Stephanie took another sip of the brandy while she waited for his reply. She didn't blame him for taking his time, it had been hard enough for her to believe Randall.

"Who is your other source?"

"I can't tell you that."

Another pause. "OK. I'll have to confirm it for myself before I do anything, and I'd need to speak to this friend of yours as well."

"I can put you in contact with him on the condition that you don't prosecute."

"You're asking a lot."

"That's the deal."

"OK. I can manage that."

"Good, then I'll send you his details."
"Thank you Delegate Vaughn.

Part 2

The Past

A noise made Josh jump. No, not yet. He needed more time. He glanced down the corridor. It was empty, the noise coming from elsewhere. He returned to his screen, fingers drumming on the desk. Why now? They were so close. Why did the bastard have to die now?

The day had started so well. News of a UN agreement was greeted first with incredulity, then with delight. Somehow, the world's leaders had agreed a blueprint for action; not the usual bullshit compromise but real, lasting change. The major news corporations were falling over themselves to condemn the agreement, but for many, especially the scientific community, it was seen as a miracle. Then came the news that the man he worked for, the stone man, had died and that their efforts had been in vain.

Josh had made the decision in an instant. He couldn't take the gamble that the stone man's family would continue their investment now that he was dead. Why would they? Fibrodysplasia ossificans progressiva was so rare that they would never get a return on their investment. Once he was buried everything would be shut down, and his work was much too valuable to be kept in storage.

It was so frustrating. They had been so close. Josh picked up the specimen jar, turning it in his hands. The foetus was small but fully formed. Any paediatrician in the country would have told you it was around 18 weeks old. They would have been wrong. The foetus had died just 12 hours after conception. His colleagues had been amazed at his results, the speed of growth was way beyond anything they had experienced. They were fools, blinkered by their preconceived ideas of what was, and what wasn't possible. If they'd had his background in oncology, they would know that the human body was capable of incredible growth rates. The challenge was how to control that growth. This foetus was proof that it could be done. He just needed a chance to perfect the technique.

A door opened down the corridor, the noise causing him to almost drop the jar. Hands shaking, Josh closed the download screen. While the threat of dismissal was no longer an issue, he still needed to get his data out of the compound. The footsteps grew louder, then Kyle walked in.

"Hey Josh. You didn't fancy it either?"

"Couldn't see the point, not now."

His colleague walked to the window, his attention captured by the sound of a scramjet roaring overhead. "Matt seemed to think we'd be mothballed."

"Matt would know."

"I've never seen him open up like that before. You know how he is; not one to say anything outside of the official line."

"There is no official line any more."

With Kyle's back to him, Josh flicked to the download screen. Two more minutes. Two more minutes and he was out of here.

"I don't know what to do. If they shut this place down…"

Josh looked up from his screen. Kyle was a good guy, not the brightest but competent. You could give a task to Kyle and you knew it would be delivered. It seemed today was a day for snap decisions.

"Why don't you come with me?"

Kyle turned from the window. "You're going?"

"Mike's right. There's no future here. In a few weeks it will be over. Going now means getting a head start on the others."

"But there's nothing out there. There are no jobs. Nobody is investing in research anymore, not with things as they are. Who wants to invest in the future when we don't even know if we have one?"

"Not everyone thinks like that. I was approached a couple of weeks ago. You could come with me if you want."

"I don't know. It's not like we know for certain what will happen here."

"They've offered me really good money, my own lab... I can make you part of the deal. All we need to do is bring our work with us and—"

"You're planning to steal the work?" Kyle stared at him, clearly shocked.

"It's my work. Our work. *They're* not going to use it. The family have never been interested in what we do. They just see us as a drain on their inheritance. Just think what we could do with the proper backing. Instead of looking to cure a disease that affects a handful of people, we could be making a difference to millions."

"It's still theft."

Why was Kyle being like this? Didn't he care about what they had done, what more they could achieve? Josh wondered once more if he was truly part of the human race or another species entirely. He didn't understand why other people allowed emotion to get in the way of their decision making. It was wasteful, counter-intuitive. It wasn't that he didn't feel emotion, it was just that he didn't allow emotion to influence his thinking. It had taken him a long time to realise that others felt differently. It was a hard lesson to learn. Still, once he had learnt, it didn't take him long to realise that he could use that emotional reflex to get what he wanted. He checked the download screen. Only seconds remained. "You think it's right to hide our work from the world?"

Kyle didn't answer.

"Come with me. Why show loyalty to a family who will drop you as soon as the stone man's body is in the ground. You don't owe them anything. What about your family, surely they should be your priority now?"

Kyle grimaced, then nodded. "You're right. It's just..."

Josh pocketed the data crystal. "If you're coming, you'd better gather up your things. I've got everything I need."

Kyle walked to his workspace, pulling out his wallet and car keys from the drawer. "So who is it that approached you?"

"A company called Aristeas."

"Never heard of them."

CHAPTER SIXTEEN
The Investigator

Jennica's apartment was on the second floor of what once had been a grand Victorian town house. The communal hall was clogged with the detritus of student living. Nico carefully picked his way up the stairs to her door and knocked.

"Who is it?"

He held up his ID to the camera. "Hello Debbie. It's Investigator Tandelli. We spoke yesterday. I need to ask you a few more questions. Can I come in?"

The first thing Nico noticed as the door opened was the cloying fug of stale sweat and refuse coming from the apartment. Debbie stood in the hallway. Her clothes were grubby and creased and she had dark smudges under her red-rimmed eyes. As she brought a tissue to her nose Nico noticed grime under her nails. She was a world away from the smiling girl pictured with her arm around Jennica.

"Have you found her?"

"No, not yet."

Debbie seemed to deflate, what little life she had flowing out with his reply. "Then why are you here?"

"Can I come in?"

She shrugged, then stepped to one side, trampling the flyers and leaflets wedged behind the door. Nico walked into the apartment. It was a mess. Dirty clothes spilled out of a laundry basket like fungus from a rotting log. Discarded plates and cutlery lay unwashed and ignored. A thick layer of dust covered everything. Debbie led Nico to the living room. On a shelf behind her was a candle surrounded by photographs of Jennica. Alongside was a hair clip and a small stuffed toy and a vase of dead flowers, a pile of petals slowly mouldering at its base. Nico moved a carton of take-out rice and sat.

"I've told you everything that happened that night."

"That's OK. I don't want to talk to you about the night Jennica went missing. I'm more interested in how she was in the days before she went missing."

"How do you mean?"

"Well, how was she behaving? Was she acting normally or strangely? Did she seem happy to you? Had she mentioned anyone she'd not talked about before? That sort of thing."

"She just seemed normal. She was working all hours but that wasn't unusual. She had a deadline, and with her break coming up..." Debbie's mouth quivered and she took a deep, shuddering breath.

"Do you know what she was working on?"

"No. She never spoke about her work. She said she loved coming back here because it was her little oasis of normality. She'd rather talk about anything other than her work."

"So she hadn't met anyone new in the weeks leading up to her disappearance?"

Debbie shook her head. "I'd have known if she'd met someone. She'd never have been able to keep that a secret."

Nico squeezed his eyes shut. He'd hoped that she might be able to tell him something new that would open up the case. Somebody must know something, but he was getting nowhere. He could feel his job slowly slipping away from him. There must be something. A girl can't just disappear like that. "You didn't talk about anything out of the ordinary?"

"No."

"Are you sure?"

"Yes."

"Come on now Debbie, think hard." What was wrong with the girl? Why was she blocking him?

Debbie let out a loud sob. "I don't know any more. I wish I did but I don't."

"You're holding something back."

"I've told you everything. Why don't you believe me?"

"There must be something!"

"Why are you shouting at me? I haven't done anything. Why are you hassling me instead of looking for Jennica?" Debbie stared at Nico, angry despite the tears. "All I read about is how the investigation has ground to a halt, or how the wrong person has been charged. You say you're doing everything but you're not. It's almost as if you don't want to find her."

"I want to find Jennica as much as you."

"How can you say that? She's just a statistic to you, a black mark against your name if it all goes wrong. But she's not a statistic; she's my best friend." Tears spilled down her face. "How can you possibly compare your feelings to mine? There is nothing to compare, nothing. You can't possibly have the faintest idea of what I'm going through."

Nico couldn't hold her stare. She was right. What was he thinking of? He was blaming her for knowing nothing when he was the one at fault. He was the one who had stalled. He was the one that was shit at his job. He got up from the couch. "I'm sorry. I'll leave now, but please, if you think of anything that may help us, give me a call."

"Get out!"

Leaving the room, Nico glanced back at the shrine. For a brief moment, the reflected light from the candle made it appear that Jennica was weeping with her friend.

CHAPTER SEVENTEEN
The Information Cleanser

Warm.

His face felt warm. Why did his face feel so warm? It wasn't an unpleasant feeling, but unusual. Reality was soft, its clarity smudged. He tried to swallow but there was nothing there. His mouth was a parched landscape, his tongue ossified. He could smell the dryness. How could he smell dry?

Drink.

He tried once more to move his tongue but it was too much. His thoughts flickered, unable to settle. There was pressure on his face. He could feel something covering his nose, cheeks and chin. A single solid thought formed, slowly, glacial in its movement from subconscious to conscious.

Where am I?

He needed to see. With a supreme effort the lids of his eyes cracked open. The world was a bright white blur, its edges flickering as his eyelids strained to stay apart. He tried his best but the effort was too much. The reddish darkness returned.

There was sound. How had he missed the sound? Whoosh, click, whoosh, click. The gentle rhythm invaded his consciousness, slow and seductive, like a lullaby distilled to its purest form. Whoosh, click, whoosh, click, whoosh…

***

He came to. There was a change. His mouth felt moist, his tongue lay in its usual bed. He tried to open his eyes but they wouldn't respond.

Where am I?

The thought came quicker than before, tighter, more angular. He couldn't see but he had other senses he could use. He worked his way around his body, looking for a response, but it was as if his head was an island, a sea of nothingness between him and the mainland of his body. A throbbing from his left hand was the only indication that it was there at all. The pressure on his face was still there. He opened his jaw slightly and his tongue felt the slightest of breezes; the chalky taste of desiccated air.

In the background the lullaby continued; whoosh, click, whoosh, click...

He was prepared this time, refusing to succumb to temptation. His ears picked up another sound, the whir of an electric servo. He listened intently as the sound grew louder. A sudden coolness on his brow caused him to flinch. There was chiming: ding, ding, ding. His brain struggled to cope with this sensory overload. What was happening? Where am I?

"Mr Jones? Can you hear me Mr Jones?" The words were soft, appearing from nowhere and everywhere; the voice of God.

Yes, I can hear you. Who are you? Where are you? Where am I?

"Mr Jones, if you can hear me, please let us know."

Yes, I can hear you. Why can't you hear me? Are you a God? Help me? Where am I?

"Mr Jones, I believe that you can hear me. If you can hear me, try to move something."

His mouth inched open, the effort left him hovering on the edge of consciousness until the whoosh click lullaby receded.

"That's wonderful Mr Jones. It's great to have you back. You've been in an accident. You're very ill. It may take some time for you to…" The voice faded into gibberish but that was OK. He wasn't alone. He wasn't dead.

Randall opened his eyes, then closed them again as the bright light stabbed into him. He tried once more and after a few seconds he was able to make sense of what was in front of him. There were a series of spotlights; their ghost images floating into view whenever he blinked. He turned and realised that the lights were not in front of him but above. He was lying on a bed in a plain white room. There was a door to the right. He moved his head left but all he could see was a blank wall. He wanted to see more but his body resisted.

"Hello?" His voice was a whisper, but it was the most wonderful thing he had ever heard. A joyous sound, a breach in his mental captivity.

"Hello Mr Jones. Welcome back." The voice enveloped him, resonating throughout his skull. He looked for its source but found nothing. Had he imagined it?

"Thirsty." The effort to speak made him cough, setting off a crescendo of pain. He luxuriated in the new sensation. Pain meant feeling and feeling meant life.

"Hold still Mr Jones. We'll get you some water." A tube moved towards his mouth. He opened his lips slightly and it slipped between his lips.

"Please suck on the tube."

His mouth became flooded with liquid joy. He swallowed, and sucked some more, his neck muscles screaming with each gulp. The harder he sucked, the faster the water flowed until, no longer able to cope, it spilled from his mouth, pooling in the hollow of his throat.

The tube retracted. "That's enough for now. We need to ease your digestive system back online."

"Where am I?" He felt water slip down the side of his neck, teasing his skin with its touch.

"You're in St Stephen's Hospital. You were involved in an accident."

An accident? He tried to remember but there was nothing there. "I can't see you."

"You are being treated remotely. We need to keep you quarantined until we are sure that you're no longer a risk."

Quarantined. He could have laughed at the irony. Is this how it feels, all that information separated from reality? A brief pang of guilt hit him. Does data have feelings? Am I culpable of some terrible crime in another form of existence?

"You may feel some adverse effects from the medication we've given you. There's a chance of hallucinations and you will remain weak for a while. Once your vitals improve we'll reduce the dosage. Until then, let us know if you experience anything out of the ordinary."

The voice continued but it was too much for Randall to take in. Black motes appeared against the red of his closed eyelids. Without understanding how, he knew that the motes were data. His mind stretched from the physical to the digital, contemplating a world traumatised by random disappearances, each one untraceable and unsolved.

The world shifted. He was journeying through the digital landscape, watching as data motes blinked in and out of existence. The glittering carpet below became mottled, its binary behaviour creating patterns observable only by him. He picked out a mote, drilling down until he could identify a face in the spark. The face was one of millions, no billions of faces; each mote searching for knowledge, connection, confirmation.

His vista changed. The faces melted, their features morphing into blank masks. The motes blanketed the ground, like pebbles on an infinite shore. Details started to emerge from these smooth stones. The shape of a nose, the tilt of the mouth. Each mote was identical, their unified images sharpening into a recognisable form. Some motes broke free like bubbles, floating upwards; in danger of becoming visible, becoming known. Panic gripped Randall. He needed to stop them, to slow this inexorable flow. He flew towards them, touching the bubbles he could reach. The contact broke the motes, sending their contents into quarantine, into purgatory. As if seeing what he was doing, the world erupted as the face inside each mote, Jennica's face, screamed to be heard. Randall flew faster, higher, his task seemingly endless. He knew he had to stop it. It was important. They mustn't see, they mustn't know.

CHAPTER EIGHTEEN
The Politician

The house printing plant was a political lifeline. Stephanie walked around the vast printing chambers, outwardly admiring the silica structures while inwardly continually reviewing her polling numbers as the footage of her visit was broadcast. The factory would employee two thousand skilled workers, providing a major boost to the local economy. It was an example of what could be achieved through private enterprise reacting to a market need, a demonstration of the type of benefits her policy could provide.

She had toured research laboratories, design studios, engineering sections and commercial offices; met new trainees and newly employed experienced engineers, shook hands with the senior management; all the time reviewing the impact of her actions with Pollscan. By the time she had cut the ribbon to officially open the plant and been presented with a miniature model of the factory—made from the same concrete like substance as the houses—she felt revived. The fightback had started. After weeks of declining polls, she had reversed the trend, just as Pollscan had indicated. Now she needed to build on it.

Sian led Stephanie to the boardroom. It smelt sharp, a freshness only found when everything was pristine. Over time, dust and detritus would dull and eventually change its atmosphere to match thousands of similar rooms around the country. That was for another day. Today was about future, progress and achievement. Waiting there were her chief donors, local business leaders who had supported her run for office. Stephanie hoped that the morning's events and the meeting location would bolster their support in the coming months.

"Thank you all for agreeing to meet me at this wonderful facility. I'm sure you agree what a positive addition to our local economy it is, something we should all benefit from in the long term. It's a good example of my campaign pledges being put into action."

"Whether it is a good thing or not, only time will tell. As for your campaign promises, this factory has been in the planning process for the last five years. It may fit your political philosophy but don't try to take the credit for this with us. We know better."

"Straight to business as usual, Patrick." Stephanie smiled warmly to take the edge from her words. Patrick Tombler had been one of Stephanie's first supporters, a fourth generation tailor who was very well connected locally. It was no coincidence that once Patrick had publicly supported her, her popularity spiked.

"Sit down, Stephanie. Please."

She looked around the room. The group seemed nervous, very few returned her gaze. Stephanie took her seat.

"There's no easy way to put this," Patrick continued. "So I'll come straight out with it. We want you to support the government's budget proposal in a fortnight's time."

Her world seemed to tip on its axis. Stephanie saw the colour drain from Sian's face. "I haven't decided how to vote as yet, Patrick."

"That's good, because—"

"It all depends on the details of the proposal, which will be published tomorrow."

The silence was unnerving. Nobody would look at her. Not a single one. Patrick cleared his throat. "We've all been put under a lot of pressure over the last few days and we need you to vote the budget in."

"What do you mean, pressure?"

"If you don't support the budget we will be forced to withdraw our funding. I'm sorry, but that's just how it is."

Stephanie studied Patrick's face. He looked drawn, much older than when they had last met. "What's happened to you, Patrick? I thought we had a deal. You would support my political effort as long as I delivered what I promised." She turned to the others. "You agreed to support me because my predecessor kept backtracking on everything he said, and I've kept my side of the bargain. What's got into you all? You're the last group of people I expected to hear this from."

"We've had a change of heart, that's all."

"For a group of people playing political brinksmanship, you look pretty unhappy." It was Sian. She could see the danger they were facing. It was impossible to be independent without financial backing. If the donors pulled out, Stephanie would lose her team, potentially lose everything. "Why don't you tell us what's really going on? Maybe there's something we can do to help."

A woman stood. "They're threatening to close my business —"

"Fiona, please." Patrick held his hand up for quiet but was ignored.

"They said we had to pull your funding if you voted against the budget. If we didn't do it voluntarily, they would make sure we didn't have the funds to support you." There was a hysterical edge to the woman's voice.

Stephanie was furious. "Who? Who said this to you? If it was somebody from the government I can assure you that I have a lot of friends in the Legislature that will—"

"It was the banks," Patrick said. "I had a call four days ago from a senior partner at my business's bank. He knew I was a donor, it's not like I'd made a secret of it, and he asked if I would put pressure on you to support the budget. I said no, of course, and told him my relationship with you was none of his business."

"Thank you, Patrick."

"That's when the threats started. He said that if I didn't do as he asked, he'd call in our loans and have our overdraft frozen. I told him that what he was suggesting was illegal but he just laughed, saying that the bank had every right to stop trading with a company that was putting its own business interests in jeopardy."

Stephanie didn't want to believe what she was being told but she knew it was true. The bastard had tried to break her physically, tried to trash her reputation, and now he was hitting her in the pocket.

"For the past few days, all I've done is talk to other lenders, but nobody is interested in taking my business. This despite us being in the best financial health in years." Patrick, normally so strong, looked grey.

"My call came two days ago," said the woman. She pointed around the room. "Arwel had his at around the same time and Stephen the day before. We all have accounts with different banks, but the message was the same. I don't know who you have upset, Stephanie, but they have some very powerful friends."

Stephanie wanted to throw her model factory through the window. The press attacks had started about a week after the assault; nothing too damaging, nothing libellous, just the odd question about her competence in some of the more radical NewsAggre's. Addy had countered with a profile on one of the local networks, portraying Stephanie as someone who had the establishment running scared by her honesty. It had worked for a while, with Stephanie's poll ratings remaining stable. The doorstepping started a few days later; Journo's asking her questions designed to provoke, hoping for her to slip up and create some headlines. This time Stephanie and the team had been prepared, handling the negative coverage with ease, but the firefighting had taken resource away from her promoting her message and her ratings had started to drop. Now this. Without funding, she would have to lay off her staff, leaving her vulnerable to attack.

"There are a couple of Journos I know. If word of this got out—"

"Please, don't do that. They'll ruin us." Patrick's hands were trembling.

She could see what he was going through. He was a good man, straight and direct. To approach her like this must be costing him dearly. Stephanie looked across to Sian, who shook her head. She couldn't ask them to risk their livelihoods for her. How could she expect them to do that? They hadn't been there. They didn't know how high the stakes were. "Thank you, Patrick, I appreciate you telling me to my face and I'm sorry you've all been caught up in this."

"I'm sorry. I was buggered if I was going to do something behind your back. I wanted to tell you right away but—"

Stephanie smiled as the flare of anger brought life back to the man who had first believed in her. "Go back to your banks and let them know that you've given me the ultimatum. I'll let you know what I decide before the vote next week." She looked at each of the group in turn. "If I do decide to go against the government, do what you think is right. I won't blame you, whatever your decision."

"Thank you for being so understanding," Patrick replied. "If there was any other way—"

Stephanie stood. "Have a safe journey home."

Their relief was palpable as they left the room, the smiles of gratitude taking some of the sting from what had happened. As Sian closed the door behind them, Stephanie sank back into her chair.

"You've got no choice Steph, you've got to stop campaigning against the budget. You've seen what they are capable of doing. We stand no chance against this, none at all. Let's go back to Gant and negotiate. They are obviously worried. Let's do this now before it's too late."

"No, Sian. No deals. Not with him."

"Why not? We're so close to getting what we want. Do you really want to risk losing the team?"

"We have enough funds for a few more weeks yet. I want to find another way out of this."

Sian looked exasperated. "There are no other ways. This is it."

Stephanie ignored her friend. "Has James dug up anything useful?"

"He said there were hints of something interesting, but he needed more time."

"Good. Chase him up. Tell him it's his number one priority. If there is anything there, I want to know. This could be our way out." Before Sian could say any more, Stephanie gathered up her things and left. There had to be something, there just had to.

CHAPTER NINETEEN
The Information Cleanser

Randall started again. The ceiling was tiled, seven and a half tiles wide by eight and a half tiles long, a total of 64 tiles. There were two ceiling hatches each a quarter tile in size, plus the eight spot-lights taking up space. Randall calculated that the number of full tiles on the ceiling was 62. On each tile was a random pattern of black dots. The tile directly above his head had 222 dots. This round number irritated Randall enough that he checked the four adjacent tiles as well. They had 217, 226 dots, 230 dots and 228 dots respectively, making an average of 225 dots per tile. Feeling more comfortable with this number, he calculated that the ceiling had a total of 13950 dots.

His boredom came crashing in once more. Randall had never been disconnected from the datasphere before, at least not that he could remember. Even though he was never immersed all day like some people he knew, the datasphere had been ever-present. Was this what it was like to become deaf, or blind? He had never felt so isolated.

As if to compensate for the loss of stimulation, his dreams had taken on a level of clarity he'd never before experienced. He'd mentioned this to the voice, but was told that the dreams were most likely an unexpected side effect of his medication. The medication that he was unaware of receiving.

Each night, Randall lived an alternate version of his life. One night he had been back at the hotel, hands shaking as he walked to the breakfast table. All conversation stopped as he approached. He started to speak, voice quivering, his words a jumble, scared of what the team would say. The warmth and concern with which he was received had been humbling. Lise called him a stupid bastard before apologising for the slap, embarrassed and never once looking him in the eye. Sylvianne smiled warmly, telling him he had nothing to apologise for and squeezed his hand. Only Robert reacted with some degree of predictability, running step by step through the argument, aping and exaggerating each twist and turn to comic effect. Randall laughed along with everyone else but was squirming with embarrassment inside.

He could almost taste the bile at the back of his throat as he nervously waited to see Seegers. Yet when they spoke, Seegers seemed almost contrite, explaining that Randall's behaviour was unacceptable, but at the same time taking some of the blame. In the dream things remained awkward between them, but they agreed that they should both move on.

Back in bed, Randall felt tormented. Each dream acted as a reminder of what had happened, yet it pained him to be so weak. Why was he being so submissive? Why was his subconscious wanting him to take the role of the villain? He had been the one wronged, not the others. They were the ones who had turned on him. His friends, the only friends he had. He could see their faces clearly each time he revisited his humiliation. Not one of them had backed him up. Not one of them had told Seegers to stop. They were all the same, rolling over to protect themselves instead of coming together against a bully. Couldn't they see that he had been standing up for them? They should have been crawling back to apologise.

Yet a traitorous part of him yearned for his dreams to be

true, to return to the comfortable life he'd once had. He hated the fact that a part of him needed friendship so desperately that he would rather demean himself to keep his friends than stand up for what he believed was right. He wanted to crush those feelings. He was on his own now. He had been alone before and he knew how to deal with it. It was better this way; nobody could hurt you if you never let them in.

He sat up. "Voice? Are you there?"

"Good morning Mr Jones. How are you feeling today?"

"Good, just like yesterday and the day before. I'm ready to go home."

"I'm sorry, but as we've explained that isn't possible. You are weaker than you think and you are still a risk to the public. We need to keep you here until your readings normalise."

"When will that be?"

"We don't know."

Randall wanted to scream. "Surely you have an idea. I can't be the only person who has gone through this."

"I'm sorry, Mr Jones, but we can't give you a timescale. You will be out of here as soon as it is safe."

"Then at least give me datasphere access. I'm bored shitless. I need something to occupy my time."

"I'm sorry Mr Jones, but you know that isn't possible. You are neurologically fragile. You've been through a major trauma. You need to remain in a calm environment until you're healed."

"Calm? I feel anything but calm. I'm so bored I could smash this place up just for something to do."

"We can give you something to ease your anxiety."

"No." He'd had enough torment from his dreams. "That's OK."

"Is there anything else I can help with?"

"No."

Randall flung himself back onto his bed. He had scoured

every square centimetre of the room but had no idea where the cameras or speakers were. He was desperate to find them, just so he could smash the bastard things up. He rubbed his hands over his newly formed beard, forcing himself to think about anything other than what had happened before his accident. Starting from the top left-hand side of the ceiling, he began the task of manually counting every single dot. His eyes followed the flow of dots from left to right, but his mind kept drifting. How was it possible for two pods to collide? It had never happened. Never. With everything centrally controlled, collisions like his were an impossibility. His thoughts moved back and forth while his eyes continued their journey, the random patterning diverting his eyes from their horizontal path. A familiar feeling tickled the back of his mind. It took Randall a moment to realise what was happening.

The dots meant something.

All other thoughts were driven from his mind. He'd been staring at the ceiling for days, finding familiar shapes in the random pattern: a lion's head, the outline of a pod; even his mothers smile if you squinted enough. Seeing patterns where there were none was a genetic trait that had enabled our prehistoric ancestors to recognise hidden danger. It was the same ability that allowed people to see shapes in clouds, or meaning in events. It was how faiths were born. This was different. Randall knew this particular feeling well. It was the same feeling he got at work, whenever he identified a pattern while sifting petabytes of data. It was the same feeling that made him so good at his job. Somewhere hidden in the pattern on the ceiling was not only a message, but a message specifically for him.

He shivered. Somebody was trying to contact him. What if it was a warning? What if he was in danger? Something wasn't right and somebody was trying to warn him.

"Mr Jones? Is everything OK? Your heartbeat levels have risen."

Randall let out a yelp, jerking around in the direction of the voice.

"Mr Jones?"

"I'm fine. You just surprised me, that's all."

"We noticed your heart rate increase. Are you feeling alright?"

"I'm fine." Randall slowed his breathing, trying to appear relaxed. "Can I make a suggestion? If you are so worried about my heart, don't make me jump like that again."

He lay back on his bed, the feeling having gone. He wanted to laugh it off, to convince himself that it had just been his imagination, but he knew the feeling had been real. Somebody was trying to warn him about something and he needed to find out what. Randall made himself relax, looking up at the ceiling once more, then beyond, clearing his mind of anything but what was in front of his eyes. He would work it out, he always did. He just needed some time.

CHAPTER TWENTY
The Investigator

"Thanks for taking the time to see me, Professor. As I mentioned, I'm trying to get a picture of Jennica's life in the hope of identifying what caused her to disappear. Anything you remember, no matter how small, will be of use."

Nico sat awkwardly opposite the Professor, his knees by his ears. The Professor reclined on a floatbed, his boyish face close to disappearing as the structure moulded itself around him. The grey sponge-like mounds were scattered throughout the room, hidden in alcoves and behind the many plants and flowers. The gentle sound of waves lapping a shore permeated the room. The Professor had explained that it was important his students felt relaxed, their minds uncluttered by the detritus of everyday living so they could fully concentrate on their work. He said that by converting the laboratory to a tranquil refuge, the students were able to focus for much longer periods.

Nico thought the Professor looked as if he was being swallowed by a brain. "What was Jennica like as a student?"

"Jennica's a fantastic analyst, one of the most talented I've seen. She's comfortable reviewing vast quantities of data, spotting patterns or discrepancies that most other analysts would miss. It is very rare for her to miss anything significant." His words came out softly, as if he was only half present.

"I thought you used algorithms to sort data."

"We do, but the skill is not sorting data to identify a pattern. That's easy, especially given the vast quantities of data we look at. The skill is in identifying the *relevant* patterns or discrepancies and discarding the irrelevant ones. Identifying large patterns is straightforward, but finding the significant smaller ones is a lot more difficult. The danger is either missing them completely, or overstating their importance. This is Jennica's skill. She can create algorithms to identify small patterns in large data samples, instinctively understanding the significance of each pattern, discarding those of little importance and focussing on those that are. It's a special talent."

"And socially? Did she have any friends she was particularly close to? Was she in a relationship at all?"

"In class she's fairly quiet, but then she's a very focussed person. I'm aware she's got a number of friends outside of class. Other than that, I don't really know."

"Was there anyone she worked closely with in class?"

"Nobody. She's a very capable student, very focussed. She doesn't need support from the others. She keeps herself to herself."

"Has that led to any resentment at all from her classmates?"

"Maybe, but classes settle down quickly into those who work alone and those who work in groups."

"No arguments or friction at all then?"

"Not that I'm aware of."

Nico adjusted himself slightly, his body complaining at sitting in such an awkward position, although he was damned if he was going to do this interview laying down. "OK, moving on to her work then, can you tell me what was she working on at the time of her disappearance?"

The Professor's voice hardened a little. "I'm sorry but I can't talk about that."

"You can't talk about it?"

"Our partners insist we keep things confidential. If the information we work on gets into the wrong hands, well..."

"I can assure you that I'm not looking for commercial secrets, Professor. I'm only interested in finding out what happened to Jennica. I would have thought that, given how highly you thought of her, you would want that too."

The Professor turned to face Nico. "Don't you dare accuse me of not caring. Jennica's disappearance has been hard on all of us here, especially for me. I would do anything to find out what has happened, but if I break any of the confidentiality agreements we have in place, nobody would ever work with us again. It would be a disaster for my students and for the University."

"And for you." That's got your attention, Nico thought.

"Yes, and for me, although I would happily trade my reputation for Jennica's safe return." The Professor made a gesture and the ocean disappeared. "When you contacted me asking for a meeting, I knew this would come up, so I contacted the partner in question, asking permission to talk openly to you. They refused."

"So Re-Life don't want their name linked to this case?"

The Professor stared at Nico for a moment, then smiled, giving the slightest of nods. "I've no idea who you are talking about."

Nico felt a tension that he had been unaware of drain away. "OK. Then without breaking your agreement, was there anything in what she was doing that you feel could be linked to her disappearance?"

"No, nothing."

Nico stood. "Thank you for your time, Professor."

"I have a question for you, Investigator." Nico looked down to where the Professor lay, the soft layers enveloping once again. "Given the evidence you have seen so far, do you think Jennica was taken against her will?"

"I'm sorry Professor, but I can't discuss case details," Nico replied, nodding his head.

"OK, I quite understand." The Professor smiled. "If there is anything I can do to help, please don't hesitate to let me know."

Nico left a little lighter as he left the room. So the delegate had been right after all.

CHAPTER TWENTY-ONE
The Politician

She could hear Sian's words but her brain refused to take them in. It couldn't be right. She'd only spoken to him the day before. Stephanie looked up to see drinks on the table. When had the waitress brought them over?

Sian used a napkin to wipe her tears. "He was found floating in the canal by two young boys. The investigative agency think he slipped. There were broken paving slabs near to where he was found."

Stephanie watched as people walked past the café. Life was going on as normal. "I can't believe it. He was so young, had so much going for him." She wanted to cry, knew that she should be crying, but the void inside sucked out emotion. *How can I achieve this without him?* "What about his family?"

"His parents have been told. He didn't have anyone else that I know of."

"Addy?"

"It's hit her hard. It's hit us all hard." Sian looked pale, agitated.

Stephanie warmed her hands on her cup. It was going to be difficult. James's knowledge and contacts had been invaluable in pulling together the vote against the budget. She needed someone to keep things going at the Legislature, otherwise the whole effort would fall apart. She couldn't allow that. She needed to hit that bastard where it hurt before—

"Steph. I'm really worried." Sian was staring at her, brows drawn together, hands gripping her napkin.

"We'll be alright, Sian. It's not going to be easy without James but I'm sure we'll—"

"It's not the bloody workload. Christ, do you think that's all I care about?" Sian threw the napkin on the table. "James is dead!"

"I know he's dead."

"Don't you care?"

"I don't have that luxury."

Sian stared at her friend as if horrified at what she was seeing. "What's happened to you?"

Stephanie said nothing, taking a sip of coffee instead.

"You need to care. I don't think what happened was an accident. I think they got to him. They must have found out what he'd discovered."

"James had an accident. He slipped and fell, you said so yourself."

Sian shook her head. "We spoke last night. He'd just finished your research and was scared at what he'd found. He called me, saying he needed to tell someone straight away. He didn't want to send anything because he was worried it would be traced."

Stephanie felt a queasiness well up inside. "What did he say?"

Sian glanced around nervously. From where she sat, Stephanie could see that the café was empty, other than the waitress standing by the bar. "James had been checking the voting records, just like you asked. He'd analysed the voting patterns of every delegate who'd publicly opposed the government over the last five years. In the majority of cases, delegates voted as they had indicated. There was only one case, abut four years ago, where a handful of them changed their position."

"They'd probably cut a deal."

"James thought that too. The delegates who'd switched miraculously delivered government investment to their district soon after the vote."

"So Gant wasn't lying when he said working with the government would be beneficial." Stephanie shivered as she felt his tongue once more on her face. She pushed her nails into the palm of her hand. No, she thought, I won't go there.

"James couldn't understand why the government decided to cut a deal for that specific vote and not any of the others. It was only when he checked the final results that he realised. If they had not cut a deal, the government would have been defeated."

"Makes sense, why expend political capital when you don't need to."

"He then checked further back to see if the trend held, and it did. Most years the vote went through as expected, the only switches taking place when the predicted voting was tight."

"So the government are well versed at bribing when they need to."

"Not one government, all of them. It didn't matter which faction was in power, the budget was always approved."

"This isn't new Sian. It's just the dirty end of politics"

Sian continued as if she hadn't heard. "They didn't just bribe, though. There were three cases where a political scandal broke out just before the vote; each time it involved a delegate or group of delegates who were campaigning against the government, and every time those involved lost their seats, replaced by pro-government candidates."

"It's not like we don't know that they'll use the stick as well as the carrot." Stephanie handed her napkin over to Sian. "Look, I know you're upset about James, we all are, but what you're talking about is political expedience. It's not nice but it's not exactly unusual—"

"Shut up a minute! I haven't finished."

The shout jolted Stephanie. She looked across to her friend and saw that Sian seemed as shocked at her outburst as she was. "Please, just listen. James felt the same as you but then decided to check up on Andy Hawthorne as we'd asked. His voting record had been immaculate—pro-government, pro-budget—throughout his term. However, when he checked his media comments, Andy appeared to have had a change of heart, especially towards the end of his term, and actively campaigned against the budget proposal of the time."

"How did he vote in the end?"

"He didn't. The boating accident occurred two weeks before the vote."

The queasiness returned and Stephanie had to swallow hard to stop herself from being sick. "It happened then? I don't remember hearing about his change of heart?"

"You wouldn't have, unless you read some of the more out-there News Aggre's. They were the only ones reporting Andy's views. None of the established players would talk to him."

"But he was always sought after for comment. The NewsAggre's loved him almost as much as he loved them."

"Exactly. It was as if he was being gagged."

Nobody held that much sway over the NewsAggre's. A few Journos maybe but the full organisation? It couldn't be right. But even as she was trying to persuade herself, Stephanie's thoughts turned to the meeting with her backers. Nobody held that much sway with the banks, either. She looked out of the window; the feeling that she was being watched was almost overwhelming.

"In the last 30 years there have been three other cases of accidental death; all long-term supporters of the government at the time, all with perfect voting records, all apparently about to vote against the budget, but with no mention or activity in the mainstream NewsAggre's."

"Why would someone kill a delegate just because they were going to vote against a government they had previously supported?"

"James wasn't a delegate." Stephanie reached across the table and took her friend's hand. Whether Sian was crying through grief or fear, the result was the same. Everything was closing in on them.

"How much sleep have you had Sian?"

"I haven't."

"Then that's the priority. I know that you've been spooked, but all you have is a small amount of data confirmed by a few dubious sources." Stephanie held Sian's hand firm as she started to protest. "I'm not saying James was wrong, but we are a long way from having to be worried. I'm pretty sure that once you've have a good sleep you'll feel the same." Sian finally nodded, her desire to believe what Stephanie was saying overcoming her grief and fear.

"Come back to mine, you can crash out for a bit while I check things out. If it looks like James was onto something, we can deal with it then, but for the moment I think the shock of what's happened so close to your last conversation may have led you to conclusions you wouldn't normally make." She took hold of Sian's hand again, putting on a smile. "This is why we make such a good team, Sian. We balance each other out." Sian tried to smile through her tears. "Dry your eyes while I pay the bill."

Stephanie stood, turning her back to the window as she walked to the cashier, hoping that Sian couldn't see how much her hands were shaking.

CHAPTER TWENTY-TWO
The Investigator

Nico stirred the pasta. His other pan was bubbling away, the tart, acidic smell of tomato combining with the familiar tang of garlic, provoking memories of his mother's kitchen. He didn't get to cook often—the family were content to use the dispenser to prepare most meals—but Nico liked the old ways and cooking enabled him to relax, freeing his mind from the day to day grind. He lifted the spoon to check how it tasted. There was a tug on his trouser. Looking down he saw Gino, his youngest, staring up at him.

"Poon," Gino said, pointing at the spoon.

"OK, but careful now, it's still a little hot." Nico scooped some more sauce out of the pan, giving it a quick blow before allowing Gino a taste.

Gino's eyes lit up. "More."

"Don't go giving him too much, you'll spoil his appetite." Fran was in the living room. How she knew what he was up to he had no idea.

"A little spoonful won't hurt," Nico said.

"More, more," Gino repeated, holding his mouth open ready.

"Sorry little man," Gino said loudly while letting him have another spoonful, "you heard your mother. No more until dinner. Go and find Maria, she's in the play-room."

Nico smiled as Gino toddled off. That boy will break hearts one day, he thought. He picked up a colander ready to drain the pasta when Corey's icon blinked into view. He stifled his annoyance and put down the colander. "Fran, can you come and take over, Corey needs to speak to me."

Fran had *that* face when she walked into the cook zone. "Can't they leave you alone just for one night?"

"You know I wouldn't ask if it wasn't important."

She snatched the spoon from his hand, nudging him aside with her hips. "That's the problem, it's always important."

"Love you," Nico said, kissing her on the cheek. He walked through the living area to his office and shut the door.

"Hey Corey, what's up?"

"Mr Chowdhury wants to know where you've got to."

Nico frowned. Was that all? "You know where I am. Nowhere. All leads from the footage have dried up, other than the charges we were able to pin on the boy. I've spent the last few days talking to Jennica's friends and colleagues, trying to find out if there was another reason why she might have gone missing."

"And?"

"Nothing. She had no enemies, no relationships as such. She was well-liked at the university, a bit of a loner but no professional jealousies that I could find. I'll keep trying but it looks like another dead end. I've one other line of enquiry to do with her work. It's unlikely, but I just want to look into that a bit further."

"I thought you said that you'd spoken to the university."

"I'm not interested in the university. I'm interested in Re-Life. That was the company she was doing the research for."

"Re-Life? That's new."

"It's probably nothing, I'm just trying to tie up the loose ends."

There was a pause before Corey spoke. "Can you just hold for a moment."

Nico felt his annoyance grow. Why were they wasting his time just to check up on progress? Surely this could have waited until tomorrow morning.

"Hello Nico. Corey has just been updating me. It sounds like you are coming to the end of the trail."

The warmth and security that had enveloped him a few minutes before was punctured by the sound of Chowdhury's voice. Was this it? The worry had always been there, ever since the disaster with Chad. It was too high profile a case for it to have remained unsolved for so long. Yet it was so unfair. He'd done everything he could. He'd gone further and worked harder than any other investigator would have in the same situation. It wasn't his fault Corey had gone public when he had. It wasn't his fault that a Delegate had attached herself to the case. "Yes, Mr Chowdhury, it's looking that way."

"Well I don't think it's necessary for you to take this case any further. You've done an excellent job to get this far but you've clearly run out of options. It's time to put the case on ice."

"There's still a couple of loose ends I'd like to chase down. It will only take me a day or so, then I'll be done."

"Leave them. I like the fact that you want to close all avenues, but you are in danger of seeing shadows where there are none. Corey will brief you in the morning. Have a nice evening, Nico."

Nico stood staring out into the night. He could hear the muffled sounds of Fran dishing up through the office door. He should be happy. He had been praised for doing a good job and was being taken off a dead-end case to work on something fresh. Instead he felt troubled. While Chowdhury hadn't been explicit, it felt like he didn't want Nico to chase down the Re-Life lead. This was against company policy, all leads must be followed up before putting a case in stasis. Then there was where the lead had come from. A delegate doesn't just provide information in confidence like that to investigators for no reason; there had to be more to it than he had been told.

Nico felt torn. He had a responsibility to his family and the agency had more than enough reasons to get rid of him if he caused trouble. The best thing for his career would be to keep his head down and do as he was told. But what about Jennica's friends and family? What about his commitment to them? He couldn't just do nothing. He couldn't just let Jennica become forgotten.

He made a call.

"Good evening Investigator."

"Good evening, Delegate. You asked to be updated on progress. Well, the case is being mothballed. We've gone through nearly every avenue available but have drawn a blank. The investigation is still open, but unless we get a new lead, I'm being moved on. I just thought you should know."

"Why aren't I being told this by Chief Investigator Akkerman?"

"I believe he'll be in contact first thing tomorrow morning." Nico hesitated, unsure whether to proceed. He could still hear Maria's voice in the background, arguing with Fran. "Delegate Vaughn, there's something else, but it is strictly off the record."

"Go on."

"I never got the chance to investigate the Re-Life connection you gave me, although I had got as far as to have the link confirmed by a second source. The case has been closed despite me not investigating the Re-Life link. It may be nothing, but leaving a lead like that is unusual and against policy."

"You think the Chief Inspector is blocking you?"

"It wasn't Corey who told me to drop it, but Mr Chowdhury."

The line went quiet for a moment. "I see."

"I want to keep the investigation going but I can't be seen to be going against the company's wishes. If more information comes to light I can quite legitimately carry on. Until then…"

"I understand, Investigator. Let's hope you have your wish."

He closed the line. That was the easy part. Now he had to hope his ability to read people hadn't let him down.

"Good evening Professor. Sorry to bother you at this late hour. Are you in a position to talk privately?"

"Hold on a moment." Nico heard footsteps followed by a door closing. "How can I help?"

"When we last spoke, you said to me that if there was anything you could do to help find Jennica, to call you."

"I did."

"Well, I need your help."

"Sure."

Randall took a deep breath. "The investigation has hit a brick wall. My biggest issue is the footage of Jennica's disappearance. It gives me nothing to work on. One minute she's there, the next gone. I've looked at it over and over again but have found nothing."

"I don't see—" started the Professor.

"I heard from a reliable source that activity takes place on the datasphere that is beyond the capabilities of crime agencies to discover. That individuals or organisations are able to manipulate or remove data leaving no trace of their activity." The line remained quiet. "Here's my problem: either Jennica magically disappeared, which I don't believe; or somebody altered all footage from that night, which I've been told is impossible. What I need to know is: can datasphere footage be manipulated without us being able to find out?"

"What makes you think I would know, Investigator?"

"You're the only person I know who might, and the only one who cares enough about Jennica to tell me."

The line went quiet. Nico waited, hoping that he wasn't wrong.

"I've heard rumours..."

"If I sent you the footage, would you be able to tell if it has been manipulated, or even better, find the missing information?"

"You put me in a difficult position, Investigator. I would love to help, but having this knowledge is in itself a criminal offence, and your agency has a reputation for prosecution. Why should I trust you, even if I could help?"

"If I send you this footage, Professor, I too would be committing a criminal offence."

"I see. Well I can't promise anything."

"I don't expect you to. All I ask is that you try, for Jennica's sake."

"I'll see what I can do."

"Thank you, Professor."

CHAPTER TWENTY-THREE
The Politician

"Is there any news on the girl, Delegate?"

"How do you feel the investigation is going?"

"Are you worried about your ratings?"

Stephanie climbed out of the pod and made her way through the crush. Addy had been busy. There was a large crowd by the house, at least ten Journos plus a number of onlookers wondering what the fuss was about. She pushed past the throng and made her way past her assistant and into the building. From the entrance hall she could hear Addy address the crowd.

"Delegate Vaughn doesn't have time to answer your questions now. She will make a statement after her visit."

Groans erupted from the Journos. "Why don't you just give up now, delegate." The shouted question stabbed into Stephanie. Yes, why not? Was revenge worth the cost? She suppressed the question. She'd come too far to stop now.

Addy closed the front door. "Her apartment is up on the second floor, you can't miss it."

"How is she doing?"

"Not good. She's had Journos going through her personal life in detail, plus every conspiracy theorist on the datasphere thinks she's involved in the disappearance. She'll be pleased to have a sympathetic face for once."

Stephanie made her way up to the second floor landing where Jennica's room-mate was waiting for her. She smiled, blushing slightly. "Hello Delegate Vaughn."

"Good morning Debbie. Please, call me Stephanie. May I come in?"

"Please." The smell of washing detergent and spring flowers greeted Stephanie as she entered. There was a trace of static in the air, tell-tale signs of a recent cleaning.

"Would you like a drink, Delegate, er Stephanie?"

"That would be most kind. Do you have tea?"

Debbie nodded. "The lounge is through there."

Stephanie went where she was directed and her eyes were immediately drawn to a shelf at the corner of the room. There were a number of photos: Jennica in the park kissing a tree, Jennica and Debbie squashed together in a bar; multiple shots of Jennica and Debbie together as children, all grins and awkward poses. One of the photos she recognised; the group shot from the first Aggre reports. She picked up the frame to get a better look.

"It's the last photo I have of her. She disappeared a week later." Debbie stood at the doorway, offering a cup. Stephanie placed the picture back on the shelf.

"You knew Jennica a long time."

"I've known her since we were seven. We were in the same class at school."

"And you both ended up studying here as well?"

"Different subjects." Debbie gestured to the sofa. "Please."

Stephanie sat, placing her cup on the floor by her feet. "I remember being excited and terrified about going to Uni. Being away from my parents for the first time, all alone. It must have been nice, the two of you having each other as company."

"It was. Jennica had always been a little shy. I don't know why, it's just that she found it hard to make friends. At school she was picked on for not conforming. The other girls used to say she was odd, but she just wasn't interested in boys or fashion. The great thing about coming here was that people accepted her for who she was." Debbie's face lit up. "We had some great times. Jennica really came out of her shell. We had a great group of friends, really good fun." The smile faded. "I wish I hadn't bothered. Then she might still be here."

"You can't blame yourself. You had no way of knowing what would happen."

"It doesn't stop you, though, does it."

Stephanie shook her head. "No, it doesn't."

One or two shouts echoed up from the crowd outside. Debbie walked across to the window. "You'd think they'd put their time to better use, like trying to find out where Jennica is."

"Just keeping Jennica in the public eye could make a difference. That's why I asked them here. I'd like to give them a statement afterwards—nothing about what we discuss today—just to keep the momentum going. Is that OK with you?"

Debbie shrugged her shoulders. Stephanie waited to see if the girl would say anything. When nothing was forthcoming, she said, "Jennica doesn't look happy, in that final photo."

"That's just how she was. She rarely let on how she was feeling."

"So there was nothing bothering her, before she went missing?"

"Have you been talking to that Investigator? Has he put you up to this?" Debbie rounded on Stephanie, her face was flushed with anger.

"Debbie? What's wrong? What have I said?"

Tears filled her eyes. "They've been bloody useless. Jennica is missing, and instead of being out there looking for her, they come here, repeating the same question as if I'm lying to them." She took another drink from her cup, her hands shaking. "I'm sorry, but..." her voice trailed off as she burst into tears.

Stephanie stepped forward and took Debbie into her arms. "You poor thing. There's no need to apologise." She stroked Debbie's hair and she sunk into her embrace, body shaking. "That's right," Stephanie said. "Just let it all out."

"You must think I'm a complete fool." Debbie was wiping her eyes, the dark smudges beneath a stark contrast to her pale complexion.

"Not at all. You shouldn't hold these things in. They'll eat away at you."

"But it's been weeks—"

"And you still don't have answers." Stephanie handed Debbie another tissue. "Do you have anyone close you can talk to?" She shook her head. "What about family? Couldn't you go back home for a while?"

"I can't. What if Jennica comes back and I'm not here?"

"I think she'd understand."

Debbie took her hand and stood. "I need to show you something. I found it after Jennica went missing. It will give you a much better idea of who she is."

She led Stephanie to a sparse bedroom. The only items of furniture were a desk, a half empty clothes rail, a wooden chest of drawers and a single bed made up with clean, plain linen. There were no pictures on the wall, just a clock and a small mirror at head height. On the desk were a handful of printed books, standing in height order. The only item that stood out was a colourful picture frame of pink and yellow flowers with the words 'friends forever' embossed at the bottom. Debbie and Jennica as children beamed from the frame. Debbie walked over to the bed and reached underneath, pulling out a small book.

"I found this while I was cleaning," she said. "I was going to give it to the Investigator, but." Her voice trailed off. Stephanie thought Debbie would cry but instead she shook herself and handed Stephanie the book. "You seem to be the only one who truly cares."

Stephanie took the book and opened it carefully. Each page was written in meticulous blue handwriting, every section headed with a day and date. What type of person keeps a paper diary? she thought. Nobody wrote by hand any more; it wasn't even taught in schools.

Stephanie closed the book. "Thank you for this. I promise not to betray your trust."

"I know you won't," Debbie replied. "Just do everything you can to find her."

CHAPTER TWENTY-FOUR
The Information Cleanser

Randall had forgotten how blue the sky could be. For a moment he felt he would lose himself in its infinite depths. He wandered around the walled garden bundled in his new clothes, his thick jacket sealed up tight, hands in pockets; the despondency and boredom from recent days evaporating in the weak autumn sun. The garden overwhelmed his senses. In his other life he would have dismissed the grounds as dismal and unkempt, but his eyes soaked up the muted browns and greens after their long diet of white. The scent of turned earth, the musty aroma of rotting leaves, the chill breeze on his cheeks; all were reminders of another time, when the outside world was a place of wonder rather than a corridor from one destination to another. He walked on pathways and the mossy grass; he touched the bark of newly-bare trees and tasted dampness in the air. Every step was a luxury to be enjoyed.

He had the place to himself, still a risk to the public according to the voice. Randall didn't care. He didn't want to meet anyone else, didn't want to speak or socialise. He wanted to use this time to reconnect with a world that he had for so long ignored. He needed to know that there was something better out there, something normal.

Since waking, his life had been a cycle of sleep, food and

observation. He knew he was being held against his will but he didn't know why. Every day the voice would speak, asking how he was, informing him of his progress and reluctantly enforcing his isolation under the excuse of health and wellbeing. Sometimes he had tried a little questioning of his own, but the voice was far too good to reveal anything. So he carried on as if nothing was amiss, becoming the model patient. His only focus was to understand the message. He had studied the ceiling each day, section by section, looking for some form of pattern. By fluke he'd discovered that the message was somehow linked to what he was thinking. One evening, frustrated with the search, his thoughts had drifted once more to the accident when the impulse to escape flooded through him. Randall had found himself on his feet and heading towards the door before he regained control. The message was clear, but he didn't know why it had been sent or by whom.

And his dreams still tormented him. The Re-Life 2 launch had been a success, his team richly rewarded for their work. He had taken time off, to take stock of his life and re-focus on what was important. He had even learnt how to paint. His dreams moved further from reality each night, his actions out of character, none more than his blossoming relationship with Sylvianne. Each morning Randall woke up bewildered by the events conjured by his subconscious.

There was a flash of movement and Randall felt something brush against his foot. Looking down he yelped as a rat scampered past. It was the first living thing he had seen for weeks. Randall shielded his eyes from the winter sun and watched as the rat raced away towards the undergrowth. After it disappeared, he stood for a moment, looking for the tell-tale signs of movement. Without warning the urge to escape enveloped him, his every fibre aching to be away. He struggled for control, a small part of him trying to understand what had initiated the impulse. There was the specific angle of a tree, the shape of the pathway he had just walked down, the grooves in the freshly turned earth; each of these elements had formed part of a cohesive pattern that triggered the reaction. He didn't know how, but someone or something had manoeuvred him to this precise spot, to this very view. And he understood the message they had sent. He needed to get away. Now.

Randall looked back to the hospital building. There was no point going that way, they had full control of the entrances and exits; if he stepped back into that building he would be trapped for good. He turned back to the direction he had been heading. Surrounding the garden was a large ivy covered wall. He casually walked towards it, pulling on the ivy once close. It was no good. The ivy came away with only a small amount of effort. Where the ivy had pulled away there were flint stones sticking out from crumbling mortar. He thought about using the flints to climb the wall but realised it would be impossible. He didn't believe he had the strength to climb the wall, regardless of whether there were enough hand- or footholds.

Randall pushed the ivy back and let out a gasp as he felt a sharp stab of pain in his left hand. Something had scratched through the dressing, causing the scar to reopen. Blood oozed from the wound. The increased throbbing strengthened his desire to escape. Ignoring the pain, he looked down the length of the wall. There were a few overhanging branches which looked too weak to hold his weight. Further down was an old, wooden outbuilding but it was too far from the wall to be of use. Then he saw it, a patch of colour grinning through the ivy near the far corner of the wall. Resisting the urge to run, Randall made his way down the wall, stopping occasionally to look at a flower or to watch a bird fly past. When he reached the spot, a quick pull at the ivy revealed an old wooden door, its hinges heavily rusted. Randall looked for a handle but there was none, just a keyhole on the right-hand side. He pushed at the door and the wood creaked but didn't budge. He tried a second time with the same result. Growling in frustration, Randall kicked the door and a part of the frame cracked.

"Mr Jones, what are you doing?"

Randall let out a yelp. He looked back to the hospital. There was nobody there but he knew he didn't have much time. He took a step back and kicked where the frame had cracked. The door shuddered but held. Randall kicked again, then a third time; showers of paint flakes floating to the ground with each blow. Despite his weakened state the flow of adrenaline allowed him to keep going, though he was breathing hard and his left hand throbbed from the exertion.

"Mr Jones, please stop immediately. You must not leave these facilities. You are a risk to the general population. Mr Jones, please stop at once."

Randall took a deep breath, then kicked out again with increased urgency. The door reverberated under the heavier blows but refused to give. Randall could almost feel the hands grabbing at his shoulders to pull him away, back to the hospital. He kept kicking, desperation driving him on, until with a loud crack the frame splintered and the door collapsed into the street behind, causing Randall to fall through the gap onto the concrete road. He lay there for a moment, stunned by his achievement. Then, ignoring the pain of the fall, he gingerly got to his feet. He was on what looked like an old service route; grass poking out of the cracks indicating the road's disuse. It was empty for now, although it was unlikely to stay that way for long. Randall ran, his only desire to be away from the hospital. He listened for the sounds of pursuit but all he could hear were his footsteps echoing off the wall beside him.

At the end of the road was a T-junction. To the right were a number of buildings, to the left the road ran straight for 50 metres before it came to a junction with a much busier road. As he watched, a blipvert appear above the traffic on the road.

"Looking for a second chance?"

Randall sprinted towards the road and away. He didn't need a second invitation. As he ran past the blipvert and on towards freedom, the message changed.

"What would you do differently, with next-gen Re-Life?"

Randall sat in front of the terminal, unsure whether to continue. Ten minutes datasphere access had cost him his jacket, but looking at the state of some of the other customers he wasn't the only person who had bartered for access. The shop he was in rented out private datasphere terminals by the minute, no questions asked. What you did within that time was your own business, but each cubicle had a tissue dispenser so the owner probably had a good idea of what usually went on. Randall had made for the Shambles as soon as he had found his bearings. It had been the obvious choice. As long as he didn't draw attention to himself he would be safe.

If he was to stay, though, he needed money and quickly. But he couldn't just get some from his account. He didn't trust the datasphere any more. Whoever had taken him were powerful. If he accessed his accounts he was convinced that they would find him and take him back to the hospital. He needed help, but the question was who could he ask? Throughout his terrifying journey here, he'd thought of and discounted nearly everybody he knew, leaving him with only one choice. Randall quietly mumbled his personal access codes into the terminal and made a call.

"Randall?"

"Steph, I need your help."

"You need my help? What happened to you helping me? Why did you call Sian to say the deal was off? I thought we'd made an agreement."

Randall felt disorientated. "I haven't called anyone."

"Don't lie. I heard one of the messages myself."

What was she talking about? "I don't understand. When did this happen?"

"About a week after we met. You said that your company had changed their mind about the missing girl and it was best that we didn't contact each other again. Bloody hell, Randall, I trusted you."

Randall tried to think back but in his mind it was difficult to separate his dreams from reality. Was this another dream? He touched the desk in front of him. It felt real, yet what Stephanie was saying sounded just like one of his dreams. The textured grain under his fingers gave Randall some reassurance. "I didn't send a message, Steph. I couldn't have. I haven't touched the datasphere in weeks."

"That's ridiculous. I heard your voice."

"It wasn't me. I had an accident, at least that's what they said."

The line went silent for a moment. "If you're making this up…"

"I woke up in this room. They said I'd been in an accident and that they wanted me to get better but they just kept me in the room."

"Who? Who wouldn't let you go?"

"I don't know. I never saw them. They kept saying they were making me better but I've felt better for weeks. Don't ask me how I know, but they wanted to keep me there and I don't know why. I'm really scared, Steph. I know this sounds crazy and I wouldn't blame you for not believing me but they wouldn't let me leave. I had to escape, but now I've got nothing. I can't access my money because they'll find me. Please, Steph, you're the only person I know who has enough power to help me."

The line went quiet. Randall felt the insidious creep of panic snake up his spine. "Steph? Steph, are you there?" She was the only one he had left. If she refused to help, he didn't know what he would do.

"Where are you?"

Randall tasted a sourness in his mouth. Why would she ask that? He could feel his hands shaking. What if she was with them? What if she was in on it? He turned, convinced that somebody was watching him, but there was just the blank locked door. Randall took a deep breath and tried to relax. He had to trust her. What choice did he have? "I'm somewhere safe. Look, I don't need much, just some money and some datalenses."

"Datalenses? How are you contacting me now?"

"I'm in a booth. I've re-routed a number of times, enough to make this difficult to trace if I'm quick."

"Randall, I don't know what's going on, but if what you say is true you need to stay off the datasphere. Send me a message to let me know where I can meet you and then stay offline. I'll do my best to get to you as soon as I can."

"Thank you Steph, I really appreciate this."

"Don't thank me. I might be the reason you're in trouble."

The icon went out and Randall was left wondering what Stephanie had meant.

CHAPTER TWENTY-FIVE
Re-Life Technician

The Technician couldn't focus. How could he, with the experiment proceeding at such a pace? Only once the results were through, once the experiment was complete, could he relax again. He had tried to limit himself to checking progress at night. Security were used to him keeping odd hours and with the bulk of staff at home he could access most areas without any suspicion. But as the clone drew closer to maturity, the compulsion to check grew. Suddenly it wasn't enough to wait until night time. The speed of development was such that he needed to monitor the clone at least two or three times a day. The problem was, if he did it remotely he would leave a trail. He needed to check the clone in situ, in one of the Gestation Unit control modules, to make sure he couldn't be traced. That was why he found himself in Control Unit 17A.

The unit was undergoing routine air conditioning maintenance, rendering it too hot for people to work there. The Technician had waited until the maintenance staff went for their break before entering. He only needed 15 minutes to complete the work, which was lucky as the atmosphere in the room was almost unbearable. Twice he'd been too slow to wipe the sweat from his brow, allowing a drop to run down his nose and splash onto the dusty console in front of him. There was dust and dirt everywhere, covering his hands and his clothes. He was even breathing the repulsiveness in. The quicker he was out of here the better.

"Excuse me. What the hell are you doing in my control room?"

The Technician spun around, stifling a scream. A young woman stood at the doorway, glaring at him. He shut the monitoring screen and stepped back from the control module.

"Did you not hear me? Who are you? This is a restricted area. You shouldn't be here."

Panic coursed through him. What should he do? What excuse could he come up with? He cursed himself for not preparing a story earlier.

"If you don't answer I'm going to call security."

Tell no-one, they had said, and be careful. If this woman ran to security, it would be the end of everything. Experimenting on clones had been banned for over half a century. He could end up in jail, his life's work in ruins, if he didn't come up with something fast. His body screamed at him to run, his legs shaking as the muscles tensed for action, but if he ran he might as well just tattoo criminal on his forehead. He could feel himself going red, his guilt on display for all to see. Get a hold of yourself, he thought. You have status here, use it.

He looked at his accuser. "I don't like being disturbed while running routine diagnostics." He took his ID card from his pocket, thrusting it towards her to disguise the trembling. "I need another five minutes to finish off. The control room will be free afterwards."

The woman took one look at his ID and her eyes widened. This is it, he thought, she's going to call security. He turned back to the control module, pretending to work; his mind frantically trying to think of a way out of his predicament.

"You're.... but.... my god, I thought you were dead."

"You know who I am?"

The woman nodded.

"Well, I'm not dead." He waggled his fingers at her. "See, fully functioning."

It was the woman's turn to colour a little, her eyes flicking between the pass and him. "What do you do here? I mean, if you don't mind me asking."

Tell no-one, be careful. He could still see the look on the agent's face as she had hinted at the consequences if he failed. He needed to shut this woman up, to get out of here before things got out of hand. He spotted the pointed shape of a thermoprobe.

"I'm sorry,' the woman continued, "it's just such a shock. You saved my life, well, your work did. If it wasn't for you, I would have died from leukaemia. I've wanted to be a scientist ever since."

The Technician hardly heard the woman over the blood pounding in his ears. Could he kill? Was he really prepared do take someone's life? Some of her words filtered through and part of him felt ashamed, reminded of how far he had fallen. "That was all a long time ago," he said. "Things move on. Now if you don't mind, I need to finish my work."

"So what are you working on?" She started to walk over to where he was sitting. "Do you need any help? It would be an honour to work with you."

A small amount of urine dripped down his leg, tickling as it tripped from hair to hair. Scared that she would notice, he pushed his seat closer to the control panel. The thermoprobe was in reach, its point catching the light. He glanced back at the woman.

"You need to go." What was wrong with this woman? Couldn't she take a hint? The pungent smell of his urine struck his nostrils. Surely she could smell it too? Sweat dripped from his armpits and down his ribcage. He was finding it hard to breathe. Go, you stupid woman, he thought. Just go will you. He moved his hand towards the thermoprobe.

The woman kept moving forward. "Honestly, I would be honoured to work with you."

"You can't. You don't have the clearance." His hand closed around the probe's handle, the ridges pressing into his palm as his grip tightened. If she moved any closer he'd have no choice. Please go away. Don't make me do this. Please don't make me do this.

"I can assure you that I qualified with—"

He turned toward her, probe hidden, ready to strike. "I don't care what you qualified with. The last thing I need is some simpering puppy following me around. I have important things to deal with. Now leave me alone."

He heard a sharp intake of breath as he spoke. "How dare you?"

"How dare I? How dare you, coming in here, disturbing my work and then not leaving when asked to. What did you think, that I'd be happy to talk? How many people do you think my work has saved? Should I just drop everything every time one of you wants to say thank you?

"The reason people don't know I work here is because that is how I like it. I don't want to work with anyone else. I don't *need* to work with anyone else. People think they help but they just get in the way, slowing everything down while I'm forced to patiently explain every little detail as if to a child. It's pathetic. Now, if you know what's good for you, you will leave. I was never here. And if any word of our meeting gets out, I will personally make sure that not only will you lose your job, but that you will never find another scientific job anywhere, ever again. Now get out."

"You arrogant shit." The woman turned and strode out of the door. The Technician slumped in his chair. The woman would never know that he'd saved her life once more. He felt sick. What had they turned him into? He could feel the urine by his ankle now, and was sure some had dripped onto the floor. Would he have done it? Would he really have used the thermoprobe? He heard a clatter as it dropped from his fingers. Sweating and urine stained, he was glad he would never find out.

CHAPTER TWENTY-SIX
The Politician

I'm not wrong, I know I'm not. There's a discrepancy in the transiessence data. It's there. Why won't the bastard Professor believe me? I've checked the data again liked he asked, but it's still there. Once the transfer starts, some of the data refuses to be transferred. The artificial brain maintains its integrity but for some reason the data doesn't go across. It shouldn't be possible, yet every time I review the data, every time I recreate the experiment, the results remain the same. There is a definite loss of data, yet once the host gains consciousness the data is suddenly there, as if it had been there all along. It doesn't make sense.

One of the earliest political lessons Sian had taught Stephanie was around the law of unforeseen consequences. The example Sian had used loomed large in Stephanie's mind as she made her way to the rendezvous. After the upheaval the country had been in chaos. To take back control, new laws were enacted increasing surveillance in public areas. The policymakers believed that with every part of the country under surveillance, criminal activity and public disorder would fall to virtually nothing. This was true, up to a point. While public order was restored, the incidences of violent crime increased year on year. What the policy makers had failed to foresee was humanity's innate need for depravity. Taking away the belief that you could behave badly without being caught was like removing the safety valve from a pressure cooker. For a small percentage of the population, the need to do wrong would build but there was no potential outlet. With their need unfulfilled, the desire to do wrong would increase to such an extent that once snapped, the crimes committed would often be far worse than the original urge. While policymakers tried to implement ever more Draconian measures to crack down on these crimes, many local communities chose a different route.

Areas within cities and towns across the country, most areas of deprivation, were quietly removed from the surveillance net. Vandalised cameras were not replaced, patrolling was reduced, a blind eye turned to petty crime. As the levels of low-level crime in these areas rose, the level of serious violent crime receded. In some areas an understanding was developed between the authorities and key crime families. The families would have a free hand to run these special areas as long as no serious crime took place. Most criminal leaders knew where the line was drawn and "policed" the areas relatively successfully. The Scrambles was one such area.

Despite this knowledge, Stephanie refused to think through the implications of what she was doing. No delegate in their right mind wanted to be seen in the Scrambles; it was political suicide. The electorate wanted their representatives to be good, law-abiding folk. The only reason for going to the Scrambles was to do something outside the boundaries of the law.

At least engineering a break in her schedule had been easier than she had thought. The shock of James' death meant that Sian had lost her usual attention to detail. She'd arranged a meeting between Stephanie and Delegate Maddison, but he'd blown her out. That call had been pretty fiery; there was another person who'd recently lost focus. Rather than concentrating on the vote, he saw himself instead as a natural leader of the anti-polling faction. With the protest march due to take place tomorrow, he'd decided to meet with the movement's leaders. It was typical Maddison, fighting for the minority against the majority. Instead of informing Sian, Stephanie kept the meeting in the diary and slipped out of the office.

The wind had an extra bite today, the cold acid-etching itself into her skin and through to the bone. Stephanie pulled up the collar of her coat. She hadn't visited the Scrambles since her student days but her memory of the place was still vivid. She walked with purpose through narrow cobbled streets, sticking to the main thoroughfares while trying her best to look as if she belonged. The overcast conditions and closeness of the buildings cast a natural gloom, partially broken by lurid shop signs.

Almost anything could be bought at the Scrambles, if you had the money. Stephanie passed signs offering drugs to elate and drugs to depress, the sale of women, men and all shades in-between; the chance to inflict pain or have pain inflicted upon you, and of course, dreamshaper. Stephanie's one and only experience of the drug had been at University, before it had been made illegal. She had been at a party with some friends when a guy she quite fancied at the time offered her a blue tablet.

"With one of these you can do anything or be anything you want," he said. "Just take one, wait 'til you feel a tingling in your hands, and watch whatever you want to feel."

Laying back on the floor, Stephanie had placed the pill in her mouth. She could remember feeling nervous as the tingling developed. She played her chosen footage on her datalenses and suddenly she was flying. She could feel cold wind rush over her skin as she glided through the air. There was a slight feeling of weightlessness as a thermal lifted her. The sense of freedom was invigorating. She could go wherever she wanted through a flick of her wing or a twitch of her tail, effortlessly gliding to wherever she desired. The longer she flew, the more in control she felt. She was at one with her new shape. She *was* a bird, a hawk searching for prey, looking to swoop on one of the lesser creature. She was the mistress of the skies. The desire to hunt was overwhelming. She was God's arrow, swift and sure in pursuit of her goal, the thrill of the mid-air snatch, the ripping of sinews as her beak plunged into the body of her prey, the hot metallic taste as the blood was released and—

It felt like a physical rip in her brain as the footage stopped. She was told later that her scream sounded like a hawk's cry. She'd had no concept of where she was, freaking out for what felt an eternity until the strangers surrounding her coalesced into friends. To her shame she had voided herself through sheer terror, but in a way she was the lucky one. Her trip had been interrupted because another student, one more experienced with the drug, had decided to watch cliff jumping. What he didn't know was the footage had been taken from a death artist. The fatal impact had seared itself into the student's brain, the neural shock causing instant cardiac arrest.

Stephanie arrived at the bar, ordered a steaming cup of anijsmelk, then sat by the window as agreed. She inhaled the aniseed steam as she watched for signs of Randall. She had expected to see the streets full of the dregs of humanity, ugly people corrupted by the filth on the inside. Instead, she realised that she could have been anywhere.

"You're late."

Stephanie jumped, the spilled anijsmelk scalding her hand. "Bloody hell Randall, you scared the life out of me."

He took the seat opposite and Stephanie was shocked by his appearance. If he had not have spoken, she would never have recognised him as the man she'd met just a few weeks earlier. Randall was not in good shape. He was pale, shivering despite his bulk, with dark smudges under his sunken eyes. His lower face was covered by a heavy beard, much greyer than his lank hair.

"I needed to get close to make sure it was you." Randall's eyes never stopped moving; one moment looking down, then at her, then behind her, then at the window. "Do you have the money and datalenses?"

"Yes, but we need to talk first. Do you want a drink?"

"No." He rocked backwards and forwards as he spoke, palms rubbing at the tops of his thighs as if to warm himself.

"You said you had an accident."

"That's what I was told. I remember being in a pod. We made a right turn, crossing the stream of traffic coming the other way, and then nothing. I woke up in a hospital."

"That's where you said you were being held."

Randall kept glancing towards the window. "They then said I was a danger to others, but I'm fine. I have been for a while."

"A danger to others?"

"Some rubbish about being contaminated at the accident site."

Stephanie shivered. For a moment she had thought he meant something else. She took another gulp of her drink. "Can anyone else confirm your story? Did anyone come to visit you, while you were there?"

Randall glared at her, before looking down at the table. "No."

"Why not? What about your friends, your work colleagues?"

"We had a falling out. That's why I called you. There's no-one else."

Randall looked up at Stephanie and she saw a world of hurt in his eyes, hurt for which she was responsible. Her actions had already led to the death of James, she couldn't cope if they led to the death of another.

"I'm so sorry, Randall. I think you might be caught up in something, something to do with me. I don't know why you are involved, but if I'm to help you I need to find out." She smiled at him but he quickly looked away. "Before your accident, you said that you would look further into what Jennica was doing for Re-Life."

"She was looking at Transiessence data."

"What's Transiessence data?"

"It's the biological and electrical data collected as part of the Re-Life process. It's what makes you, you. It's used to create the artificial brain, where your personality is held until the clone is grown. Once the clone's brain reaches maturity, they start to feed data to it from the artificial brain. She thought there was a data transfer error in the first few moments after activation. She blogged that the data levels didn't balance initially but came back in balance quickly afterwards."

Stephanie nodded, as if she understood. So he was being truthful about that, at least. "So Jennica thought the data that makes you, you, wasn't being transferred to the clone."

"Right."

"Isn't that a big deal?"

"Maybe, but the discrepancy level, if it existed, was tiny. It would be like breaking an elephant apart, putting it back together and finding it was missing two hairs off its head. My guess is that there was a measurement error."

"So you think she made a mistake."

"*She* thought she could have made a mistake, that's why she posted it up in the first place."

"And if it was confirmed there was a transfer issue?"

"No idea. My best guess is that it meant somebody's birthday gets forgotten." Randall looked out of the window and froze, mouth open. Stephanie turned her head to see what he was looking at but there was nothing there. She turned back to Randall and his face looked ashen.

"Have we finished? I really need to get going."

"There's just one more thing—"

Randall grabbed her wrist. "I need the money and datalenses. Now."

Stephanie snatched her hand back. "Don't you ever do that to me."

"I'm sorry, I really am. Please Stephanie, I need your help."

She looked at him for a moment, her old friend, her old lover. The man seemed terrified of her. What had happened to him? She reached into her pocket and placed a package on the table. "There should be enough money here to last you a couple of weeks."

"And the datalenses?"

"They're in the bag too."

Randall grabbed the packet and got up from his chair. "Thank you." He leant forward and Stephanie automatically jerked backwards, almost falling off her chair in an effort to get away. Randall looked across at her, his face shocked. "I only wanted to kiss you on the cheek." With tears welling up in his eyes, he ran out of the door.

CHAPTER TWENTY-SEVEN
The Investigator

A few years ago in a speech to his employees, Deepak Chowdhury joked that his agency had been built on a solid bedrock of domestic abuse. He went on to say that it was a sad indictment of society that despite millions of years of evolution, if you were ever unfortunate enough to be attacked during your lifetime, the perpetrator was likely to be somebody you knew or even loved.

Nico stared once more at the case details. It fitted Chowdhury's profile in all its tawdry details. A couple met when young, became lovers, then the woman became pregnant. As the pressure built they fought, verbally at first as the woman looked to exert her independence and the man struggled to accept she had changed. They compounded the situation by having another child—lack of sleep adding fuel to the fire—and the arguments turned to bullying and the bullying turned to violence. The agency were brought in after the man was admitted to hospital with a fractured skull, broken jaw and collarbone, 12 cracked ribs and severe bruising of the face and abdomen. He didn't want to press charges but the law was clear; the pattern of domestic abuse was difficult to break due to most victim's refusal to prosecute. Now the state took the decision out of their hands.

The case was a goldmine. Nico knew what to do—the

policy was clear—he just didn't like it. He had interviewed both suspect and victim. His questions having just one goal: profit. Had they spoken to anyone about their problems? Any friends or government agencies? Did any of the physical or verbal assaults take place in front of the children? With each and every discovery, the charges increased and the profit margin rose. Chowdhury always maintained that for domestic violence to flourish, it must be aided by collusion, incompetence or wilful ignorance; all of which were billable in one form or another.

Nico developed the charges meticulously, desperate to prove he could still be an income-generator for the agency. The work wasn't taxing though, leaving his mind free to wander. Was this really what he had become an Investigator for? Was it right to ruin lives for the sake of profit? Part of him wanted to rebel, to say enough was enough, but he knew what that would mean for his family. For Nico, when faced with a choice between morality and family, there was only one winner, no matter how he felt.

He finished his report and made the call.

"Hello Professor."

"Let me call you back."

The icon disappeared. Nico reclined in his chair. Maybe he'd had company. Moments later an anonymous call came through.

"Are you out of your mind?"

"Professor, I—"

"Have you any idea what you've done? I shouldn't even be speaking to you."

"But—"

"I'm going to send you something, then I never want to hear from you again. You didn't send me anything, we haven't spoken about anything. Do you understand?"

"Look, if you're worried—"

"Worried? You've no fucking idea! I'm not worried, I'm

fucking terrified. I've learnt things this week that I had no idea existed, things that shouldn't be possible. The only reason I'm sending you this is so I can be rid of it."

As the call icon went, a message icon appeared, winking at him as if filled with malevolent intent. He had no idea what had scared the Professor, but the fact he was scared wasn't in doubt. Was the message even safe to open? Maybe he should just delete it? Nobody would be any the wiser. That was the safest course. Delete the mail and be done. Nico went to speak the command and then stopped. What if it had been Maria who had gone missing? What would he do then?

The file opened. Inside was the original footage he had sent to the Professor. Confused, Nico played the file.

He watched as a pod pulled up at the end of a familiar street. The scene was one he recognised but the angle of the footage was new. Where had the Professor got it from? Jennica stepped out of the pod and walked towards her home. She paused for a moment. From her actions she appeared to be talking to somebody out of sight, her arms gesturing, pointing in the direction she's heading. Nico felt himself sucked into the footage until it became his whole world. He'd traced every bit of footage available, so why hadn't he seen this before? As he watched, the conversation appeared to be over and Jennica continued down the road. The footage flicked to a different angle, something very familiar. It was taken from behind Jennica, from a camera in a solicitor's office close to where the pod stopped. It had taken Nico days of negotiation before they had released the footage. He watched as she approached the trees where she disappeared. Nico knew this footage well, having viewed it what seemed like a million times, yet in all the times he'd watched it he'd never seen the figure under the trees, just visible despite their dark clothing. In the original footage Jennica walked under the trees and was lost in shadow, but here Nico could clearly see the figure as she walked past. With a gasp, Nico stopped the playback. Had he seen that

correctly? He rewound the footage and ran it forward at half speed. Yes! As Jennica walked past, the figure glanced down the road, directly at the surveillance camera.
 "Got you."

CHAPTER TWENTY-EIGHT
The Information Cleanser

Randall waited in the alleyway until Stephanie left the café. Despite everything, his body betrayed him whenever he saw her. He had wished it had been possible to spend more time with her, but it was better for the both of them that she was gone.

All through their meeting he'd felt that familiar nagging feeling. He couldn't work it out at first. He had looked around the bar, staring through the walls into the far distance, hoping to get a hint of whatever message had been left for him. It was only while he was looking out of the window—his mind drifting back to earlier times—that the warning had coalesced in the pattern of bricks above the doorway opposite. The message was simple. They're coming.

He hadn't had time for the heart-to-heart he had been hoping for, to ask why she had dumped him so long ago. The need to be away overcame everything. It was critical that he left, for both their sakes. But the look on her face when he had tried to kiss her cheek goodbye had slashed across that ancient wound with an intensity in total disregard of time. Did she really think he would hurt her? He didn't have a chance to raise the question. Given how much effort they had used to find him, he knew they wouldn't be too far away. So he left, to escape capture and to avoid being betrayed by his own emotions.

Randall clenched his teeth hard to stop the chattering and waited. After 20 minutes he decided that his flight had been successful, and made a circuitous route back to the hotel he'd spotted earlier. After checking in under an assumed name he went up to his room and closed the door. His relief was palpable. The room looked as if it had been decorated during the last century. 1970s porno chic was not to his taste, but the room was clean and secure. He set the lock then lay down on the circular bed that dominated the space. The sheets felt soft and smelt of roses, so different from the antiseptic smell of the hospital. His energy leeched from his body, causing him to sink deeper and deeper into the mattress.

It was night when he woke. The room was bathed in a flamingo pink light coming through the open curtains. As had been the case for weeks now, sleep had given him no respite. Randall lay on the bed, trying to work out what his dream had meant. He'd been on a date with Sylvianne at Capaldi's, an Italian restaurant that had recently opened in the city. While he'd always thought Sylvianne attractive, whenever they had spoken she had always maintained her professional facade. Not in his dream. She was playful, charming; she had even teased him about his dress sense. They shared food, the taste of each mouthful so vivid that it made his mouth water just thinking of it. He could still feel the Chianti warming his cheeks and softening the rough edges of their interaction. It clearly had an effect on Sylvianne too. During dessert, she had stroked the back of his calf with her shoeless foot. By the end of the meal they were holding hands, Sylvianne softly biting her lower lip as he said what a great night he'd had. He paid the bill—at 237 globals it was not cheap—and there was time for a quick kiss and cuddle before he walked Sylvianne to her pod.

Remembering that final dream embrace brought the

reality of his situation crashing in. He was alone, friendless, unsure if he could trust the only person who could help him and all the while hunted by persons unknown. A sense of despair welled up from deep within and for a moment Randall almost surrendered. How could he continue to exist in this way, always looking over his shoulder, expecting to be snatched out of society at any moment? Then he thought back to his weeks in the hospital, his alternate existence.

He turned on a side light and pulled up the room service menu on the room's datascreen, ordering a pizza and a drink. He then picked up Stephanie's package. He put the money to one side and pulled out the datalenses, fingers trembling as he opened the packaging. If he wanted to have any chance of finding out what was happening, he needed to take a risk. Lying back on the bed, he slipped in the lenses and started hunting.

Initial progress was painful. Randall couldn't risk opening his profile as he usually did. It was far too traceable. He needed to create firewalls and security loops before that would be possible. Instead he had to use the datalenses on their vanilla settings. He felt like a child learning to walk. The oral and eye commands he had so patiently built up since starting school were gone. Without the security in place it was unsafe to access his profile, but without his personalised data the datalenses would have to be taught everything from scratch. Unable to wait, he had visited a couple of NewsAggre's, keen to look for any information on his accident. Pod accidents were rare, collisions between pods unheard of. His accident should have been big news, easy to find, yet because of the settings it took minutes to achieve the most basic tasks. Randall growled in frustration as he tripped over the most simple things, unable to stop his muscle memory from executing actions that had no response. Realising he couldn't continue in this way, he set about building security to protect his identity and location.

The last slice of pizza was cold by the time Randall was happy with what he had put in place. Providing he was quick, nothing and no-one would be able to trace him. As a final measure, he let loose a few counter-tracking agents. But it was still with some trepidation that he loaded his profile. The transformation was dramatic. The baby steps from earlier were gone. He was quicksilver, as fast as thought itself. Randall went back to the NewsAggre's, looking for any reports on his accident. There was nothing. He searched for signs of cleansing but again drew a blank. Having hit a wall he started filtering back, day by day, until he came upon something he recognised. A number of news stories chimed with things that he already knew, yet the timings were all wrong. Re-Life 2 had been launched to great acclaim. That was no surprise, but he recognised quotes from the CEO despite knowing he had been in the hospital at the time. He dismissed the thought as coincidence. Perhaps they just sounded familiar because he'd heard something similar in the past. The news that Jennica Fabian was still missing reassured him a little. At least Stephanie's questions made sense.

Randall thought hard, trying to pierce through the haze to when his accident took place, but his memories failed to solidify. The colour green was predominant but he had no idea why. Had he been riding through the park at the time? Thinking back to that time was frustrating, akin to grabbing moonlight. Instead of wasting his time further, Randall checked his messages, confident he could determine when he went missing by looking at the earliest message on his unread list. His message box was empty. Stunned, he stared at the emptiness for a few seconds before fear swept through him and he shut everything down. How was that possible? It was unthinkable that he hadn't received anything since he'd been offline; at the very least he should have received prompts from work, or messages from Seegers asking where the hell he was. The security on his messaging system was one of the best available. If somebody had broken into his messages, was there anywhere left that was safe to access?

He lay quietly on the bed as he thought. His mouth was dry yet he had run out of drink. Not wanting to risk room service again, he walked to the bathroom to fill his glass. The water was tepid and had a slightly metallic taste, but it was better than nothing. Randall splashed some water on his face, trying to clear his head. Was it safe to continue? Was it safe not to? Back in the bedroom he re-accessed the datasphere using the datalenses' vanilla settings, laboriously checking through the security processes he'd set up. Everything held. He checked the trackers. Again nothing. Satisfied that to the best of his knowledge nobody had been alerted to his activity, he attempted to access his company's system.

User access invalid. User already logged on in another session.

He gripped the bedsheets as he felt the room spin. That couldn't be right. Employees had to sign in via a neural command linked to their Re-Life profile. The security system was based on each individual's neural fingerprint, impossible to break or duplicate.

Randall tried to access once more.

User access invalid. User already logged on in another session.

What was going on? He paced the room, rubbing his hands over his face as he thought. There must be a glitch in the datalenses' neural connector. It happened occasionally with some of the cheaper models. A moment of doubt surfaced. Maybe Stephanie was part of a plan to stop me. Thinking back to their meeting, Randall remembered Stephanie having an odd expression on her face when she thought he wasn't looking. Had she set him up?

Furious at the thought of her betrayal, Randall lashed out, smashing his fist into the wall. Pain from his knuckles shot up his arm, electric spikes of agony sharpening his senses, clarifying the truth. He smashed the wall again, his mind blazing with humiliation. Why did they always let him down? Why? With each blow, the agonising, beautiful pain cleansed him, washing out the dross of fear and self-doubt. There was no point in complaining about fairness; he was where he was. What he needed to do was deal with it.

As quickly as it had erupted his fury passed. Randall sat for a moment, catching his breath. If his company's system had been compromised it would be madness to try to gain access again. At the same time, he still had no idea who was after him and how long he had been held. He needed to try something else.

Banks. He laughed out loud as the thought hit him. How could he have been so stupid? The banks had the most secure systems known. He could look at his bank records and see the last time he had been micro-billed for datasphere access. Randall ran through the security routines once more and logged back via his profile. He accessed the banking module and checked his account. The list contained typical, everyday expenses: multiple pod charges, home entertainment costs, groceries, hotel bar bills, restaurant bills, cash withdrawals, salary payments; the list went on and on, including page after page of datasphere access charges. The pattern repeated, day after day, nothing excessive but with no signs of a break. He didn't understand. How was this possible? He felt the room sway and had to lean on the wall to stop himself falling. Nothing seemed real anymore. Backwards and forwards he scanned through the list of transactions, looking for something, anything out of the ordinary. Little speckles of light appeared in front of his eyes. It felt as if someone was sitting on his chest. It wasn't right, none of this was right.

Randall made a whimpering sound. He'd known this disorientation before, when he was a child. He had gone upstairs to see his parents, walked into their bedroom, and found his father hitting his mother with a strap, her yelps muffled by a gag. Randall had rushed forward, grabbing his father's arm in an attempt to stop him hurting her further, but his mother had just shrieked and his father had shouted at him. He could still feel the tears as his mother pushed him out of the door, telling him never to come into their bedroom without knocking again. His world had changed then. His comfortable childhood shattered, trust in his parents evaporated.

His eyes flicked down the list of charges but what he saw just confirmed that the world wasn't as he thought. He wanted to understand, he truly wanted to understand, but what he was seeing was impossible. He wanted it to go away yet he couldn't stop looking. Each impossible entry felt like the crack of leather on his mother's backside, leaving an angry red welt on his psyche. Part of him couldn't look but another part couldn't resist, powerless against the wrongness of what was in front of him.

And then he saw it. A charge from four days ago:

Capaldi Restaurant - 237 globals.

Those four words burst the dam, and Randall went under.

CHAPTER TWENTY-NINE
The Politician

I finally managed to access the source documents today. Why they made it so difficult I've no idea. All I'm trying to do is understand what is going on. Not that it helped. The missing/reappearing data appears to be purely electrical with no link to any biological activity at all. How is this possible? Part of me thinks it was a scanning glitch, but I've reproduced the results twice now and it doesn't explain how the data reappears without being transferred. So on top of everything we now have unaccounted electrical activity in the brain. What is going on?

"Please. You can't do this to me."

"I'm sorry Stephanie, but the answer is still no. Don't you realise what is happening? The populous are rising. They see what is happening and they aren't prepared to stand for it."

"You promised me your support."

"Stop wasting your time on the budget and join me instead. If the anti-polling movement gets enough momentum, we can tear this corrupt edifice down and start again, just like our forefathers."

"Don't be a fool. You'll fail. Too many people like the new system. The polls show—"

"Do you think the people who operate the polling system don't understand how to rig a vote?"

"Please, Bobby. If you can't do it for me, then do it for James."

"And play into their hands? I'm sorry, Stephanie, but I did warn you. I'm not the one responsible for that poor boy's death."

Stephanie walked out of Maddison's office. Bastard! How dare he blame her for what happened to James. He knew as well as she did who was responsible. But the barb had stung because it had echoed her own thoughts too closely.

Outside the Legislature, crowds had gathered to protest against the global electoral system, pillorying those that entered or left the building. The whole city was on edge, either angry because of the voting system or scared about the planned march. The datasphere was heading towards boiling point as normally calm people became spooked by rumour and insinuation.

She climbed into the nearest pod and headed home, ignoring the crowds and their fears. The bastard was winning. Since James had died, Stephanie had struggled to keep the anti-budget voting block together. With Maddison pulling out, it looked like her attempt was doomed. On top of that, the ongoing Journo attacks were having an effect despite Addy's best efforts to counter. Her rating was sinking and there was still no break in the investigation. She refused to stop fighting, but she was tired. It felt like the rising surge was becoming too strong, she was doing everything in her power to keep going, but if things continued as they were, at some point she would slip under. The thought of Gant celebrating yet another victory made her want to scream.

She was jerked back to the present as the pod slowed to a halt. Stephanie queried the datasphere. It seemed that domestic security had started shutting down the main arteries into and out of the city in preparation for the protest march. A number of road blocks had been set up to protect the wealthier suburbs. Stephanie activated her security override and the pod started moving again. Other people were not so lucky. A row of pods stood silently by the side of the road. At the front, a woman holding a baby was remonstrating with a helmeted trooper. Anger, anxiety and fear were mixing to produce a toxic atmosphere. All it needed was a spark. That was when she got the call from Addy.

"Where is she?"

"She's in the back. She's... she's not good."

Stephanie leant forward and gave Addy a hug. "Thanks, Addy. I think you've done enough for today. Why don't you get yourself home while you can. Things are starting to get a little crazy out there."

"Are you sure? I can always stay for a bit longer."

"Go, before I change my mind." Stephanie smiled to herself as Addy collected her things. At least someone was still keeping it together.

She could hear sobbing as soon as she walked into the bathroom.

"Sian? It's Steph. Can I come in?" She eased the cubicle door open. Sian was sitting on the floor shaking, arms wrapped around her knees. Stephanie knelt beside her friend and took her in her arms.

"Hey, come on now. Nothing's worth getting like this."

"Don't. Please don't. I can't stand it."

Stephanie refused to let Sian push her away. "It's OK, Sian. I'm here for you."

"Stop it. I've had enough. I can't do this any more."

"Of course you can. We're all going through a tough time but we'll pull through. You'll be back to your best in no time."

"You don't get it, do you? It's my fault. It's all my fault."

Stephanie stroked her friends hair. "Don't be silly, Sian. We were all involved in pulling together the strategy. We're a team. We succeed or fail together."

"Please, you're not listening..."

"Think back to why we are doing this. It was you who showed me how the political system was out of kilter, how the politicians were serving their own interest and not those of the electorate. I have you to thank for giving me the kick up the backside I needed. We're here to do good, Sian. We are the good guys."

"Get off!" Stephanie found herself falling backwards as her friend pushed her away. "You don't understand. I killed him. It was my fault. I killed James!" Sian's face was pale, her red-rimmed eyes wide, almost disbelieving as the words spilled out. For the first time Stephanie noticed the faint red criss-crosses covering Sian's forearms, some crusted with fresh blood. There was a red-smeared blade on the cistern lid.

"Oh Sian, what have you done?"

Sian looked at the floor, the words coming slowly, her breath ragged. "You wouldn't listen. I tried to help, but you wouldn't take any notice. I had to do something." Sian's body shook as she spoke, her chattering teeth making it difficult to understand her words.

"Nothing is worth harming yourself for."

Sian continued as if she hadn't heard. "They said they

wanted to make a deal. They would invest in the district, support my vision if I let them know what you were up to. I had no idea what they would do. I had no idea..."

Stephanie felt as if she had been punched in the stomach. No. Not Sian. "Who said this? Was it Gant? Please tell me you didn't talk to Gant?"

Her friend nodded.

Stephanie wanted to scream. After all she had done to reassure Sian that she had nothing to worry about. She done her best to protect Sian from the truth of what had happened to James and keep her focussed on their goal. Stephanie had realised her insistence that James look into the voting patterns had most likely led to his death. She knew it hadn't been an accident, but she'd had to suppress her guilt because she couldn't afford to lose focus. Yet all along it had been Sian, her so-called friend, who had betrayed him. Just so she could be proven right. "You stupid idiot. You told them about James, didn't you. You told them about what he was doing, what I'd asked him to look into."

Sian took a step towards Stephanie, arms outstretched. "Please, Steph, I didn't know. Please."

The slap hit Sian full in the face, knocking her to the floor.

"How could you? You, of all people. What did they offer you? Money? A chance to work for them? Come on Sian, what did it take for you to betray your friends?"

"Nothing. I didn't take anything. I thought we could make a deal."

"Then you're a fool as well as a traitor." Stephanie looked at her former friend, barely suppressing the disgust she felt for the woman she had once looked up to.

"Please, Stephanie, I want to make this right."

"You can't."

"Please."

She looked pathetic, grovelling on the floor, her face covered in snot, spit and tears. To think she had looked up to this piece of shit. "Get out of here. Take your things and go.

I never want to see you again."

She pulled Sian up and dragged her to the corridor. "Don't you ever contact me again."

Stephanie watched Sian leave and then stormed down the corridor to the waiting room. The bastards were all as bad as each other, corrupted by the slightest promise of power, its necrotic effect rotting the flesh from their principles. She should never have got involved in the first place. She hated it, the whole rancid mess.

A call flashed onto her datalenses.

"What?"

"Is now not a good time?"

Stephanie took a deep breath. "How can I help you, Investigator."

"How well do you know Randall Jones?"

Stephanie felt the room shift slightly. How had he found out? She should never have met him in the Scrambles. "I told you, he's a friend from university. Why?"

"So you know him well?"

"Not really well. We lost contact. He only got back in touch recently to talk about Jennica."

"So you don't really know each other that well?"

"Look, Nico, I've had a really hard day. Can you just get to the point."

"Randall was involved in Jennica's disappearance."

Her stomach flipped. Bile hit the back of her throat. First Sian, now Randall. Stephanie sat before her legs gave out. "Are you sure?"

"Positive. I've just sent a file over. It's a still from new footage of Jennica's disappearance. I'm sorry, but it looks like you've been used."

The old Stephanie screamed at herself to disown him, to run away from what she'd done. She needed to protect her position, protect her reputation. But she was tired of it all, of having to deal with other people's lies and deceit. She wasn't going to become part of it. She was who she was and she had done what she had done, and if she was to be judged, it would be with a clear conscience.

"I met with him, with Randall, yesterday afternoon."

"Where?"

"The Scrambles."

There was a brief period of silence. "If you don't mind me asking, what were you doing in the Scrambles?"

Stephanie told the Investigator everything. The meeting, what he had said, how he had appeared, the fact that she had given him money and datalenses, nothing was left out. As she spoke, her queasiness disappeared.

"Did you believe him, about the hospital?"

"I know he believed it. He told me the truth about the transiessence data as well. Either he's a very good actor or there's more going on here than we know. I don't believe it's as straightforward as you say."

"I'm sorry, Delegate. I know he was a friend of yours and I'm sure this is a shock, but I've got hard evidence that proves his involvement."

"I understand, but I'm convinced we're only seeing part of the picture. Please try to keep an open mind." Stephanie didn't think for a minute he believed her, but she was past the point of caring.

"Where are you at the moment?"

"In my office."

"Are you alone?"

"I was on my way out."

"You should go somewhere safe, at least until we catch Jones. Can you send me your home address. I'll make sure somebody keeps watch over your place, just in case."

"I don't think he's after me. If he was, he had every chance yesterday to do something about it."

"Still…"

"OK."

"Thank you, Delegate." The icon blinked out.

Stephanie felt like a piece of driftwood, battered by forces beyond her control. Too many things were happening at once to take in. How had she allowed things to get to this state? She looked outside. It was starting to get dark. The protest march would have started by now. If she wanted to get home, she would need to leave soon.

The street was empty. Stephanie pulled her coat to her chin, turning up the heating while fishing in her pockets for gloves. The thickening mist made it hard to see to the end of the road. She walked towards the main thoroughfare; it would be easier to pick up a pod from there. The polling icon popped up at her command but she stopped herself from opening it. What was the point? Word would get out about her link to Randall. Gant would make sure of that. It was over. He'd won.

A pod turned into her street. Stephanie almost laughed. Looks like my luck is finally turning, she thought. At her signal it pulled across to her side of the road. She walked towards the pod when the doors peeled back. Two large men got out.

"Wow, that was quick. Did Investigator Tandelli send you?"

The shock of pain stunned her. One of the men had slapped something across her mouth. She tried to pull away but they were either side of her, forcing her arms up behind her back and slipping something over her wrists. There was more pain, this time from her shins as they kicked her legs from under her. Stephanie struggled against their grip as they dragged her along the path, her screams blocked by the gag. In panic, she looked up and down the street but there was nobody there, the mist concealing what was taking place. Within seconds she was bundled into the pod, landing face down on the back seat. Stephanie heard the doors seal and felt the vehicle move away.

"Lift her up, would you please. That's no way to treat a delegate."

Everything slowed at the sound of that voice. Stephanie could feel her heart lurch as it attempted to break free of her ribs. Instinct made her want to curl up into a ball, to hide away from what was happening, but two cruel hands gripped hold and hauled her up by her armpits. She tried to slump back but the hands were callous and she was forced to remain upright between her two assailants. Her eyes betrayed her, unable to stop themselves, they locked on the person opposite. Zachary Gant had a broad smile on his face.

"Hello, Stephanie."

Part 3

The Past

"This is ridiculous. How am I meant to work in these conditions?"

Josh threw down his tools in disgust as the emergency lighting flickered on, bathing the room in a soft, red glow. It was the second power outage this week. He tapped the sensor on the side of his eyewear, the impact resonating through his earpiece.

"Place call. Trial lab."

He waited a moment, unsure whether the power outage was local or regional. Then the call tone kicked in. It was a local blackout.

"Trial lab, Ben speaking."

"Ben, it's Josh. Have you been hit too?"

"Yep, everything's ground to a halt."

"Any accidents?"

"No, all golems remain standing. Looks like your adjustment worked."

Josh breathed a sigh of relief. "That's great. Once we're back up, run the sequence from the beginning." They had lost two golems during the last blackout from asphyxiation. The synthetic brain controlled the golem via a neural receiver planted in the hippocampus. If the signal was lost between the two, all body functions shut down. In response, Josh had developed a holding routine that he'd uploaded into each neural receiver. Now, if the signal was lost the golems would still freeze, but the program maintained basic organ functionality until the signal was restored.

"Er, Josh, hang on a minute. Something's going on."

Josh sat back in his chair. He hoped Ben hadn't spoken too soon. If they'd lost another golem, Kyle was going to go berserk. Still, it served him right, thought Josh. If he hadn't spent all his time brown-nosing his way to the top, I would be leading the project, not him.

"Josh? I think you need to get down here. Something strange is going on."

He let out a sigh. "OK, I'll be right down."

The team were frantically trying to get things in order by the time Josh got to the labs. He watched as staff set up the trial sequence within each of the rooms, guiding the golems back to their prearranged start positions, all the while looking to reassure them that everything was OK. Microphones relayed snippets of conversation to the observation gallery.

"I don't understand. What am I doing here?"

"You had a fall, Mr Jenkins. Why don't you sit down for a minute, get your breath back."

A two way mirror allowed Josh to see into their fabricated world, each element a replica of their original home. Not surprisingly, a number of golems looked anxious, clearly concerned about what had happened. If any of them became unmanageable, their handler had the ability to switch off the neural signal, but it didn't look like it would be required. This batch of golems had been selected for their docility. The original volunteers had been unaware that the neural scan and stem cell extraction procedure had nothing to do with a cure for Parkinson's disease but had instead been used to create copies of themselves. Josh had agonised over the ethics of what they were doing, but in the end decided that the golems were nothing more than very large tissue samples. If they weren't linked to their artificial brain, they were just lumps of meat.

He turned a corner and saw Ben ahead, staring into another test room.

"So what's up?"

"It's subject Alpha Two." Ben replied, pointing into the room. "When the power went off, it didn't stop like the rest of them."

Josh turned to see what Ben was looking at. An old man, late sixties, was sitting in his armchair stroking a tabby cat. There was a cup of tea on the table beside him and he was nodding his head to the music being piped into his room.

"What happened?"

"It started shouting, swearing about the power outage and how everything had gotten worse since the oil ban."

Josh smiled to himself. The golem had a point. The sooner the Sahara array was online, the better. "You haven't got both the original's and Alpha Two's signals feeding in to the same synthetic brain again, have you?" It had happened once before and led to some very awkward situations as the two sets of memories merged, shared dreams being the least of the problem.

"Certain, although it wouldn't make any difference. Everything in this place is fed from the same generator. When the power went, every other golem just stopped."

Josh felt his pulse quicken. Theoretically there had always been a possibility that a golem's brain would start to function separately from the artificial one.

"Can you turn the signal off again? I'd like to see it for myself."

Ben turned to him, grinning. "It's off. Alpha Two is running on its own power, so to speak."

Josh looked back at the old man. Alpha Two was one of the earliest test subjects, having been online for six weeks. Was that it? Was that all that was needed, enough time for the brain to interpret and take ownership of the neural sequencing? He rubbed his face with his hands. If he was correct, Alpha Two was proof that you could transfer a personality from the original host, via an artificial brain, to a clone. He'd created everlasting life.

"Get Alpha Two to the scanning group as soon as you can. I want to know exactly what is going on in that brain. Set up a series of memory tests. We need to speak to the original donor. Find out details of his life that nobody knows, then see how many answers Alpha Two can remember." He turned back to Ben. "What are you still doing here? Go. Now!"

Ben turned and ran down the corridor. In the test room, Alpha Two smiled to himself as the cat purred contentedly on his lap, blissfully unaware of the storm he had just released.

CHAPTER THIRTY
The Information Cleanser

She looked so beautiful, sitting there on the edge of his bed. How had he ever thought of her as cold and calculating? He stroked the line of her cheekbone with the tips of his fingers before sliding them down her neck. Goosebumps rose in response to his touch. She placed her hands on his shoulders and pulled him down, the sharp tang of raspberries on her lips. Her legs wrapped around his hips. Worrying that he would crush her, Randall rolled the two of them over until Sylvianne straddled him from above, hips gyrating as instinct took hold. Light spilled in from the doorway, leaving her body in silhouette. He lifted the bottom of her sweater, stroking her stomach as he raised it higher. The same moment he leant forward to kiss her breasts, Sylvianne bent down causing their heads to collide; the impact causing them both to burst into giggles. For a moment they pause, each waiting for the other to continue. Then, with a new found urgency they quickly undress, not wanting to delay any longer.

Whether overcome by shyness or just looking for an opportunity to tease him further, Sylvianne dived under the covers. Laughing, Randall joined her, the fact that he hadn't removed his socks adding a little to the absurdity of the moment. How had this happened? A good question, the part of him drifting above thought, observing the scene; how *had* this happened?

In the darkness, Randall explored Sylvianne's body as she explored his. They started gently, stroking fingers, the palm of the hand, across thighs, breasts, back, the nape of the neck; the kissing grew in passion, intensifying the depth of their contact. Unable to wait any longer, Randall rolled Sylvianne back on top, gasping as she raked her nails down his chest. She rocked her hips backwards and forwards, each movement teasing him, delaying the moment until with a shudder he felt himself inside her. She arched her back, the movement moving him deeper, and ground herself against him; each contact causing shivers of delight. Randall stroked her sides, his thumbs caressing the underside of her breasts before cupping them in his hands, his arms steady so her nipples could rub against his palms as she moved.

Slowly, ever so slowly, the speed of her motion increased. Randall moved his hips, looking to match the rhythm of Sylvianne's dance. Cautiously at first, but with more confidence, the two of them drew themselves down to that animal place, pushing themselves closer and closer; their joyous movement, the taste of salt and sweat, nothing in the world mattering except now, this moment, this perfect union of flesh.

Looking up, Randall saw Sylvianne clench her jaw, her top lip curled as she came ever closer. The shadows and movement caused her features to move and blur, one moment distinct, recognisable, the next subtly altered. Lying on the bed Randall was lost in the moment, but the part that watched was unable to take his eyes off Sylvianne's face; first frowning, then biting her bottom lip as she got closer, ecstasy in reach. The shadows started to play tricks, as first she was Sylvianne, then with a movement she became Jennica. The observer watched in horror as his lover oscillated between Sylvianne, approaching her climax to Jennica, not in joy but in pain, distraught. As the rhythm got faster, the changes more frequent: Sylvianne, Jennica, Sylvianne, Jennica; ending with a shriek that could have been agony or ecstasy.

He could smell the scent of Sylvianne's body when he came to. Randall breathed in deeply, hoping to take in more of her musky smell. Rolling over, he reached across to stroke Sylvianne's back when cold shock shot up his forearm. Confused, he opened his eyes to see the underside of a sink above his head. A moment of fear hit him; please god, don't let me be back in the hospital. The bathroom there has white tiles, but this room was the wrong shape, plus in the corner there should have been a shower module instead of an olive corner bath. Hanging beside the sink was a large brown and orange fluffy towel. He turned his head and looked into the adjacent room, through a doorway that by rights shouldn't be there. There was a large circular bed with a tiger print bedspread and with a moment's recognition it all came flooding back. He was in the hotel, or he had been in the hotel all the time; he wasn't sure which. So how had he ended up on the bathroom floor?

The room swayed as he got to his feet before stabilising. The back of his head felt incredibly sore. He went to the basin, and ran the tap, the cold water splashing his hands, stinging his knuckles and the gash on his left hand. He looked at the wound. It was red and angry around the edges, and when he touched it brownish-yellow puss oozed out. Deciding to park the problem for another time, he filled the sink and dunked his head, the cold jolting his system awake. By the time he was finished the water in the basin was a pinky brown colour. Randall glanced at his reflection in the mirror before quickly looking away, not wanting to recognise the man staring back at him.

In the bedroom, the bed had been pushed to the opposite side of the room from the window, bedclothes a rumpled heap by the headboard. Looking around the wreck of the room, the full misery of his situation hit him.

He was hurt.

He was being hunted.

He was alone.

Loneliness consumed him, infusing his every cell with the knowledge that there was nobody that cared. In 40 years of life, he'd managed to remove everything good, push away anyone who'd loved him, leaving him alone with nothing. He felt skinless, every nerve ending exposed to the pain of being alone. The dream of Sylvianne had felt so real, that sense of being held so intense it had erased reality, at least for a while.

Why had he met Stephanie? If he hadn't met her, he would never have re-awoken these dormant feelings. Now, his every failure had come back to haunt him: Jane, his ex-wife, unable to play second best to his career; Stephanie, dumping him a few weeks before his finals, never explaining why; his mother, so demanding that he was never able to meet the high standards she required. It felt as though life intended for him to remain alone. Randall laid back on the bed and cried as he hadn't for years.

He thought about ending it all there and then, daydreaming about which method to use. The thought of running a warm bath and cutting his wrists was enticing, except the knife that had come with his pizza was too blunt to do any real damage. There were more than enough drugs on the house menu to finish him off, but the hotel knew he was alone and Randall was sure they wouldn't sell him the quantities he needed. Eventually he conceded that these thoughts were pure fantasy. There was no way he could kill himself, and even if he had overcome his cowardice there was no escape. Re-Life would see to that.

He couldn't get the dream out of his head. It had seemed so real. Yet now, lying on the bed, he wasn't sure if what he was experiencing was real or yet another figment of his imagination. The after effects of whatever they had given him at the hospital had broken down the barriers between dreams and reality. Randall realised that if he was to get through this, he needed to cling to the physical, to trust only what he could see or feel.

He was real. This room was real. His bed was real. The walls and doors were real. That was his start point.

He couldn't trust the datasphere. Until he got access to his company's systems and checked what could be proven to be real, he couldn't take anything at face value. A wave of loneliness hit once more as yet another comfort was taken from him, and he teetered on the brink of despair. How could he do this? Would he have to live like this forever?

He was real. This room was real. His bed was real. The walls and doors were real.

At the sound of the words, his despondency receded. Those small concrete truths gave him a foundation to build on, a foundation that he could trust. Now he needed to broaden the list.

He couldn't trust his memories, that much was clear. His dreams were so vivid that he struggled to tell dream from reality. The restaurant bill was a good example. Had he dreamt it or had it actually happened? He couldn't see how it could have happened, but his memory of that evening was tangible. He couldn't trust his recollection yet at the same time, the charge was on his bank statement. Not just the right restaurant, but the right amount. How could they have known what he had dreamt?

Each doubt, each element of uncertainty dragged him inexorably towards madness. If his dreams felt so real, how could he trust that he wasn't dreaming now? His heart pounded against his ribcage. Was anything real or was it all in his head?

"Stop it! Stop it!"

He wouldn't let it happen. Not now. Randall refused to give up the control he'd just gained. He got up from the bed and sat on the floor, back firmly against the outside wall.

He was real. This room was real. His bed was real. The walls and doors were real.

He couldn't carry on disbelieving everything he once knew. He needed to make sense of his memories, sort out what he could trust and what he couldn't. What he was feeling was not normal, but he remembered what normal felt like. He needed to use the techniques he'd learnt at work to help him through this crisis, to break the problem down into smaller, more manageable pieces.

The rightness of this thought shone brightly, firing synapses recently clogged with despondency. He pushed the thought a little further. When he had first woken at the hospital, they'd said he'd had an accident, yet he couldn't remember it and he couldn't find any trace of it on the datasphere. If the accident hadn't happened, he must have been taken, just as he thought. He knew he was on shaky ground—it meant that he had to trust a small part of the datasphere—but again it felt right. He wasn't going mad. He *had* been held against his will. Randall felt his excitement rising. So he had been taken, but the question was why? What did they want from him?

Randall stopped himself. Don't go there, he thought. Not yet. Those questions were unknowable. Stick with what you know to be true. Stick with the timeline. Focus on *what was real.*

His time in hospital had been a blur. They had given him medication; he knew this because what he was now feeling was part of the side effects. What if the medication had also caused his memory loss? Had that been a deliberate plan? Had they tried to confuse him, hoping his confusion would lead them to whatever it was that they wanted? There was a warm glow of rightness as he confirmed another piece of the pattern.

With each mental breakthrough, the picture became clearer. They hadn't been successful in breaking him at the hospital, so they needed to find another way to weaken his mental state. That was why it had been so easy for him to escape, and why he hadn't been picked up yet. They were waiting for him to crack, happy to sit back until he did.

Randall sat on the floor, focussing inward, trying to understand what was happening. He laughed out loud. The feeling had returned and this time he didn't have to scrabble around for a meaning. Another message had been left for him.

Find the proof.

Since arriving at the hotel he had tried his best to ignore the decor, yet it seemed it had been laid on especially for him. With his conscious mind elsewhere, his subconscious had deciphered the tiger stripe and leopardskin patterns. He needed to access the datasphere and find out which records had been adjusted. Then he could filter the truth from the lies. He needed to access his company's systems. The question was, how?

What about Lise? Would she help? The thought hung there, teasing him with its simplicity. Lise could check the records for him. She was more than capable of seeing if they'd been adjusted.

Would she do it though? They hadn't exactly parted on the best of terms and she'd made no effort to contact him in the meantime. Then again, if she had tried when he'd been at the hospital, she probably thought that he had been ignoring her. Randall worked the thought backwards and forwards until he realised that he had no other option. Steeling himself for another rejection, he made the call.

"Hi Rand, how are you?"

The familiarity of the greeting, the normalcy, put him on edge. He had expected anger, resentment, even being told where to go, but not this.

"I... I need some help, Lise. I need you to check something for me."

"Christ, only you could contact a girl the night before her

wedding and ask her to work."

"Wedding?" Something wasn't right. This whole conversation wasn't right. "What do you mean?"

"Have you started drinking again?"

"No."

"Then stop pissing about. It's my wedding tomorrow and I expect you to be there."

Randall paused, trying to catch his bearings. "Look, Lise, I'm in real trouble. I need you to check to see if someone has hacked into my bank account."

"Now I know you're winding me up. What is it, some joke about wedding gifts? Are you going to pretend you've run out of cash?"

"Lise, stop it. Please. I need your help."

"Very funny, Rand. Look, I don't have time for this. I need to get some sleep before tomorrow. Tell Robert nice try, but you're going to have to do better before you catch me out."

"Stop. Lise, you're the only one who can help. Lise?"

The icon had disappeared. The groundwork he had so carefully assembled shook. Reality had decided to bite back. Randall struggled to make sense of the conversation he'd just had. With no other option, he decided to ignore it. It had never happened. Maybe later, when he had all the information to hand, it would make sense. For now, it had never happened. It was clear that there was nobody else. He only had one option left.

Find the proof himself.

Randall collected his things from the bed, unlocked the door and walked out into the hallway.

CHAPTER THIRTY-ONE
Re-Life Technician

The Technician had waited for something, anything, to let him know his work was appreciated but the days turned into weeks and there was still no contact. Had he been asked to create the clone or had he imagined the whole thing?

He felt tired, so tired that he thought his flesh may slip from his bones. He wasn't built for intrigue, his life had always revolved around the peaceful confines of the laboratory. Everything in its place, that was how he liked things. The uncertainty and chaos of the past few weeks threatened to overwhelm him.

He slapped his cheeks in an effort to keep awake. He had to concentrate. Nothing must go wrong. An alarm would sound if anybody approached the room; like any good scientist he had learnt from his previous mistakes. He checked once more then punched the instructions into the console.

Deploy the clone

Three small words, yet the impact was startling. A great weight lifted from his shoulders. He had to stop himself from laughing out loud as he was hit by a wave of giddiness. He had done it. At last he would find out whether the impossible was possible.

***

A section of the ceiling eased open and a large, glutinous sack prolapsed into the room. Clear secretions dripped onto the plinth below. The sack rippled as a clear, lozenge-shaped capsule spilled onto the plinth, a trail of tubes and wires sliding in its wake. Within the capsule, half hidden by the multitude of umbilicals, was the clone.

Looking out from the control room, the Technician studied his child for the first time. Physically, it was a disappointment. Gestated to its middle years, the original clearly had an indolent lifestyle. Its arms and legs were flabby despite the exercise regime the clone had been under. Its stomach rippled as the holding fluid, agitated from the drop, sloshed around inside the container. The skin was near translucent, veins clearly visible mapping its lifeblood. The Technician wondered if all parents felt disappointment when first seeing their offspring, as if reality could never match the ideal. It was a stupid thought. He knew from the template that the original was no Adonis. Still, it was a shame that a duplicate was needed, rather than a renewal. That would have opened up more possibilities.

Irritated at his inability to control his thoughts, the Technician slapped his cheeks vigorously. He continued through the checklist: immunisation complete, exposure to common viruses complete, physiological check complete, neurological check within parameters. The last point was the most important. Everything rode on his ability to adapt the template without altering the neural fingerprint. If he had made a mistake, the memory transfer would fail. He yawned. It was time. The Technician took one last look at the capsule, then keyed in the initiation code.

The gelatinous sack retracted, leaving the snaking umbilicals hanging from the ceiling. In the centre of the chamber, the plinth slowly leant back, allowing the capsule to move from the vertical to the horizontal. Holes opened in its base and the embryonic fluid drained away. The cap at the top of the capsule broke free, allowing the web of tubes and wires to slither back into the ceiling. A piercing green light flared briefly. Once gone, a faint line appeared in the previously unblemished face of the capsule and it neatly separated into two identical pieces, exposing its contents to the atmosphere for the first time. The Technician watched the clone's chest rise and fall. It would be some time before it woke from its induced coma.

He keyed the command to release the aural block. For the first time, the duplicate's brain would have access to the external world directly. A few more keystrokes and the verification procedure started.

"Dog."
"Father."
"Birthday."
"School."
"Carrots."
"Winter."

With each spoken word, the system compared the clone's neural impulse to that of the original. The myriad of factors associated with each word produced a unique synaptic pattern depending on what had happened during a person's lifetime, forming a person's neural fingerprint.

The Technician caught himself tapping his foot on the floor. The wait felt like an age as the system analysed the clone's responses. Any deviation from the pattern on file and the memory transfer would be classified as unsuccessful. One by one green lights appeared on the screen in front of him. He felt his excitement rise. It had worked. He'd changed the balance of a person's brain chemistry without affecting their neural fingerprint. He was a genius.

Flushed with excitement, the Technician donned his face mask and entered the birth chamber. Standing beside the capsule, careful to avoid the solid excretions, he ran his fingers along the clone's blemish-free skin. A trail of goose-pimples rose wherever his fingers touched. He justified this contact as a test of the body's natural reflexes, but this test didn't appear on any checklist. For the Technician, the physical contact turned theory into reality. At that moment the full implications of what he had done hit home. Was it right for him to have done what he did, or should he have left the duplicate unaltered? He ruthlessly quashed these doubts. It was far too late to stop now.

He made his way around the plinth, removing the air and waste tubes from the clone as he went, careful to ensure that no damage was caused. Once complete, he took a few moments to contemplate the body before him. It still amazed him that he could create a perfectly-formed middle-aged man within the timespan of a few weeks. It was so easy, why people bothered with biological conception any more he had no idea.

Back in the control room, he turned on the laser array. Multiple streams of red light began the process of adding all the skin defects that had occurred during the original's 40-plus years of life. Once finished, the clone would be indistinguishable from its original. Smoke arose from flesh as the laser etched a belly button. The Technician smiled to himself. It may be a useless relic and totally unnecessary, but it was amazing how much people missed their belly buttons.

CHAPTER THIRTY-TWO
The Investigator

"I'll arrange a meeting with Mick O'Driscoll," Corey said.

"I was thinking of just going in. I know where Randall's been, he shouldn't be too hard to track down."

"This isn't a suggestion. Wait until you get my confirmation before setting off."

Nico looked through the pod window but thick fog prevented him from seeing anything but light and shade. The weather showed nature at its most impressionistic. The protest march was happening over the other side of the city, but everywhere else was quiet. The roads were empty. Most people had ignored the government's advice and left work early. A sense of disquiet echoed around the empty streets, as if the city itself was holding its breath in apprehension. Nico shivered. It wasn't his problem. All he had to do was get to Jones.

Progress should have been quick, but it didn't take long before his pod was pulled over at a road block. The doors peeled back and an IS trooper peered in.

"No admittance except for residents or those on official business."

Rivulets of water trickling down the visor of the Trooper's chitinous helmet. Her voice sounded fuzzy, as if the moisture from the fog was affecting the speaker. Nico broadcast his ID. "I'm going to a meeting near the Scrambles."

The trooper said nothing, the helmet remaining fixed in Nico's direction. There was something malevolent about the insectoid gaze. Nico felt guilt well up inside, and despite having nothing to hide he found himself sinking further into his seat as each second ticked by. The trooper nodded finally and waved his pod on. As the doors sealed, Nico spotted more of the squad, dark silhouettes surrounding a spider-like mass, its smooth body glistening above its many jutting legs. He was glad to be moving on.

The pod was stopped three more times before eventually pulling over for good, an electronic voice informing him that under section 21b/337 of the civil disobedience act, it was unable to travel further. Cursing the protesters and their timing, Nico got out and walked the last few hundred metres to his destination.

The thickening fog reduced visibility to just a few metres, making everything beyond unknown and unknowable. Shapes emerged out of the gloom as he walked, every step taking him back to a time when uncertainty was king. The shaggy facades of buildings appeared as childhood monsters; bare tree branches clawed hands, looking to snatch you from your bed. Nico was in a part of town he knew well, but the fog cloaked everything familiar and he was at his destination almost before he realised. It was not as if there were signposts to the Scrambles, there were no archways proclaiming a welcome, yet the boundary between the main city and the Scrambles was as clear as if it had been painted in fluorescent colours. On Nico's approach, three shadows emerged from the gloom.

"Sorry mate. No-one's allowed in." It was the largest of the three, his voice soft for a man of his size. "You'll have to come back tomorrow."

Nico stood his ground. "I've got an appointment."

The speaker stepped closer. "I said, we're closed. Now bugger off."

"Tell Mick O'Driscoll that Nico Tandelli is here to see him. He's expecting me."

The man stared into space, as if his controlling signal had been interrupted. After a moment, he smiled. "Be safe, *Investigator*."

Nico walked past the heavies and into the Scrambles, the smile making him aware just how much the men wanted to express their feelings in a more physical manner. It took all his self-control not to look back.

He found the address without a hitch. As he approached, the door opened and he was guided in with a minimum of fuss, blinking to adjust to the hallway lights. The moment he had stepped into the building, Nico lost access to the datasphere. It wasn't unexpected, but it was disconcerting. From the outside the house had looked like one of many similar buildings along the street, its facade dirty and unkempt. Once inside, though, the wealth and importance of the man living there was clear. A long hallway led from the entrance with a set of stairs rising on the right-hand side. Paintings and antiques were displayed tastefully wherever you looked.

He was guided along the corridor and through a set of double doors on the left-hand side. The room contained floor to ceiling shelves full of leather-bound books. It was another display of wealth and taste; only the eccentric read books made of paper. On the other side of the room was a large, open fire; logs crackling in the grate. Two antique sofas faced each other in the centre of the room, a small table between them. Sitting on one was the man he had come to meet: Mick O'Driscoll, King of the Scrambles.

Nico waited while O'Driscoll stared into the fire. He was a short man, slim, with no remarkable features. If you had walked past him in the street you wouldn't have given him a second glance. Only the cut of his suit and his brand of dataglasses gave him away to be anything more than what he appeared. As the fifth O'Driscoll to head the family since they first came to the Scrambles, Mick had overseen a change from the brutal regime of his father into a more commercially-focussed organisation. Not that he wasn't able to become physical when required; O'Driscoll's two older brothers had mysteriously disappeared after his father's sudden death, along with four of his father's trusted lieutenants. Still, the Scrambles had never been quieter than at present.

Nico stood wondering how to announce his presence when Mick O'Driscoll turned, gesturing to the seat opposite.

"Please, sit down. I believe this is the first time we've met, Mr Tandelli." His accent was plummy, the benefit of his expensive education. His father may have been a thug but he knew what was best for his children. Nico sat himself down, his hands and ears stinging from the heat of the fire.

"I hope you didn't have too much trouble getting here?"

"Not really, Mr O'Driscoll. I had to walk the last part but it was fine."

O'Driscoll looked over his glasses at Nico. "Please, call me Michael. Whenever anyone says Mr O'Driscoll, I look for my father. It's quite disconcerting." He smiled an odd smile. "I don't really understand what is happening with the country at the moment. All these demands, people clamouring for supposed rights. Useless, of course. You'd think they'd know by now that the whole game is rigged. Wouldn't you agree Nico?"

"I wouldn't know. I tend to stay away from politics."

"Except recently I believe…"

Nico shifted uncomfortably. Seemingly unaware, O'Driscoll's attention was drawn back to the fire. "We all go this way no matter how much you try to stop it. Ashes to ashes, dust to dust. It makes us question why we bother to struggle so hard, given the pointlessness of it all." A spark spat from the grate, landing on a patterned rug. It smouldered for a moment before extinguishing, a few wisps of smoke remaining to distinguish the burn from the singe marks surrounding it.

"What I don't understand is why they allow it? What's in it for them? That's the problem with the long game, unless you know the goal it's bloody difficult to understand." O'Driscoll turned to Nico. "He's not here, the man you're looking for."

"I haven't said why I'm here."

"Randall Jones, aged 41, Data Cleanser for Re-Life. He arrived here before lunchtime yesterday, went to the Old Street datasphere lounge where he sold his jacket. Two hours later he met with a woman at the Oranje Bar before booking a room at the Hotel Aphrodite. Unfortunately for you he left the hotel an hour ago, and was last seen leaving the Scrambles via Jessops Street."

"How the hell do you know who I'm looking for?"

"Save your anger for another time, Investigator. If you want to catch your suspect you'd better get a move on. I hear things are a little bit dicey where he is heading, especially for upstanding members of society like yourself."

Nico hadn't needed the warning. It was a virtual straight line from Jessops Street to Arrhenius Park.

O'Driscoll leant forward. "It's none of my business, but you should know that they're leading you by the nose. Unless you're happy to carry on that way, start looking at the bigger picture."

"Do you know anything about Jennica's disappearance?" As Nico spoke, the double doors to the room opened.

"Good luck with your hunt, Nico. Try to stay out of harm's way."

Nico felt torn. Was O'Driscoll playing with him or did he know something? He wanted to stay, ask more questions, but O'Driscoll was right. He had to be quick if he wanted to catch up with Jones. "Many thanks for your time, Michael, it's been most helpful."

The King of the Scrambles didn't appear to notice, his attention was back on the flames.

The cold bit into Nico's face. As he stepped out of the front door the datasphere blinked back on. He'd need it. The fog seemed worse than when he had entered. Nico went to bring up his map of the area when a call came through.

"Hey Corey, I've got some news. Jones left the Scrambles an hour ago and was last tracked heading out via Jessops Street. Can you access the security cameras in that area? I need to trace where he's got to."

"Stop what you are doing and head to the address I'm about to send through."

"What? For christ's sake Corey, he's got an hour's head start on us. If we don't trace him soon we could lose him."

"Just do as I ask—"

"No. Are you mad? We've spent weeks trying to crack this case and now that we're close, you want to pull me out again? What's going on? Do you actually *want* me to solve this?"

"We've picked up a signal from Jennica's datalenses. *She's* the priority now, so stop moaning and go get the girl. We'll meet you when you get there."

CHAPTER THIRTY-THREE
The Politician

The potential implications of what I've found haunt me. If it's true, it indicates that there's a part of us that cannot be transferred, cannot be removed or replicated. It means that Re-Life isn't a continuation as was promised but just a duplication of life, as related to who you are as your shadow or reflection.

I'm becoming obsessed with the data. What is it? Why has it never been spotted before? It seems to indicate that there is more to who we are than is contained within our biology. How can that be and what does it mean?

✷ ✷ ✷

Although she knew they had been travelling, the effortless glide of the pod and the lack of visual stimulus made it hard to tell that they were moving at all. The longer the journey took, the deeper the pit within her grew. He was there. In striking distance. The man who had assaulted her, corrupted her friend, killed a colleague and god knows what else. Every time he looked at her she had to suppress a wave of terror and revulsion, but Stephanie refused to give him the pleasure of a reaction. Somehow, someway, he would pay for what he had done.

It was a small mercy that Delegate Gant had withdrawn into himself; quiet mumbles and small gestures showing that some still had access to the datasphere. Stephanie hated the fact that her eyes kept being drawn towards him, especially whenever he caught her looking. She wanted to stamp on that greasy face until it was unrecognisable; wrap her hands around his throat until his eyes bulged. Her fear fuelled her rage until the heat had burnt out, leaving the cold, purity of hatred. She knew that she could do nothing to him now; how could she, a small woman between three hulks? Instead she chose to use the only resource she had left: time. There were too many strands to pull together. She knew that they were linked but she needed time to think through what had happened, to form a whole from the scraps she had discovered. Somewhere in these disparate pieces of information was a route to vengeance.

The doors peeled back. Stephanie looked up as the two bodyguards left the pod. Gant leaned close.

"Ladies first."

She spat in his face. "Cunt."

For a split second Gant's fury glistened, revealing the monster within. Then the mask returned. "Bring her out," he said, wiping her saliva from his face.

The mist from earlier had now solidified. The only point of reference being a pale glow in the distance. Stephanie breathed in the air, grateful to be away from the pod's musky interior. There was a salty tang that for a brief moment took Stephanie back to childhood visits to her Grandparent's house. Their village had been bordered by salt marshes. If she was this close to the sea, they must have headed east; there were no other coastlines close enough to the city.

"This way." Gant walked down the driveway, each step crunching as he went. With no other choice, Stephanie followed.

Out of the gloom she was able to make out what looked like a modest, two-storey dwelling. Rather than entering, Gant turned left, disappearing around the side of the building. Stephanie turned the corner to find a bright glow ahead, the sharp line of the wall clearly delineated against the glowing softness of the fog. In front of her was a large white patio, a box hedge on its left-hand side. To her right was a large wall leading to a kitchen. Another glass wall on the far side of the patio led to some form of seating area. What drew her eye though was not the house, the minimalist decor, the gardener carefully trimming at the box hedge or even the large black table with matching chairs that stood in stark contrast to the predominantly white background, it was who was sitting at the table: Richard Asquith, Prime Delegate and leader of the country.

Asquith stood as she approached, his features lit up by that all familiar smile. "Stephanie," he said, "so good of you to come. I do hope the journey wasn't too much of an inconvenience."

Stephanie stared at him, ignoring his outstretched hand.

"Please, Stephanie. Don't be like that. I can understand you're angry. I would be too. Unfortunately there was no other choice. Give me a few minutes to explain myself. If you're still mad after that, by all means go ahead and report me. I won't deny a thing."

Her icy calm solidified. Stephanie wanted to punch Asquith in his posh, handsome face. It had always angered her when people of a certain background brought their entitlement with them in everything they did. She had seen it so often at the Legislature; jumped-up shits who had no interest in who they represented behaving as if the world was their playground. Asquith may act all compassionate in public, but she'd heard enough stories to know that he was no exception.

"Zachary, would you mind awfully getting us some refreshments? What would you prefer, Stephanie, coffee, tea, or something a little stronger?"

"Tea, white, no sugar." She was thirsty. There was no point denying herself out of spite.

At Asquith's gesture, Gant went into the kitchen. The two bodyguards moved to either end of the patio, becoming dark smudges as the fog enveloped them. The only other person on the patio was the gardener, clipping away at the hedge with pruning sheers, face partially obscured by a wide brimmed hat. The occasional snip as the gardener picked off stray growths was the only sound Stephanie could hear. Unbothered by the gardener's presence, Asquith sat at the table, gesturing for Stephanie to join him.

"How long have you been a delegate Stephanie? Six months? A year?"

"It's been four months."

"Only four?" Asquith seemed taken aback. Stephanie knew not to be fooled; he was a consummate actor. "It didn't take you very long to get to grips with the place. From my side, it seems like I've been hearing your name mentioned for months. You've had my advisors worried for quite a while. They seemed to think you're plotting to unseat me."

"They're wrong."

"Really? So how did you think it would end, then, if you had managed to vote down my budget proposal? Do you think my coalition partners would just sit there and accept the defeat? Of course not. They would have torn me apart."

"If you had wanted to talk about the vote, you could have just called."

Asquith smiled. "The vote has been taken care of. You played a good game, I'll give you that, but you were finished the moment Bobby Maddison got involved with these protests. It was a small matter to dangle the carrot in front of him. His ego did the rest. He couldn't miss the chance to head the protests. Now all it needs is the odd nudge here or there for them to turn violent. By the end of today, you'll struggle to find anyone who'll vote alongside a man who unleashed such violence against the public."

"I don't believe Bobby Maddison is your stooge."

Asquith laughed, the sound a whip-crack against the eerie quiet. "Bobby? God, no. He'd rather eat a shit sandwich than support the government." He leant back in his chair, taking a few moments to compose himself. "It's just that he's predictable. Once you know which buttons to press, it's easy. Of course, this should come as no surprise to you, seeing as you've pressed the same buttons yourself."

Stephanie shivered, the thought making her feel very uncomfortable. Was she really the same as Richard Asquith? "I don't understand, then. You know you've won. It won't be long before my poll rating sinks below my rival's. Why did you bring me here, to gloat?"

There was that smug smile again. Stephanie could feel her fist clenching. "That's where you've made your second mistake. I wasn't the one who arranged this meeting."

"You're pathetic, you know that? You kidnap me from outside my office, bundle me into a pod bound and gagged, drive me to the middle of nowhere and now sit here denying all responsibility. Enough games. If you didn't arrange this meeting, who the fuck did?"

"I did."

Stephanie turned to find the gardener looking back at her. Asquith walked to the end of the table, pulling back a chair for the gardener to sit. Recognising the question in her eyes, Asquith said, "It's true. She asked me to arrange this meeting."

The woman took off her gloves and removed her wide brimmed hat, placing them on the table in front of her. She had the appearance of someone who had spent their whole life working the land. Stephanie guessed she must have been in her late fifties, her cropped grey hair accentuating her pale blue eyes.

What surprised Stephanie the most was the way that Richard Asquith deferred to her, his body language almost obsequious; a mirror of how Zachary Gant had behaved towards Asquith himself. As the thought formed in her mind, Asquith said, "I think I'll just pop and find out what has happened to that tea."

The gardener sat staring at her. Even if the Prime Delegate hadn't have behaved as he had, it was clear that this was someone used to authority. Her gaze seemed to last an age, much longer than was comfortable. Eventually, she spoke.

"So *you* are Stephanie Vaughn. Have you any idea how much trouble you have caused us?"

Stephanie remained very still. The woman had one of those mid-European accents still common among the first generation of refugees looking to escape the chaos caused by the Upheaval. Except for her bejewelled hands she looked innocuous, yet someone who had that sort of power over Asquith and Gant was someone to be feared. "I'm very sorry, but who the hell are you?"

"I know, it's a little unfair. I know so much about you yet you haven't a clue who I am." She smiled, but Stephanie felt little reassurance.

"Do you work for the government?"

She laughed "Me? No. I am no-one; just a messenger."

"A messenger for who?"

Her smile deepened. "That is the better question. I would be happy to tell you, in fact I would be more than happy, as I do hate secrets. The problem is, once I tell you, there is no going back."

"You make that sound like a bad thing."

"I can't answer that. Many have found the knowledge enlightening; others less so. What it means to you, who can say?"

"And if I don't ask?"

"Then we have a conversation, you will help us, and you will never hear from us again. You will go back to your wreck of a political career. After that, who knows? What we find, though, is that most people, like the Prime Delegate, are very happy they did ask the question. We can be most helpful."

I've heard that before, Stephanie thought. "Before I decide, what was it that you wanted to talk to me about?"

"Jennica Fabian and Randall Jones."

"Do you know what happened to Jennica?"

"Yes, and we know your role in protecting Randall. In a way, this is why I'm here. We need to sort everything out." The woman's smile slowly faded. "So, Stephanie - what is it to be?"

The enormity of the moment hit Stephanie. People had died for knowing the wrong things. James had died. She thought back to what he had found, that the delegates who had died had all been about to vote against their own party. It had never made sense. Why not just kick them out in disgrace as had happened to so many others before? Now she realised why they had to die. They had the knowledge that was being offered to her. The gardener hadn't lied. It truly was a one-way street.

The sound of laughter drifted through from the kitchen. Stephanie turned to see Asquith and Gant together; two privileged men laughing at the world. Gant looked across to see her staring at him. He smiled, raising his cup.

Watching the two of them revel in their privilege, Stephanie realised there was only one way forward. She turned to the gardener. "OK. I want to know. Who are you and who do you work for?"

The gardener smiled again, this time with warmth. "My name is Indigo and I am here on behalf of Global Governance."

CHAPTER THIRTY-FOUR
The Information Cleanser

The orange glow pulsed malevolently in the night ahead. This was the first time Randall had seen anything other than grey or black since leaving the Scrambles. Grateful for the warmth of his newly purchased jacket, he did his best to remain in shadow, stopping whenever anyone was near; hoping the combination of fog, lack of light and lack of movement would prevent him from being seen. He could sense it when people approached and was able to hide as they emerged from the fog like echoes of memories, observed for a moment and then gone. His relationship with the fog was ambiguous. It was a help, no doubt about that, but the vague abstractness of its form induced feelings similar to those when he sensed a pattern. Somewhere, his brain believed that the fog was a message, or the patterns in the fog were messages.

Randall stopped, the thought striking him cold. Could that be so? Was it even possible? He thought back to when he'd had these feelings before: in the hospital room, urging him to escape; in the hospital gardens, leading him to flee; in the bar, warning him not to trust Stephanie; even at the hotel, leading him to his current destination. Despite its apparent absurdity, the idea trickled around his cerebellum, seducing him with its simplicity. He couldn't ignore the facts.

Somebody was looking out for him. Somebody cared.

The pulsing orange light strengthened as he moved closer, highlighting bare branches of the trees lining the street. Noise overcame the dampening effect of the fog, sometimes rising, sometimes falling; a muted drone with an occasional yelp or whoop the only moments of clarity. Randall needed to keep heading in this direction—it was the shortest route to where he was heading—but forward meant people, and people meant... what? What would seeing other people mean? His instinct was to run away. He felt safer alone, unseen. Another part of him questioned this wisdom. What was more suspicious: a man found sneaking in the dark or a man walking through a crowd? He had his coat, his hood and his guardian angel. He tried to wash all thought out of his mind, to sense the message he was being sent. What should he do?

A hand grabbed his shoulder. Shrieking, Randall spun to face his attacker.

"Woah! Sorry mate, didn't mean to scare you."

He could just make out the girls face in the flickering orange light, eyes wide open in shock. She'd raised her hands as if to protect herself and Randall lowered his fist; a fist he hadn't even realised he had raised.

"We've been sent out to collect the stragglers. You need to get back to the main group. This place is crawling with security. Word is, they're picking us off one by one, using the fog to hide their work. It's best to be back at camp, safety in numbers and all that."

For a moment Randall prepared to run and take his chances in the dark. Then he thought about what the girl had said. If security were everywhere he was pretty sure he knew why. She was right. His best bet was to go with her to camp—whatever that was—and hope that he could use their numbers to hide.

The girl had started towards the glow, so Randall followed. "What a day, eh?" she said. "Which group did you come with: the unions? The anarchists? You look a bit old to have come with the students."

"I came on my own."

"Really? Good for you."

Randall couldn't help feeling envious. The girl couldn't have been more than 18 and had everything in front of her. She seemed to float down the road, so great was her excitement at the adventure she was having. Life is so simple at that age, he thought. There is right and wrong and that's it. He remembered being 18, leaving home and breaking away from his parent's influence. He had learnt so much about life back then, forming opinions that were so solid as to seem inviolate. Randall was taken back to university, his blood racing as they debated candidates and policy. She'd drawn him into her world and he'd been enthralled. His family had never been political, each generation inheriting their views from their parents. To suddenly find that there was another world of opinion out there, viewpoints at odds with how he'd been brought up but equally valid; it was intoxicating. That was until she had spoilt it, had broken his heart and shat on the remains.

"Are you feeling OK?" The girl was staring at him.

Randall suppressed the anger he felt at Stephanie's betrayal. "I'm fine."

There was the smell of burning long before he could see what was ahead. The road ended at a T-junction and Randall knew that ahead of him lay the beautiful Arrhenius Park. What he found was a chaotic sprawl of humanity and squalor, the glow of camp fires leading off in all directions. A group of people nearest to the junction were burning refuse, sitting close and warming their hands regardless of the black smoke belching into the air. Randall felt stunned. Arrhenius Park was usually a tranquil spot, popular with families who would let their children run around or feed the ducks by the stream. There were people from every generation. Looking from fire to fire, he could pick out the old and the young, small family groups, even a mother with a baby. Who in their right mind would bring a baby here he thought.

Uneasy at remaining where he was, Randall followed the girl's lead and went further into the chaos. The deeper into the camp they went, the harder it became to breathe. A black miasma lay over the park making it impossible to see further than a few metres. One or two people drifted out from the murk but the majority headed inwards across the park like themselves. The further they went, the louder the noise from ahead became.

"Let us through!"

"Fucking scum, get out the way!"

They had left the campfires behind by now and were heading through an area of darkness towards a much brighter, harsher light.

"I don't like this," the girl said. "It was like a carnival when we started out, everyone peacefully marching together. It's different now."

Randall could feel it too. The energy emanating from the crowd ahead was palpable; there was a blackness to the mood. The feeling was a familiar one; it reminded him of the miasma that had descended when he'd been told that the promotion wasn't his. There was a similar feeling of disappointment, anger and betrayal. This is what he could sense now, betrayal.

The girl stopped, grabbing his arm. "I don't think we should go any further."

Randall shrugged. "Go back to the campfires then. I want to see what's going on."

This was what he had been looking for. What better place to be invisible than here, mingling with this seething mass. He surged ahead, shouldering past a few stragglers. He could make out a press of people ahead of him, a long line eight, possibly ten people deep, disappearing into the fog. Enormous lights hovered in the air before the crowd. Randall felt the hairs on the back of his neck rise. This was where he should be, he was sure of it. He just needed to get himself into the middle of the throng and wait for everything to kick off.

He didn't have to wait long.

CHAPTER THIRTY-FIVE
The Politician

Is this electrical activity what makes us who we are or am I attributing causal effect without proof? It seems too much of a coincidence that on death this activity, this data disappears, only to reappear once consciousness is reestablished. Is this the very essence of who we are? Sentience has yet to be explained by science. We know what it is but the how and why is still a mystery.

"Global Governance? You're in the security business?"

Indigo laughed. "I guess I am. That is a good way of putting it. We are a security company, only a little different to most."

Stephanie couldn't understand why Indigo looked so

amused. "So that's the big secret. You work for a security company, and if I guess correctly, you have a number of delegates in your pocket, including the Prime Delegate."

For some reason, this seemed to amuse Indigo even more. "You remind me so much of myself before I joined." She looked across to the kitchen. "We'll have that tea now."

Stephanie watched in wonder as Asquith hurried out, bringing a tray of drinks to the table. He carefully passed a cup to Indigo, then a second to Stephanie. There was a strange look on his face as he handed her the cup, almost sympathetic.

"Let me ask you a question," continued Indigo. "How much do you know about the lead up to the Upheaval?"

"Just what I learned at school. We knew that human activity was causing climate change yet did little about it. There was a lot of talk, agreements that were circumvented and delay followed by delay to get any form of substantial agreement. It was only after the frequency of so called natural disasters of the Upheaval last century that the evidence became too obvious to ignore. Even then the political classes were too under the thumb of big business to act. Then everything changed when the Miracle was signed at the UN."

"Very good. You've just highlighted one of the roles of Global Governance: information security." Indigo stirred some sugar into her tea. "The Miracle: over 200 of the world's leaders locked in discussions for five days, forging an agreement that would save humanity. It was a wonder of diplomacy, still raised as an example of humanity's ability to pull together in a time of crisis. Total bullshit, of course, but a necessary lie." She placed her teaspoon onto the saucer. "You were correct about one thing though, the signs of impending disaster were there and nobody of influence was prepared to do what was necessary. To call them leaders is an insult to leadership. You can count on one hand those that were prepared to stand up and tell the truth; the rest were too scared."

"My Grandmother said that the corporations were the bad guys and that the politicians were just weak."

Indigo blew on her cup, the rising steam a small addition to the ever-thickening fog. "Yes, big business did pervert the discourse and I'm sure there were one or two politicians under their sway. However, the reality was that the politicians never forgot to whom they owed their power. The issue was that because of this, very few politicians were willing to sacrifice their political career by telling voters that things would get worse. That's the biggest problem with democracy - those in power will do anything to stay in power, and the best way to stay in power is to give the electorate what they want. The democratic process failed humanity when it was needed the most."

"But democracy won. Every country in the world uses some form of democracy." Stephanie heard a noise from behind. Asquith and Gant were walking back to the table. She shuddered at Gant's smile, and it took all of her self-control not to fling her tea in his face.

"You have to think back to the time in question," said Indigo. "Democracy needs difference to thrive. The stronger the ideological differences, the more likely any tension between differing viewpoints will lead to a compromise that meets the needs of the majority. Sometimes this balancing act fails, and the political path see-saws between one stance or another, but in the long-term these are small obstacles on the road to progress. All this changed towards the end of the twentieth century. Ideological debate died with the fall of Communism. Capitalism had seemingly won and democracy turned into a beauty pageant. Politicians came to power who had no real world experience. Politics stopped being a calling and became a career. Having never existed outside of the political bubble, these politicians needed help to understand how the real world operated. That was where big business came in.

"The biggest problem, though, was that the people had been sold a lie. For years they had been promised that if they worked hard and saved hard, they would retire on a pension far outstripping what their contributions could deliver. Pension funds became major shareholders, initially looking for secure growth on their assets, but as the realisation dawned that they couldn't meet their long-term obligations they changed focus to new industries that delivered growth unachievable by the more established industries. This didn't stop the established industries from trying, however. Businesses became less interested in stability and more interested in short-term profit as they competed for market funds that were in the hands of the pension funds. Assets were stripped, millions were laid off as once solid industries became ever more desperate to deliver growth. This led to lower pension contributions which ramped up even more pressure on the pension funds. It was a mess. Pension funds were scared they would fail to meet their commitments, businesses were scared the pension funds would pull their investment if they didn't produce ever increasing profits, governments were scared that big business would pull out and destroy their nation's economy if they were seen to legislate measures that harmed profitability, and the electorate refused to vote for politicians who proposed legislation that could damage the comforts they had been promised. This edifice remained sustainable only through the exploitation of our planet's natural resources, but anybody with intelligence could see that it couldn't last. Sadly, nobody was strong enough to stand up and say 'enough is enough'. Even when Mother Nature started to complain, the fear of losing power prevented politicians from doing what was right, so they did nothing."

Stephanie looked pointedly across to where Asquith and Gant were sitting. "It doesn't sound any different from where we are today."

Gant's laughter roared out into the night. Indigo raised

her hand, just a little, and he immediately quietened. "Around this time some extremely wealthy individuals decided that something needed to be done. They could see the system was unsustainable and decided it was time for a change. They put out feelers for like-minded people, quietly pulling together a network with vast resources of wealth and influence. Unlike in the past, what made this group of individuals different was that they were not interested in taking power. Most had stepped back from the businesses they had built which allowed them to rise above established short-term thinking. They saw that a mechanism was needed to ensure a safe future for their children and their children's children, one that couldn't be corrupted by short-termism. They called themselves Global Governance."

As Indigo paused to take a sip from her drink, Stephanie struggled to take in what she had heard. If what this strange little woman had said was true, everything she knew about the world, everything she had been taught and had believed to be true, was a lie.

"The detail of what happened next would take too long to tell. Needless to say, Global Governance built their resources until they were ready to take control. The Upheaval was the tipping point. The effects of climate change had been visible for years but nobody had prepared properly for the speed at which the sea-level rose. Whole countries were lost. The weather patterns changed and much of the world's food producing areas became either dust bowls or swamps. The basic infrastructure started to fail in even the least vulnerable nations. Many countries introduced isolationist policies, hoarding their resources to provide for their own and exacerbating an already grave situation. For the first time since the industrial revolution the lights went out. Food was scarce, civil unrest increased. The financial markets were in chaos and many countries were on the verge of collapse."

"The whole of civilisation was at risk," Gant said.

Indigo nodded. "The UN called its now famous

emergency meeting. During the debate, many heads of state, including 'Saint' Doleman from the UK, were concerned that their military would take control. The world was teetering on the brink of the abyss and the politicians knew it, yet still they were unable to overcome their own petty squabbles." She slapped her hand on the table. "If ever you needed proof that democracy is a flawed concept, that is it.

"With shares at rock bottom, Global Governance bought out the world's major banks. At the UN, the Chinese delivered an ultimatum, either agree to the proposed way forward—our proposal—or they would call in their debts. Each government had to support the building of a unified, global plan, encompassing a new renewable energy infrastructure, recyclables, food production, security, political systems; it was a new approach to end the petty internecine squabbling that had so blighted humanity in the past. In return, we supplied the investment in the form of long-term bonds and the expertise to deliver through a portfolio of companies we had so patiently developed. We called it a Marshall plan for the world. Everybody else called it the Miracle."

Stephanie sat stunned by what she had been hearing, scared about what all this meant for her. A part of her wanted to go back, to say no, to not know what she now did. The sheer enormity of the deceit was staggering. It didn't seem possible.

"How have you managed to keep this secret? Surely, nowadays, with the amount of information available to everybody something would have leaked?"

There was laughter from Gant. "Who do you think controls what information you get to see and what you don't? Who do you think runs the datasphere? The UN?"

"Delegate Gant is correct," Indigo said. "The datasphere was created by Global Governance, run under charter by the Global Development Bank to be neutral and available to all. Its forerunner, the internet, had been swallowed piece by piece by corporate interests and nobody trusted it. The people wanted a new, totally neutral and, most importantly, free network. Within a few years, the internet had died and only the datasphere remained. As it became central to the way we live, so has Global Governance. We have the ability to control what you know and what you don't."

"But that's terrible."

"It could be terrible, in the wrong hands, but I would remind you of one of the first things I told you. Global Governance have no interest in power. We do not want to control the world. We just want to ensure the future remains safe for our children and their children to follow. For the most part, we do not interfere in people's lives. Our activity is visible and accepted as standard business or politics. It is just not carried out under our name. We are a force for good."

CHAPTER THIRTY-SIX
The Information Cleanser

Randall pushed his way forward, ducking under arms and squeezing through gaps as he used the confusion to camouflage his movements. The closer he got to the front, the harder it was to make any headway. Steam rose from those in front and the musky smell of damp cloth was almost overpowering. Randall found himself squeezed between those pushing from the back and the protestors giving resistance at the front. The undulating ground made it difficult to see what was happening. He pushed past two large protesters and stopped.

The mass of people ended five metres in front of him. Ahead was an area of dead ground, mist rising from the darkened earth. Facing them was the enemy, a double line of Internal Security, menacing in their stillness. Those at the front held clear shields over two metres tall, their edges interlocking with their neighbour's to form a transparent wall curving off left and right, the ends quickly lost in the fog. Each shield was propped up by two rods, forming an A-frame at each side. Writing scrolled along the front of the shields.

Do not touch, electrified barrier

It was an eerie sight. Randall couldn't remember the last time IS troopers had been deployed, certainly not during his lifetime. As he looked across he felt nervous. The troopers were wearing insect-like polycarbon armour and helmets. Across the polished surfaces rippled the reflection of the warning, the moving light highlighting ridges and curves.

There was a movement in the crowd. Protestors to the right surged forward, crushing those in front against the shield wall. A bright flash and loud crack was followed by screams piercing the night air. The line of protestors flew backwards leaving a number of figures prone. Randall could see a ghost image of the protesters hitting the shields. The smell of singed hair assaulted his nostrils. A few seconds later, the first rock sailed through the air and over the shield barrier.

"Fucking bastards, let us through!"

Another rock crashed against the barrier, then a third. Within moments the air was full of rocks, their staccato impact causing the shield line to vibrate, the electronic warning dancing as it journeyed down the line.

"Where the hell did those come from?" Randall muttered to himself.

"Students were pulling up cobbles from Exeter Street as soon as the shield wall went up," a protester beside him said. "It's not the only surprise they'll have today either."

As the text on the shields jerked around, Randall sensed another message trying to break through. He blinked to clear his eyes but the shadow from the earlier flash remained. Another wave of rocks hit the line, and the images merged, the message suddenly becoming clear.

Smash the bastards

Randall shook his head. When he looked back the message had gone, the original warning back in place.

The stones kept coming. A second set of shields were being held, forming a roof over the troopers further behind the line. For some it was too late. Randall saw a number of troopers carried back from the IS lines.

A large wooden pole emerged from the crowd behind

him. Randall grabbed hold, passing it hand over hand to the front. The long end protruded from the protesters and wobbled towards the immobile IS wall. As it reached their line it was manoeuvred against the foot of the shield wall. Too late, the IS lines realised the protestor's intent, but trapped behind the wall they could do nothing. The protesters holding the pole started to push. Randall joined them, pushing with all his might. A glance down the line showed other poles being pushed against the shield wall in a coordinated attack. Randall redoubled his effort, digging his heels into the earth to stop himself from slipping. Cheers from in front grabbed his attention. The shield wall in front was wobbling. The crowd roared. On the other side of the shields, troopers pulled desperately on shield handles, looking to use their weight to keep the A frame legs on the ground.

The noise intensified, a mix of anger and delight. With a loud crack, the warning message went out and the shield collapsed forward, the sudden movement causing Randall to fall to the ground. Protesters charged past as Randall stumbled to his feet. People were flying through the breach, spraying like the spittle from a zealot's mouth. With its structural integrity weakened, other sections of the shield wall fell until the IS troopers, knowing they were overrun, simply gave up; the fog swallowing them as they retreated. The main block of protesters surged forward, trampling over broken shields as they chased after the troopers. Randall let them run. He felt tired from his exertions, his fatigue acting as a pressure valve, deflating the anger he'd felt moments earlier. Let the youth discover what's hidden in the fog, he thought.

After the noise of before, the world felt very quiet. Randall made his way forward. He could see the bodies of a protester and an IS trooper, their arms wrapped around each other as if in an embrace, blood mingling as it pooled beneath them. To his left a protester was being carried back to camp screaming, one leg at an unnatural angle. Two teenage girls sat cross-legged on the floor, hugging each other.

A crack rang from up ahead. Within moments the shapes of protesters started to emerge from the fog. A loud metallic groan echoed through the murk followed by a low rumble that caused the ground to vibrate.

A shape came hurtling towards him. "Get away! Run!" The man rushed past Randall, his eyes wide with terror.

Randall smiled to himself. This was the moment he had been waiting for. He ran off to the right, along where the original line of protesters had been. He needed to use the chaos to skirt around the security forces and away from the protest. The datasphere was offline so he had to rely on his memory of the park. An impossible task given the fog and disorientating lights. Still, he had to keep moving if he wanted any chance of escaping.

Shapes flew out of the fog. Randall dodged past a young boy but then found himself knocked to the ground. The figure on top thrashed around, his hands pushing Randall's face into the dirt. He couldn't breath. Panicking, he lashed out with his feet and fists, his whole existence pared down to a scramble of arms, legs and teeth. Then, the pressure disappeared and the person was away. Randall pushed himself up, worried that if he stayed on the ground he would get trampled by others. Things were getting out of control. He needed to get away, and quickly.

It took him 20 metres before he realised that he'd lost his bearings. Materialising out of the fog in front of him were a line of troopers, stun sticks banging against shield as they advanced. Interspersed between the lines were nightmarish machines. Large ovoid shapes lurched forward, their multiple legs pounding through the carnage on the ground as spotlights scanned ahead. Randall ran.

He had only run a handful of steps when the booming stopped. Not wanting to look back Randall kept going. The only sound he could hear was the blood pumping in his ears.

Second Chance

A hint of a breeze pushed at him from behind. The skin on his arms and head started to tingle and he could feel the ground vibrate under his feet. Randall snatched a glance back to see what was happening.

Each of the giant machines had dropped to the ground, their fronts opening like giant maws; depths in shadow, unfathomable. A low hum, almost inaudible, flowed from these holes. As the volume increased, so did the pitch. Randall's skin itched as if burnt. Too late, he realised what was happening. He started to run once more. The sound from the hellish machines intensified and a dull ache spread around Randall's body. His stomach cramped and he stumbled. The tone increased again and his muscles turned to jelly, his body hitting the ground hard. The noise never stopped, but increased in intensity. Randall was surrounded by sound. It was a physical presence, squeezing his flesh, pushing all breath out of his lungs. The tone rose higher and his body screamed. His bones vibrated, each joint sparkling with agony as cartilage failed and nerve endings ground on bone. His back felt on fire, his spinal cord pummelled by each vibrating disc. The world was pain, and pain was everything. Wave upon wave crashed through his central cortex, overwhelming in scope and threatening his sanity.

Within the pain Randall performed an invocation in his mind; a rhythmic counterpoint to each pulse of agony, the words looping around, all other thoughts gone.

"Please stop, please stop, please stop, please stop..."

On and on it went, the agony, the litany, his very existence pared down to those two intertwined themes. Randall had never thought of himself as brave, but as the agony continued, he plumbed the depths of his cowardice, knowing he would do anything, say anything, just so it would stop. Nothing mattered any more. Nothing was more important than release. An inhuman keening emerged from his mouth, his final communication to the world.

Something tugged at his leg and the world fell from

underneath him. Over and over he rolled, the pain diminishing with each revolution.

He hit water.

The shock of the cold caused air to burst from his lungs. Randall panicked, thrashing around in the murk as he looked for a way out. He pushed out with arms and legs, only to find his hands digging into sediment. It took a few moments to manoeuvre his legs underneath himself and he stood, bursting out of the water and gulping in a deep breath. He was standing waist deep in a stream, the high embankments either side protecting him from the agonising noise above. By the lip of the bank, a number of protesters bravely crawled out into the agony and pulled people down to safety.

A voice shouted down to him. "Get up here and give us a hand."

Randall looked up to see a man beckoning to him. Not a chance, he thought. He needed to leave, to get away from here. Gritting his teeth against the cold, Randall waded downstream and away from the carnage.

CHAPTER THIRTY-SEVEN
The Investigator

The city was in chaos. The pod network had been taken offline leaving thousands stranded. On the security system, Nico saw reports that the protest had turned violent. The population was turning on the authorities.

His lungs were burning. The outline of two figures emerged from the fog, one giving a small shriek of surprise as he ran past. Then they were gone, sucked back into the mist. More figures emerged, alone or in groups, all doing their best to jump out of the way as he ran past. Each time fear etched their faces. Within minutes, the trickle of people turned into a flood and the road became filled with people. Some ran past laughing, thrilled by the excitement of it all. Others, those older, more worldly-wise, looked anxious, scared even. A number were in tears.

The fog echoed to the sound of shock and disbelief. Nico slowed as he wove his way through the tide. A group of girls shouted at him as he made his way past.

"What are you doing?" one said. "Turn back. They've gone mad."

Nico continued to push through. He didn't stop to ask who 'they' were; he didn't have time. Their shouts faded into the distance as he ran on. He had only one goal. He needed to get to Jennica.

Slowly, the flood of people turned to a trickle, then the trickle evaporated. Quiet enveloped Nico once more. He slowed to catch his breath as nausea threatened. Whatever the people had run from was up ahead, but he had no choice but to carry on.

An outline of the street overlay his vision. The signal from Jennica's datalenses glowed like a beacon in the distance. Nico assessed his options while sucking in large gulps of air. He could stay on the main road for a few hundred metres before taking the next turning right, but he spotted a short cut through an alleyway. Nico made his mind up and started off again, his legs feeling leaden despite the brief respite.

The entrance to the alley was overgrown, the vertical gardens of the buildings either side overspilling. Nico ran a couple of metres before his feet caught something and he hit the ground hard. A wave of pain shot around his body. Swearing, he gingerly got to his feet. He turned back towards the alley entrance and saw the outline of a body lying across the alley entrance. The boy must have been in his early teens, his face swollen, blood pouring from his nose and mouth. Hands shaking, Nico checked for a pulse.

"Hello? Can you hear me?"

There was the shallowest of movement from the boy's chest. Nico leant closer until he could feel the boy's breath on his cheek. He felt torn. The boy needed medical attention, but his priority was clear. He had to get to Jennica before they lost the signal. He stayed with the boy for few a moments more, sending an urgent message to the emergency services. Sorry, he thought as he got back to his feet, but that's the best I can do.

Emerging from the alleyway, Nico spotted a young woman, lying on the ground, eyes staring up into the dark; her purple hair plastered to her face and neck, skin glistening with moisture. Laying by her side was a member of Internal Security. The side of his face was distorted, smashed in by a blood-covered rock by his feet. Shards from his broken helmet were embedded into his face, his left eye hanging out of it's shattered socket by it's optic nerve. The two of them couldn't have looked more different, but they were both as dead as each other.

Nico looked around in panic but all was quiet. He shook, his stomach flipping as his mind sought to reject what he was seeing. What was going on? This wasn't his city. Things like this didn't happen here. Glancing down the street he saw other shapes, their true form shrouded by the mist. Rocks and stones lay scattered across the road. The fog seemed to close in. The silence roared in his ears as he listened for the sound of others.

It was at that moment he saw a single child's shoe among the debris. A small piece of purity amid the carnage. Nico walked over and picked it up, his heart skipping as he realised that Gino had the exact same pair. Not Gino, please, he thought, before calming himself. He had spoken to Fran before he had left. They were safe at home, far away from here. He turned the shoe over in his hands, staring at its perfect form, before walking to the side of the road. He placed the shoe carefully on top of a low wall, making sure that it could be easily seen, forcing himself to believe that someone would come back for it. Someone had to, he hoped.

CHAPTER THIRTY-EIGHT
The Information Cleanser

Randall crept up to the glass doors. A shiver rippled through his body and he clenched his jaw hard to stop his teeth from chattering. His feet felt clumsy, numb from the cold and tired from his panicked escape. He'd been jogging on and off since he'd got out of the water but the cold had eaten into his bones. He needed to get inside before it finished him off.

He looked into the study. The lights were off, but enough light spilled from an open door to show that the room was empty. A movement caused Randall to jump back. He had seen the back of somebody's head, poking above the sofa in the next room. They must be waiting for me, he thought.

The urge to flee nearly took him, but he viciously quashed the impulse. This was his last chance to find out what the hell was going on. If it was a trap, then at least he was prepared. If nothing else he would go down fighting.

He edged back along the wall until he could see into the house. Music was playing. It was Scattered Future, one of his favourite songs. If he could hear it from outside, it would be pretty loud in the house. Randall backed away from the doors and out into the garden. He lifted the top of a small stone bird bath. The scraping seemed loud enough to wake the dead. Randall tried to take the key from its hiding place, his numb fingers fumbling a few times until he finally picked it up. He returned to the doors and used both hands to place the key in the lock. Very slowly, he pulled the handle down and opened the door. The heat and noise from inside enveloped him. Stepping into the room, Randall was overcome with the sense of familiarity.

He crept to a shadowed corner, desperate to remain quiet despite the music from the other room. Warmth seeped through his clothes causing painful pins and needles in his extremities. He needed a chance to think. Getting here had been his goal but he stupidly hadn't considered that somebody would be waiting. In the lounge, the song was reaching its peak, a series of atonal chords complementing lyrics that described the agony of a culture with no home. The first tendrils of panic crept up his spine. Looking around, Randall's eyes fixed on a trophy by the edge of the desk. He reached for it, light reflecting from a plaque near its base proclaiming "arsehole of the year." Feeling comforted by the trophy's heft, Randall crept towards the lounge doorway. A stolen glance showed that the person hadn't moved. He scanned the room but there didn't appear to be anyone else around. Eyes focussed on the back of that head, he slipped into the room, feet sinking into the soft flooring. Randall realised he had never felt so alive. He was terrified and exhilarated at the same time. His sense had never felt so heightened. His hands and feet throbbed in time to the music, the corners of the trophy base dancing with each pulse. Randall caught the stench of stagnant water from his clothes. A final keen of despair broke out over the music and Randall raised the trophy to strike.

The head turned.

"What the—"

Time stopped. The song faded into the background. For a nanosecond Randall struggled to keep hold of himself, the universe appeared to distend before snapping back into shape.

Randall brought the trophy down hard, hitting the head

with a sickening crunch.

CHAPTER THIRTY-NINE
The Politician

It seems strange to use a religious term but I can't think of a more suitable word than soul. I don't know whether mother would be delighted or disappointed if she knew what I was thinking. If this data really is our soul she'd be the first one to say I told you so, but then she always maintained that science couldn't answer everything. I'm not sure she would be as happy when I pointed that out.

Richard Asquith coughed and everybody turned towards him. Blushing slightly, he said, "Now that the history lesson is over, I think it's time to let Stephanie know the reason we dragged her here."

Indigo turned to Stephanie, her face softening. "You might be surprised to learn that we have been following you for some time. We became aware of your potential after we found traces of your little program on the datasphere."

"I've no idea what you're talking about."

"Please, Stephanie, don't lie. You agreed to full disclosure. You have a smart little algorithm that can predict future electoral behaviour based on past evidence, allowing you to propose scenarios and predict their impact on your polling figures. Am I correct?"

Stephanie felt the last remnants of belief that she could control what was happening vanish.

"It's a smart piece of coding, in fact one we have yet to reproduce. We only become aware of it by identifying its tiny markers, then following its trail to you and cross-referencing what it accessed with your actions. Once we'd realised what you had developed we kept an eye on things to see how well you performed. Up until recently, you haven't disappointed us."

"Until recently?"

"Your algorithm is only as good as the factors you ask it to consider. You were able to win your election because the factors impacting on your district were limited. Once you attempted to influence the national scene you fell foul of factors you weren't aware of. Your second issue is that you became distracted by events that had no influence on your overall goal." Indigo paused for a moment. "Why did you become interested in the missing girl?"

It was the way both Asquith and Gant refused to look at her that confirmed Stephanie's suspicions. That poor girl. What had Jennica got herself involved in? "I needed something to boost my numbers and the case seemed a safe bet. If the girl was found, I would look good. If the case remained unsolved, I could bash the Investigative Agency and my popularity would rise. I couldn't lose."

"Sadly for you, things got out of hand."

"You could say that."

"The problem is," Asquith said, "this case is more sensitive than you think."

"Why? What interest do you have in a research student?"

"None. She just happened to be in the wrong place at the wrong time."

"So this has nothing to do with what she discovered about the transiessence data?"

There was a flicker of a reaction from Gant and Asquith, just for an instant, but it was Indigo that looked most surprised.

"I don't know what you are talking about," Asquith replied. "Our problem doesn't lie with the girl but with your friend, Randall Jones. It's his situation that needs resolving."

Stephanie placed her hands on her lap so the others couldn't see them shaking.

"We need to find them," said Gant, "before their situation becomes public knowledge."

"Them? What do you mean them?"

Indigo glared at Gant. "I told you that we have been working towards putting the mechanisms in place for a safe future. Our first priorities were to secure food production, have enough housing for all, more employment and sustainable utilities, among others. As the situation improved, we focussed on security and health. Humanity's biggest fear is the great unknown: death. This is where Re-Life comes in. The next phase of Re-Life will lead to a new era of stability. By controlling death, we can control the population. If committing serious crime means losing the right to live forever, who would take that risk? The fear of dying is removed for billions by the new, cost effective process and the world will become a much safer place." There was an almost evangelical note in Indigo's voice as she spoke. "However, for it to work people must have total faith in the process. Sadly, an error has led to the clone of Randall Jones being activated while Randall is still alive. We believe the clash of their combined stored memories has driven one or both of them mad, leading to the death of poor Jennica Fabian. We need you to help us resolve the issue. It has to be you, you are the only one he will trust."

Stephanie felt sick. "Poor Randall."

Asquith leaned forward. "Yes, it is a real pity."

"But I don't understand. How could you not have known that there were two of them if you control everything?"

"We are still trying to get to the bottom of it," Indigo replied, "and believe me, we will find out what happened. We think that some form of trauma triggered the automatic activation process. That is one of the reasons why it is important to get to them, so that we can learn what happened. It was only when the two of them tried to access their work system at the same time that we knew we had a problem. By the time we traced his signal, Randall had moved on. We lost him for a time—today has been very trying from a security perspective—but our last information shows that he is heading home."

Interesting, Stephanie thought. You can't control everything. "So why don't you just catch him there?"

"Because he is already home. The two of them are about to meet."

"I still don't understand? Why do you need me? What can I do to help? Why can't you send in the security forces instead?"

"We need you to let us know which one is the original." Indigo smiled at Stephanie. "You are the only person within our organisation that has any knowledge of Randall Jones."

Our organisation. The words stung Stephanie as if she had been slapped. She was part of this organisation whether she liked it or not.

As if reading her mind, Indigo said, "You belong to a very exclusive club. Why don't you ask Richard or Zachary if they regret joining us?"

Stephanie looked at Gant again, a smug smile plastered over his face. All the time she had been here, the realisation grew that Gant thought they were now friends; that by being in on their secret somehow absolved him of what he had done. How many people have you killed or assaulted, knowing that nobody could touch you? What other evil have you done, hiding behind your friends? She wondered if he had always been like this, or whether power had rotted away his principles too. Had it done the same to her? She thought about it, but then realised that thanks to Gant there was nothing left of the person she used to be, and how could power corrupt revenge?

She took a deep breath. "Could we have a word alone ?"

Indigo nodded, gesturing for Asquith and Gant to leave. Gant looked as if he was about to object but one glance from Indigo was enough, and he left.

Once alone, Stephanie said, "If I understand correctly, you need me otherwise things could get messy."

"That's correct."

"You also need my algorithm, because you can't reproduce it yourselves."

"It would be helpful,"

"OK, I'll do it."

For once, the smile lit up the whole of Indigo's face. "I was hoping you would say that—"

"But I want something in return."

"You are in no position to bargain."

"You didn't bring me all this way just to kill me, so I must be of some value."

Indigo stared at her for a moment. "Why are you not scared?"

"That's what I want to talk to you about."

CHAPTER FORTY
The Information Cleanser

The pain from his temple enveloped his skull. He tried to move but was overcome by a wave of nausea. It felt like the world's worst hangover. Had he been drinking again? No. He'd promised himself never to touch another drop and he knew he'd kept that promise. He'd been on the wagon now for nearly two months. A trickle crept down his forehead, travelling to the bridge of his nose. He tried to lift his hand but it was stuck behind his back. He pulled harder but his opposite shoulder wrenched backwards. In a panic, he opened his eyes and a cascade of stars swamped his senses, sending shafts of pain down his optic nerves. His yell was blocked by something in his mouth.

His right arm exploded in pain as it was struck, again and again; a rain of blows on his upper arm and elbow.

"Shut up if you want to live."

The pain was incredible. He tried, oh god he tried, but he couldn't control his sobbing. The blows increased, this time on his legs, each impact sending shock waves through his body. His skull felt like it would implode.

A knife materialised in front of his eyes.

"I won't tell you again."

Instinct took hold and his body stiffened. He could feel the cold metal against his throat and tried to pull back. A small squeak left his throat but he managed to control himself.

"I'm going to take your gag off. If you make any noise I'll stab you in the eye. Do you understand?"

Randall nodded, the movement sending another wave of nausea through his body. That voice was familiar; where had he heard it before? Sparks swam in front of his eyes as his head was shaken. With a gasp he drew in a lungful of air as the gag was removed. "I don't know what you want," Randall said, "but take what you need. I don't have much, but it's yours."

He felt another blow, harder than before, this time to the back of his head, the impact making his teeth crack together. His skull was a self-perpetuating cycle of pain. Randall couldn't believe such agony was possible. Then, gradually, the pain subsided. He could taste blood in his mouth.

"You don't speak unless I tell you to, understand?"

Randall nodded, bracing himself for the expected attack.

"This can't be happening. It's impossible. Tell me, what's going on? Who is doing this to me?" The voice travelled as the person moved behind him.

"Sorry?"

Another blow, this time on his ribs. Randall screamed in pain.

"Don't piss me about. What's going on? Who are you?"

"Randall! My names Randall! Please don't hurt me."

Blows rained down, his nerves screaming with each impact. Randall felt his mind slowly drawing back, his vision starting to fade. Pain receded and his face felt warm. He wanted to sleep. He could feel his body shaking with each impact but it was if a soft blanket had been placed between his body and his brain.

A slap to the face woke him.

"What's your name?"

Pain flooded his senses once more. "Please," Randall whimpered, "I don't know what you want. I don't know what to say. I'll be whoever you want me to be, just please stop hitting me." Snot dribbled down his face, mixing with tears and the blood in his mouth. I'm going to die, he thought, I'm really going to die.

"I don't want you to make things up, I want you to tell me the truth. Who are you?"

"Don't kill me, please."

"Just answer the question."

"Randall."

The pain was sharper this time, setting his shoulder blade on fire. Randall felt warmth trickle down his back. My god, he thought, I've been stabbed. He cried out in frustration. What could he do? What did this monster want him to say? He couldn't think, the pain in his head was immense. His arms hurt, his ribs hurt, breathing hurt. He knew he was going to die. If this was the way it was going to end, he would rather it was over quickly. A calm descended as he came to peace with his situation. His weeping stopped.

"My name is Randall Jones."

The yell was primal, a shriek of pain and fury. Randall braced himself for the killing blow but it never came.

"Why are you doing this to me? What do you want?"

Randall started to answer and then stopped, realising that the questions weren't aimed at him. A shadow appeared above him. He flinched, sure that this was would be the fatal blow. Fingers dug into his cheeks, yanking his head upwards.

"Look at me and tell me what you see. Look at me!"

Randall looked up and gasped.

"No, that's... who are you?"

Laughter erupted from the monster's throat.

CHAPTER FORTY-ONE
The Investigator

What had happened to his city? How could people change so quickly? Every street had revealed its own set of horrors, every turning another shocking scene. The emergency network was going into overdrive, each message saying the same thing: the protesters were out of control. The people had turned feral.

Nico stretched his arms high to relieve the stitch in his side. What had been an ache in his ankle had slowly turned into a short stabbing pain as he continued to push forward. Not far now. His datalenses picked out Jennica's position as a beacon drawing ever closer.

The yellow glow of distant streetlights lit up the gloom ahead. Nico sped up, the sound of his feet pounding on the ground and the harshness of each breath blocking all other sounds. This must be the junction he'd been looking for. Nico kept his head down, determined not to look ahead but to focus just a metre in front; concentrating on placing one foot in front of the other. He would take a breather once he got to the junction.

His months of investigative work were finally bearing fruit. Despite the horrors he had witnessed as he'd moved across the city, Nico felt a tingle of excitement. He had a chance to show that even on the bleakest days, some good could be found. All he needed to do was to get to Jennica.

The fog thinned slightly and Nico broke through into light. He staggered to a halt, hands on knees. His legs felt like jelly and his face burned. He really needed to get fit again.

Nico looked up. In the middle of the crossroad was a barricade of three Internal Security pods, the gaps between sealed by large clear panels. The set-up was similar to the checkpoints Nico had passed on the way to the Scrambles. That was where any similarity ended. Surrounding the pods, sprawled in hideous poses, were bodies. Lots of bodies.

A group of young men lay close to where Nico stood, their charred faces visible despite the scarves wrapped around their heads. Over to one side he saw an old man slumped on top of a woman in what looked to be a protective pose. Beside them was a mother holding her baby, a bloodied blanket failing to hide the horrors underneath. A loud crack broke the stillness followed by laughter. The screech of a dying animal could be heard in the distance.

Nico looked to the checkpoint. Two Internal Security troops were beating a man with batons, the blows cracking his head against a pod. Beside them, a girl was being held down, each arm and leg secured by a trooper, her nakedness highlighted in the bright security lights. Kneeling beside her, a trooper had his trousers pulled down to his knees. The girl struggled against the four men but they were far too strong; the metallic sound of amplified laughter spilled out from the trooper's helmets.

Fear gripped Nico as reality came crashing in. He started to back away, desperate not to make a sound. A part of him wanted to report what he had seen. It was a horrific crime, shocking not just in its scale but because of who the perpetrators were. How could people that were sworn to protect do such a thing? If he reported it now maybe he could save the two that remained alive.

He couldn't bring himself to do it. He was outnumbered, unarmed and close to the point of exhaustion. The troopers may not have seen him approach but they would know somebody was out there as soon as the report was filed. His thoughts drifted towards Fran and the kids. He'd heard rumours of what happened to people who complained about Internal Security, the intimidation they had been forced to endure. He'd dismissed them at the time, but now he was all too certain that they were real. He couldn't risk anything happening to his family. The guilt hit him hard, but he couldn't get Gino out of his head, his big eyes full of trust, expecting Daddy to protect him.

Nico sidled back until he was on the very edge of the junction, the fog transforming the checkpoint to a shapeless blur. He worked his way around the edge of visibility, judging that if he struggled to see the checkpoint, the checkpoint would struggle to see him. Step by step he crept ever closer to the right-hand exit, ignoring the sounds coming from the checkpoint. A group of bodies lay in his path. As he stepped over one, the accusation in the man's lifeless eyes bored into Nico's soul.

A shriek pierced through the murk followed by another loud crack. Nico stopped. What followed was a silence more terrifying than any scream. Arguing erupted from the checkpoint. For a moment Nico thought they would come to blows, then one took command and the troopers started to disperse. One walked towards where Nico was standing.

His instincts screamed for him to run, but he knew that if he did he would be spotted immediately. Nico forced himself to stand still. Step by step the trooper continued in Nico's direction, its outline solidifying the closer it came. Nico began to shake. It's alright, he told himself, you're in the shadow. He can't see you. The trooper took three more paces. The faint sound of radio chatter broke the silence. There was a gentle patter as water dripped from branches onto the earth below. Nico ignored the trickle of sweat sliding down his nose as he concentrated fully on the shadow in front of him.

The trooper continued forward, then stopped, the insect-like helmet looking straight at where he was standing. Nico looked at the trooper. The trooper looked at Nico. A crackle of static erupted from the trooper's radio and without a second thought, Nico was off, running as fast as he could into the night, faster and harder than he had ever run before. He knew he couldn't run far, he was almost spent in the rush to find Jennica, but he had no other choice.

Blurred shapes flew past him as he made his headlong charge from the checkpoint, the superimposed map letting him know which direction to run. The burning in his lungs quickly changed to daggers and the stitch had returned with a vengeance. Nico screamed at himself as he fought to keep going. He had to get to Jennica, that was where the team were. That was safety. Sweat stung his eyes, making his journey even more treacherous. Was it his imagination, or was the sound of boots pounding behind him getting louder? He turned his head to get a better look just as the street lights went out. In desperation, he initiated a mayday signal but before it could be sent his datasphere connection disappeared.

Terror gripped him as darkness consumed all. Without the map, he had no way of knowing where to go, no way of reaching safety. Nico slowed down, his vision swarming with the ghostlike traces from the datasphere map. He had a moment to compose himself before he heard the sound of boots. Nico searched in desperation. There must be somewhere around here to hide, he thought. He spotted a slight lightening of the gloom up ahead. Without thinking he ran towards it, driven by fear. Within moments the fog had thinned enough for him to see that the light was coming from a house. There was a family sitting around their dining table, light spilling out through their unshuttered window.

"Help! Please, you've got to help me!" Nico ran up the path and banged on the window, desperate to get their attention.

One of the women let out a sharp scream, dropping a plate of vegetables. The other, a startled look on her face, shouted at him through the window. "Go away, leave us alone." The sound was muffled through the glass but there was no mistaking the anger in the woman's voice.

Nico struggled to catch his breath and the world started to spin. "Please," he gasped, "I'm desperate."

The woman at the window hesitated. A baby's screams pierced the air. Her partner mouthed something, shaking her head. Nico dropped to his knees, crying at the unfairness of it all. He'd done nothing wrong. He'd just been doing his job. He turned back towards the window to make one last desperate plea when he felt a sharp pain at the back of his neck. His head hit the ground with a thud. Nico smelt the acid reek of vomit. He tried to get up but his body wouldn't respond; he couldn't even cry for help. Out of the corner of his eye, he made out the shape of a boot. Then even that was denied him as something was placed over his head.

CHAPTER FORTY-TWO
The Information Cleanser

Randall stared at the man in front of him. Why did the impostor keep claiming to be him, even when he thought he was going to die? Did he think he could confuse him, make him doubt himself somehow?

"I... I don't understand?" the man squinted as he looked up. He was pitiful. Dried blood matted his hair where his scalp had been split. Snot and blood trailed down his left cheek, and he reeked of piss.

"I don't understand either," Randall said.

The man grimaced for a moment as he shifted his weight. "Who are you?"

"You know who I am."

"But you can't be."

"You're good, I'll give you that." Randall leant forward, showing the man the knife again. "What are you doing here?"

The man tried to move back, wincing as he did so. "This is my house, I've lived here for years. You can check my pockets for the keys if you want."

Randall felt his anger rise once more. "Why are you lying? I've lived here for ten years, not you. This is my house. What are you doing here? Who gave you my face?"

"Please. Check my pockets."

Randall reached down and pulled out a set of keys. They were his keys, the keys he had lost after the accident.

"I lost these. Where did you get them from?"

"I've always had them."

"Who gave them to you?"

"No one."

This time there was no containing his rage. How dare this impostor come into my house, take over my life and then deny everything. Randall's grip on the knife tightened. It would be so easy to finish him off. Just one stab, that was all. This man was one of them. They'd made his life a misery and now they had to pay. But then how would he get the answers he needed?

"Look," said the man, "let's think for a minute. You said you lost the keys. When did you lose them?"

Randall ignored the voice. He was just trying to confuse him. He needed to work this out for himself.

"Please, I'm trying to understand. I've never lost these keys. I always keep them in my pocket. Always the same pocket."

Randall stared at the man. How *had* he known which pocket to search? He'd gone straight for the right one. Was that just luck? "I lost them in the accident?"

"What accident?"

"The pod accident."

"Pod accident?"

Randall punched the man in the ribs. "You know what happened, that's why you're here."

"I don't, please, I don't know what's happening." He looked to Randall, his eyes full of tears. "Please... the accident... when did it happen?"

"You know damn well. You must have waited until I'd cut all ties before jumping in."

The man went pale. "Cut all ties? You mean at work?"

Randall kicked the man again. "Don't act the innocent."

"I know what happened to me!" he shouted. "I don't

know anything about you."

Randall knelt next to the man and pushed his face to the floor. Why was he being so stubborn? What did he think he had to gain? He took the knife and held it against the man's throat. "OK. Tell me about you."

The man started gabbling, giving his name, how old he was, who his parents were. Randall pushed the knife closer to his throat. A trickle of blood ran slowly downwards along the blade's edge. "Let's start with the last clear thing I remember. I had an argument with Thijs."

"About Stephanie. It was about Stephanie Vaughn. Thijs pushed me to chase Stephanie. He didn't believe I was trying hard enough. He wanted more progress on the Jennica Fabian case, because I'd quarantined something she'd written while working for Re-Life. We were worried that the investigation would link the girl to Re-Life—"

Randall stared at the man. How did he know this? Who told him? Only three people were aware of the link between Jennica and Re-Life.

"—because it could end up screwing up the launch of the next-gen Re-Life process."

"Who told you about this?"

"Nobody. Nobody told me. Please, listen to me. This is my life. Thijs and I argued and I said some things to him and the others before storming out. I was angry and frustrated. I felt betrayed. I left the office, went back to the hotel and got blind drunk. The bastard had humiliated me in front of my colleagues, my friends. At least that's what I thought. It took a couple of days to realise what an idiot I'd been. By that point I knew I had one of two choices. Either I run away from what he said, or confront the truth. I went back to the office and apologised. It was hard, but it was probably the best decision I've ever made."

How could the man know this? How did he know how he had felt? Randall felt his grip on reality weaken. The old fears were returning. He needed facts. He needed things he could focus on, to ground him, to make everything certain again.

"What happened after you went back?" Randall asked.

"We agreed to stop our involvement with Stephanie. I had to eat humble pie with the team, but they were brilliant; far more understanding than I'd expected."

A familiar feeling overcame Randall, as if he had taken a step back from reality. He knew this. He'd seen this before. A pattern was becoming clear. Always before it had been about something external, but this time he felt a transformation happening on the inside, like a butterfly emerging from its chrysalis. The realisation struck that he could become what nature had always intended. He just had to push a little further. "What, all the team? Even Sylvianne?"

"Yes, even her."

"Why say it like that?" Randall asked the question, but he already knew the answer.

"I'd been wrong about Sylvianne. I thought she was cold, purely career minded. But she was different when I came back."

"What do you mean, different?"

"Warmer, as if seeing me at my lowest point let her see me as something other than her boss."

"And you became close." Randall said.

"Yes."

"Close enough to start dating?"

"Yes."

"Nice Italian meals?"

The man looked confused. "How do you know that?"

"At the Capaldi Restaurant? Costing 237 globals? Followed by fucking in the bedroom upstairs?" The man looked terrified, but Randall didn't need to wait for further confirmation. He already knew the answers and he knew what was going on. They had warned him in the hospital it might happen but he hadn't believed them. Yet for once they hadn't lied to him. The click of pieces falling into place was almost audible. It explained everything.

Randall brought his knife down, severing the rope tethering the man's hands and legs.

"Get up," he said, grabbing the man by his hair.

The man yelled as Randall pulled, but managed to roll onto all fours. "Where are we going?"

"Home," Randall said. "We're going back home."

CHAPTER FORTY-THREE
The Politician

Was religion right all along? Do we have an everlasting soul? But if it really is our soul, why is the data different from host to clone? If what I've found is consciousness, does this mean that there is no continuity of self, that the clone is nothing more than a copy after all? And if it is truly a soul, why does it come back changed?

Stephanie shivered despite her heated coat. The light had come on as soon as she walked down the pathway, its sensor not hindered by the fog. She paused for a moment, staring at the door. It was just a door, yet Stephanie knew that it meant so much more. Walking through would change everything. If she walked through that door, it would complete her transition.

She pushed the buzzer and waited.

The journey back with Asquith had been quiet. It was strange how suddenly things could change, how quickly the balance of power could shift. If you had spoken to her a few weeks back, the thought of having access to the Prime Delegate, alone, for nearly an hour; she would have given anything for that opportunity. Instead, the two of them kept silent. Stephanie knew she should have been overjoyed with what had happened. After she had explained her terms and why, Indigo had been quick to react. The look of shock on Gant's face as the security guards threw him to the ground was wonderful. It was only with the crack of their weapons that the finality of her request hit home. She refused to flinch from the consequences of her actions, but instead of the wholeness she had thought revenge would deliver, she felt an emptiness inside. Asquith had thrown up at the sight of his dead friend. It seemed that the Prime Delegate was happier ordering hearing about death second-hand. Later, in the pod, Stephanie occasionally caught Asquith looking at her. Whenever she looked back he'd glance away, out into the fog, refusing to meet her gaze. Should she be happy that the Prime Delegate was scared of her?

There was no answer to the buzzer so she tried again. Get in, identify the real Randall, make the call. It should be simple but—

"Hello?" Stephanie recognised the voice on the intercom. So they had been telling the truth, at least this far.

"Randall, let me in. It's Stephanie."

There was a moments pause. "Stephanie? What are you doing here?"

"Please let me in. I think I know what's going on and who's after you."

"Stephanie? Of course. That makes sense. OK, wait there. I need a few minutes to get changed"

Stephanie felt a moment's uncertainty. Randall had sounded remote, almost disconnected. What was she getting herself into? She looked back down the path to the fog-shrouded street. Somewhere out there were the pick-up team. At least she hoped they were.

The front door buzzed. With trepidation Stephanie walked into the dimly lit hallway.

"I'm in here."

The living area was brightly lit. There were two large sofas close to a burner with a rug between them; the fire from the burner giving plenty of warmth and light. Standing opposite, wearing a purple robe, was Randall. His hair was wet and the robe clung to him, as if he had failed to dry himself properly, but it was the same drawn face she had seen in the Scrambles, his eyes unable to remain focussed on one place. Stephanie noticed a bag of pills on the mantelpiece. Was that dreamweaver?

He rubbed at his hair with a towel. "I'm really glad you appeared. Would you like a drink?"

Stephanie smiled her warmest smile. "I'm fine for the moment, thanks."

"Can I at least take your coat?"

"In a minute. I just need to warm up first."

His smile dropped just for a moment before quickly returning. "Of course. Sorry for keeping you waiting." He gestured for her to sit and took his place on the couch opposite.

Stephanie made a show of glancing around the room. "It's a nice place you have here." Where was he? Where was the other Randall? They said both would be here.

"You said you knew who was after me."

So much for small talk. "I don't know for certain."

"But you have an idea."

Stephanie nodded. "They said you were out the night Jennica went missing?"

Randall frowned. "I've no idea."

"Are you sure? It was the night I got elected."

Randall's eyes dropped to the floor.

"Randall, this is really important. I need to know if you were out that night."

Randall's gaze remained at his feet.

"Please Randall. Some people have told me that you were."

"So why bother asking?"

"Because I need to hear it from you. Were you out that night?"

He nodded.

"Can you remember what you did, where you went?"

"I got drunk." Randall looked uncomfortable, his hands clenched together on his lap. The front of his robe hung open to reveal a torso covered in bruises. Stephanie stifled a shiver. Had she got it wrong?

"Do you often go out and get drunk?"

He shook his head.

"So what was so special about that night?"

He looked up, staring. "I needed to forget."

"Forget?"

The look Randall gave Stephanie made her realise that something was very wrong. "I needed to forget you."

CHAPTER FORTY-FOUR
The Information Cleanser

Randall could see confusion on her face, that beautiful, horrible face he'd never been able to forget.

"Why? We haven't been in contact for over 20 years. Why would I even be in your thoughts?"

He smiled inwardly, marvelling as his brain played its tricks. He'd always thought Stephanie was intelligent, way too good for him, but the last 24 hours had changed his opinion. What an idiot he'd been.

"Because you were all over the datasphere. Everybody was talking about you. Stephanie Vaughn takes the district from nowhere. The rising star of the Legislature. Your image was everywhere while I sat here alone, working in a job where I wasn't respected with a group of people who either took me for granted or despised me." Randall felt calm as he spoke. For the first time in a long time, everything was clear. "I hated you for your success, and I hated myself for feeling that way. So I went out to get drunk and forget, to get away from this place and my failures."

She reached forward. "Randall, I'm sorry. I didn't realise."

Stephanie's words twisted into him, shattering his calm facade. "Don't give me your pity. After all these years don't you fucking dare!"

Stephanie recoiled as if bitten. "It wasn't... I didn't mean it like that..."

"You have no idea, do you? What you put me through."

"No, Rand, I don't. I was young and stupid. I'd never allowed myself to open up to others so I had no idea the pain I was causing. It took me a long time to learn that lesson. I'm sorry."

Randall realised that he was on his feet. He sat back down, head spinning. The block that he'd kept in place for over 20 years had been breached and rage and self-loathing was seeping out. He thought about what she had done to him, how she had wrecked his life, and he wanted to lash out. Yet when she looked at him, her eyes focussed purely on him, he realised that he still meant something to her. That feeling he'd had in the park when she hugged him, it wasn't fake. This was why he needed her here, to resolve those feelings, to heal him. If he wanted the pain to go away, he had to let her take the lead. But it was confusing. His memories felt jumbled. He didn't know what to believe any more. He'd thought he'd found the answer, but now he wasn't sure.

"What happened after you got drunk? Did you go anywhere else?"

Stephanie's voice broke into his thoughts, blurred sounds that took a moment to clarify. "I went home."

"You went straight home."

Did he? He couldn't remember. The pressure in his head was becoming unbearable. He could taste blood in his mouth. Was it his blood? What was happening? He tried to focus on the question. What *did* he do that night? All he could remember was waking up the next morning.

"I don't remember."

"Randall, if I'm going to help, I need the truth from you."

The damn burst and rage sprang up inside him, boiling over, burning out all rational thought. "I said I don't fucking remember! I don't know! Stop asking me all these questions!"

She looked at him, terror in her eyes. "Please, Randall,

you're scaring me. Please sit down."

"You just won't listen, will you? I said I don't know." He could feel his fists clenching. The urge to lash out was almost unbearable. "Why do you want to know? Tell me the truth now."

"They said you'd killed Jennica. I've even seen footage of you at the scene. I think you're being set-up but I needed to hear it from you."

At last. Randall relaxed. "Do you want to know what happened?"

"Yes."

"I thought I was going mad. My dreams... things I would never do. They didn't make sense. Why would Sylvianne like me? She hated me; she'd never sleep with me. Why did she turn into Jennica? Was she hurting or enjoying it? Nothing made sense. I had to come home, to find out what was happening, and I have. Everything's clear now." Telling Stephanie the truth made Randall happier than he had felt for a long time. The suppurated abscess in his soul was being lanced, and it felt good. He smiled down at her. "They told me I would have visions, that I would see things that weren't real. At first I didn't believe them, but then I started to see the messages. I got scared, really scared. How were they doing it? Who was talking to me? But then I realised that the messages were helping me. I thought I was being guided by a guardian angel, but I wasn't. It was me all along. I came home because I knew the answers would be here and I was right. I came home and saw a vision."

"What did you see?" The way Stephanie looked at him made Randall smile again. Despite the anxiety in her eyes, he knew she understood.

"I saw me, how I wanted to be; the me from my dreams. I didn't realise what was happening at first but then it came to me. I needed to reconcile myself, inside." You need to come clean, he thought to himself, tell her everything. "I would never hurt anyone, Steph, not in a million years—"

"I believe you Randall. I know you would never hurt anyone."

"But part of me must have done, part of me must have done something to that poor girl. I dreamt her face. I could see me, sitting there, the bad me. It couldn't go on. I had to deal with it, make sure the bad me would never attack anyone again. It was never me that did these things because I'm me. Something else did what it did, but I'm back in control and it will never come back."

"What did you do?"

"You don't have to worry, it's gone now. I've stopped it."

"Randall, please, tell me what you've done."

Of course, he thought. This would be the ultimate test. This would prove everything.

"OK," he said. "I'll show you."

CHAPTER FORTY-FIVE
The Investigator

Nico used to have nightmares about dying. He could never remember why he was going to die, or how, but in the dream he always had time to think about what dying would mean. Every night for weeks he would wake up alone, in the dark, terrified at the endless nothing that awaited him. He lay there, every atom of his body shaking with fear, terrified at the thought of the abyss, the nothingness that he couldn't avoid. His 11-year-old self would cling to his teddy bear, whispering "I don't want to die, I don't want to die," squeezing his eyes closed as he struggled to overcome the existential terror. Every night. For weeks on end. Every night the same.

He had wanted to believe in an afterlife. He'd tried to use his mother's strength of faith. On Sundays he would go to church along with many other families he knew. Most of the families were survivors of the Upheaval, using faith to help make sense of what they had lived through. Nico had tried to throw himself into the ritual and ceremony, to find comfort in the words, but in his heart he knew that it was play-acting. He didn't really believe. So his nightmares continued, week after week, until he found a way to suppress the corrosive thoughts, using the act of living as a buffer against the thought of death.

Now, laying helpless on the cold, hard floor, Nico realised he had never truly come to terms with death. All his control was gone. The abyss had opened up inside him and he could feel his flesh cool as his very essence slipped down like grains of sand in an hourglass.

Nico railed at how unfair it was. He had done nothing wrong. He was one of the good guys. He had led a good life, committing himself so that society remained safe and whole. It wasn't fair that he was the one to stumble upon the checkpoint. After all the good he had done, why had fate chosen him to observe that horror?

His mind was stuck in a loop, a vortex fuelled by fear, spewing out thought after thought with no coherence. What if he told them he hadn't seen anything? Could he rely on his status as an Investigator to save himself? What about Fran, the children? My god, not the children! They wouldn't hurt the children would they? Surely they'll be safe at home? What will they do to me? I don't want to die. Please, don't kill me. I don't want to die. I don't want to die.

Time stretched as Nico's world shrunk. Deprived of stimuli, he was forced to grab hold of anything solid as a tether to reality. He embraced the feeling of the fibres of his hood tickling the tip of his nose. The mustiness of the hood's material became a heady perfume, each element to be assessed and identified. Even his breath became something to celebrate, proof that death was yet to take its hold. He needed to experience the now, no matter how bad a position he was in. The piece of gravel in his back, a pinpoint of pain in his hip, the sound of his own heart; with each element Nico gradually calmed himself, accepted his situation, and used the opportunity to experience all of what it meant to be alive.

The loud metallic squeal shattered the silence. They were coming for him. A brown, muted light made its way through his hood. There were footsteps, then silence. Nico could hear someone breathing and tensed. The side of his face smashed against the floor as his hood was yanked away. The bright light stabbed into his retinas. This was it. Death had arrived. Nico wasn't prepared, he never would be. The icy fingers of terror grasped hold.

The room slipped into focus. He could see a whitewashed wall, mildew creeping up from the concrete floor. He was trapped inside his numb body, his eyes the only thing he could control. There was a scraping sound. Fear ratcheted up a notch. Who was this person? Would they hurt him? Did they have a knife? Would they slit his throat? His mind reached a new level of panic but his body remained still. Then Nico felt a sharp sting on his neck which was followed by a high, keening sound. It was a pitiful sound, made worse by the fact it was coming from his throat.

"Give it a minute and you'll be able to speak."

There was a knock followed by a screech as the door opened once more. Nico attempted to move his lips. His mouth was so dry it was like rubbing sandpaper over bark.

"I don't care about your fucking orders, the prisoner is staying with me." There was a loud slam and the footsteps returned.

Nico let out a croak, waited a moment, then tried again. "Water."

"Later. We need to have a little chat first. My name is Oscar."

"Water."

"You can have some once you tell me what you were doing running from a checkpoint."

"Nothing." Nico squeezed the word out, a faint whisper, hardly audible.

"Don't lie. I know exactly what happened. You ran because of what you saw. You ran because you were scared."

"Saw nothing."

"What you saw were people obeying orders. What you saw is what happens when people provoke too much, get a bit above themselves. It was bound to happen sooner or later."

Nico felt the man's breath on the back of his neck. "Let me ask you a question. A family owns a dog. Its been with the family since it was a puppy. This dog loves the family and wants to protect them. Now the family don't respect their pet so the dog ends up covered with fleas. These fleas feed off the dog, use its blood to sate their own desires. Every time a flea bites the dog, the dog's mood gets worse. The family don't do anything about the fleas so the biting increases, but the dog is a good dog—it's there to protect the family, so the dog tries its best to ignore the irritation. But the biting doesn't stop. It goes on for week after week until the baby of the house, seeing its favourite play-mate, decides to give the dog's ears a good yank. So my question is, who's to blame when the dog crushes the baby's skull in its jaws, the dog or the owners for ignoring the fleas?"

In his mind's eye, Nico can see the checkpoint, the piles of bodies and the bare, splayed legs. He can see the stained baby blanket and the mother sprawled on the ground. The stench of death is still in his nostrils.

"You see, this has been coming. Too many people think they know better than those protecting us. They keep prodding away, complaining about this or moaning about that, forgetting about where we were not so long ago. Well, finally the protectors have had enough. Tonight was a turning point. Once the full horror is made known and the violence blamed on the protestors, control will be restored and everybody can get on with their lives."

So it was true. The government knew what had happened. They not only knew, but they instigated it. It was horrific, monstrous. The state was there to protect the people, not abuse people to protect the state.

"So now we come to you."

Nico's sense of disgust was quickly overwhelmed by fear. They knew he'd been at the checkpoint. They knew what he'd seen. They even confirmed it. He was as good as dead.

"By rights we shouldn't be having this conversation. You know too much. But despite my better judgement, you are to be released. Seems somebody high up is looking out for you."

Nico couldn't believe what he was hearing. It was impossible. Then he thought about holding his children again and felt tears sliding down his cheeks. "Thank you."

"Don't thank me. Because of you, I've missed an important pick-up. Right now I'm so pissed off I'd prefer it if you were dead."

Relief was once again replaced by fear. His body shook as the full realisation of his future hit home. Even if they didn't kill him now, he would be watched for the remainder of his life. He'd seen too much to be allowed any freedom. His whole life would be put under the microscope.

Nico turned his head to face Oscar. The man looked familiar and it took a few moments to place him. That was when true terror hit him.

"This is how it will be. You saw some protesters going on the rampage, attacking anything or anyone in their path, including innocent civilians. You managed to capture images of those involved at risk to your own life. Once you report what you saw you will be hailed as a hero."

"OK—"

"I haven't finished. The case that you are working on has been solved. Jennica Fabian was abducted and killed by Randall Jones. He hid her in a sealed contemplation room, then covered his tracks using his specialist skills. Your colleagues are at the scene now. As lead Investigator in this case, you will sign off these findings. Do I make myself clear?"

"I don't understand. Why are you telling me this?"

"You have no idea what you are dealing with, do you? This is not a game. Too much is at stake to be fucked up by someone like you." Oscar paced the room, his footsteps echoing off the walls. "I don't know if you are more intelligent or more stupid than they originally thought. You were told to stop the investigation yet you decided to ignore the warnings and do your own thing. That wasn't meant to happen. You were picked to screw up the investigation, or at least do as you were told. Instead, you had to keep pushing. Why couldn't you have left everything alone like you were supposed to?"

Nico said nothing. He knew the answer. It wasn't because he couldn't let Jennica down. He felt an obligation to her, but that wasn't what had kept him going. It wasn't as if he had to find her because it was the right thing to do, even though that was a factor. It wasn't even his promise to her housemate. He had continued because he needed to know that he could still do it, that he wasn't a failure.

"You have a lovely wife and two beautiful children."

"No, please no."

"You love them very much, don't you?"

"Please, not my family."

"I asked you a question. You love them very much, don't you?"

"Yes."

"We will be watching you. If you think of going public with what you saw, or changing your story from what we've told you, the next time your family step foot outside the door, something terrible will happen. This is not a threat. It will happen. It won't be a quick death. It will be slow. They'll be in great pain. We can do that. We can arrange anything. I think you know this by now. You will be able to visit your family in hospital and watch them writhe in agony until they die, knowing that you put them there, that you were the one responsible. Now fuck off out of here before I change my mind. Have a nice life, Nico."

CHAPTER FORTY-SIX
The Politician

I try my best to pretend that everything is alright. I go to the labs and work as if nothing is bothering me, but it's all a sham. I can't stop thinking about what it all means. Are we really extending life or are we developing soulless copies of ourselves? What does this mean for humanity? How will we ever know the truth?

I've arranged to go away, somewhere remote. Hopefully it will do some good, bring me back down to earth. I've posted a blog so others can check the data. I'm hoping that I'm wrong and that somebody will spot the flaw. I've never hoped to be wrong before.

What had happened to poor Randall, the bumbling kid she knew from University? What had they done to make him end up like this? He beckoned to her and Stephanie followed. A rank smell drifted up into her nostrils and she almost gagged. It was coming from his bandaged left hand. Something was badly wrong. She went to speak but Randall manoeuvred her forward and headed towards a side door.

"When we met in the park I was convinced you still had feelings for me." His voice was calm, detached. "It was good to see you again. It had been a long time."

"Randall? After our meeting, did you mention to anyone else that Jennica was working for Re-Life?"

"No."

"What about your boss?"

"Thijs wanted it kept quiet."

They stopped in front of the door.

"I don't think you took Jennica. I think somebody is trying to set you up."

"You've said that already."

"Yes, but someone in government, somebody high up, asked me about Jennica and mentioned Re-Life when there was no way they should have known about the link." Please Randall, she thought, trust me.

"It's OK, Steph. I've worked it out. Open the door to the bathroom. You'll see."

Randall let go of Stephanie and gave her a gentle push forward. The door loomed in front of her. Controlling a shiver, Stephanie steeled herself and pushed. The door opened a crack and then stopped. "It won't open."

"It must be my dirty clothes." Randall stepped forward and gave the door a kick.

The blow forced it to open a little further. A sliver of light entered the room. Randall kicked at the clothes wedged under the door and pushed again. The wedge of light expanded. The clothes on the floor were soaked in blood. A thick layer of blood lay congealed on the tiled floor, smeared where the clothes had been dragged by the door. Blood splattered the walls, the spray reaching as high as the ceiling in places. The smell of shit and piss clashed with a cloying, charnel stench and Stephanie covered her face with her hands. There was too much blood for it to be Randall. She didn't need to know any more. She needed to get out. Stephanie stepped back but Randall was behind, pushing her forward.

"See," he said, "I told you I'd dealt with it."

The far end of the bathroom was shrouded in darkness. Stephanie pushed back once more but his body remained immobile. "Please, Rand. I've seen enough."

"No. Not yet. You said you wanted to know. Well now you know."

Randall flicked a switch and Stephanie fell to her knees, violently retching. At the far end of the bathroom, arms and legs bound tightly together, was the clone. Its head was a seeping lump of flesh, teeth grinning white through streaks of gore.

Stephanie turned her head but Randall grabbed hold of her hair to pull her head back round. "Don't look away now."

What she saw defied comprehension. The clone's face had been sliced off. A large knife gleaming proudly from an eye socket. On the far wall, the face had been reassembled; a mosaic of flesh tesserae, blood and matter dripping down the wall. A yellow layer of fat spilled out from a wound on the neck. There were further gaping holes in the shoulders and torso. What clothing was left was soaked in blood.

Stephanie's mind recoiled. She cast her eyes down, away from the corpse, but the sight of her own vomit sinking into the congealing blood sent another violent spasm coursing through her body. Panic took hold and she kicked backwards, her legs slipping in the coagulated mass as she battled against Randall's grip.

"It took me a while to realise what needed to be done. My problem was that I was looking at specifics. As soon as I pulled my inner focus back, the pattern became clear. My mind had become fractured. I'd do things but have no memory of them. The hospital gave me medication. They warned me that I would see visions. I didn't believe them but it turned out that for once they weren't lying. I do see things. Different facets of my mind made flesh. I was scared at first, but then I realised that by confronting these visions I could deal with them. I could heal myself."

Randall stared into the bathroom, his eyes still for once, his face almost serene. "I know this is hard for you, Stephanie. I can see that. But it isn't real. It's just my mind's way of coping with what I've done. The bad part of me, it needed to be dealt with. That's what I've done."

"He was your clone."

Randall laughed. "I know why you're saying this, Steph, but it won't help."

"There was a mix up and your clone was activated. That's why I came here, to help."

He pointed to the body. "You think this is real? You think I would really do this?"

"You have, Randall. You've killed him. You've killed yourself."

Randall remained quiet. Stephanie tried once more to get away from the room and the madness, but her feet kept slipping in the blood and vomit. From the back of the bathroom came a soft sucking sound as a large slice of cheek slowly curled over itself and fell from the wall.

"You're wrong, Stephanie."

"Randall, you need help. I can help you. That's why I'm here."

"It's just a vision, a hallucination. Confronting your

demons can be a violent experience. The drugs are just making me visualise it, that's all."

"Think, Randall. If that was the case, how can I be seeing what you're seeing?"

Randall knelt down beside Stephanie and whispered in her ear. "I wondered when you would realise." He pulled her head back, stroking her cheek with his left hand, the smell of corruption overpowering.

"It's strange," Randall continued, "it must be a result of what happened before. The bad part of me could never admit what he was, despite my best efforts, yet you..." He tapped her gently on the nose. "It wasn't until you appeared at the door that I realised. My love for you had turned bad, gnawing away, making me empty inside. I could never love anyone else, never care deeply enough, because I had never recovered from what you had done." He smiled at her, almost tenderly. "I idolised you. So much so that I couldn't see the damage you had caused. I locked it away inside, refusing to acknowledge it, but of course it had to come out somehow.

"I'd dealt with the symptoms but I hadn't dealt with the cause. That's why you're here. You're the catalyst, the reason I fractured in the first place. You're a physical manifestation of my deepest neurosis. I need to deal with you too, otherwise it will only happen again."

Randall pulled Stephanie forward by her hair, dragging her through the horror. "No! Stop! Please stop!" She tried to grab Randall's leg but missed, landing heavily on her shoulder, her face inches from the blood and offal. There was a loud crack and daggers of pain shot up Stephanie's arm. She needed to send out the code, but the pain was overwhelming.

"I know you don't want to go and I don't really want to lose you, but it's for the best. Without my feelings for you, I'll be able to move on, to have a better life."

Stephanie's mind was filled with agony. She felt helpless as she was pulled inexorably towards the corpse of the clone. Randall grunted as he pulled the knife from its skull, drops of matter falling from its tip. He looked down at her, sadness in his eyes. "Goodbye Stephanie. I did love you, you know."

He pulled her up by her hair and the pain in her shoulder abated just long enough for her to shout. "Gemini! Gemini!"

A large explosion rocked the room. Randall looked up, startled, seemingly unsure of what to do as smoke poured into the bathroom. He looked down at Stephanie one last time, smiled, then drove the knife into her neck. The pain from before paled before the agony that now assailed her. Stephanie's head rocked back and she saw Randall's arm raised for a second thrust. Another crack sounded and he flew backwards, slamming against the far wall. Without his support, Stephanie collapsed to the floor.

There was a buzzing in her ears and the world started to fade. She tried to move but couldn't. She felt thirsty. A warmth enveloped her. She wanted to see what was happening but it felt so comfortable where she was. Yes, she could rest here for a while until help came. She could hear yelling but it seemed so far away. Sleep, that was what she needed. Ignoring the pulling on her limbs, Stephanie closed her eyes and slipped into darkness.

CHAPTER FORTY-SEVEN
Re-Life Technician

The porter's uniform was too tight, the trouser bottoms failed to reach his ankles and the jacket arms rose about three centimetres above his wrists. Doubt gnawed at the Technician as he pushed the trolley through the tunnels. How could he have been so stupid? It would be typical for all his hard work to be undone by a poorly-fitting uniform.

He took a turning to his right. There was a chill to the air here and moisture glistened from the beige wall tiles. The Technician made his way down the tunnel, chuntering as he went. According to a sign he had just passed he was heading towards an exit, away from the old Northern and Central lines.

The shuffling of his feet matched with the beat of his racing heart. Not long now and he would finally be free. Once, at the start, he had hoped that by completing the task he could regain the status he had lost. Now all he wanted was to go back to his laboratory. It was safer there, a world where he had total control. What had he been thinking, pining after past glories? He was as bad as the idiots who had retained those old wall signs. He would go back to his laboratory and focus on what he did best. He already knew what he would work on. He had successfully transferred a personality into an adapted clone. If he could create the conditions to produce a neural imbalance without affecting the original's memories, surely he could adapt other areas of the brain to improve cognitive reasoning and increase the brain's natural power. Who wouldn't want to come back as a more intelligent version of themselves?

The trolley jerked to a halt, jarring his wrist. The two right-hand wheels had caught in a gap between the floor and the wall. The Technician tried to pull the trolley back but the wheels were jammed tight. He pulled again, tugging at the trolley with his full weight. Pain shot up his arm from his wrist. The Technician let go of the trolley handle, cursing. This couldn't be happening! He felt like screaming. He was so close. Only another few minutes and it would be done. He grabbed hold of the handle with his good hand when a waft of roasting pork assailed his nostrils. Looking down, he saw that the clone's left hand had fallen loose from the trolley and was resting on a heating pipe. With a yell he jumped forward and pulled the arm back, the clone's hand coming away with a tearing sound. Where the hand had touched the heating pipe the skin had fallen away revealing the pink flesh beneath.

The Technician felt like crying. The clone had been perfect, beautiful. He checked the tunnel in both directions, his datalenses showing that a security patrol would be in the area in five minutes. A moan escaped his lips. It couldn't end like this; it *mustn't* end like this. He reached across the clone and placed its left arm back on the trolley. The was nothing he could do for him now, they would just have to deal with it later. Ignoring the patch of skin sizzling on the pipe, he ran to the front of the trolley and placed the handle in the crook of his arm. With his teeth gritted, he straightened his legs. The trolley didn't move. He strained harder, using every ounce of his energy in the attempt to free the trolley. Stars appear in front of his eyes. He could smell blood in his nostrils. Then, with a wrenching sound, the wheels came free.

Second Chance

The Technician sat next to the trolley, panting. He'd done it. He'd actually done it. He checked the patrol timings again. They were still four minutes and 20 seconds away. He started to laugh. There's no greater fool than an old fool, he thought, especially one who thinks they are cleverer than everybody else. The complexity of what he had achieved was stunning, yet it could all have been undone by a crack in the floor.

"You took your time old man. Quickly, bring it over here."

It was cold in the loading bay. Mist formed as the man spoke. Another man stood next to the transporter pod, his back to the Technician as he kept watch outside. To the Technician they looked like the type of men more used to using their muscles than their minds. He pushed the trolley forward. The thought of interacting with these men brought on flutters of anxiety. Keep going, he thought, once this is over you can go back to normality. His limbs still trembled from his earlier exertions. It had all been too much. He needed to get back to his lab, get back to anonymity.

The speaker pulled back the cover to reveal the clone's face. His eyes glazed for a moment before he pulled the cover back.

"This is the one, Randall Jones. Let's get him on board. Quickly now."

"The online process went well," the Technician said, struggling to catch his breath. "All checks came back within parameters, and there were no adverse reactions to the adjustments that were requested."

The speaker looked at him, blankly. Why did he look so familiar?

"I had a slight accident on the way here," the Technician continued. "The clone has a burn on his left hand that will need some attention."

The doors peeled open and the transporter pod sank to the floor. Inside, the Technician could see respirators, feeding tubes, bio-monitors; everything that was needed to bring a clone online.

The speaker nodded his thanks towards the Technician and he suddenly remembered why he recognised his face, surprised he hadn't realised earlier. The speaker looked like the clone, close enough to be cousins. He raised his hand to point out his observation when he felt a sharp crack on the back of his head.

"Take care not to leave any trace." It was the voice of the speaker. "We don't want the same shit-storm as we had when we took that girl."

"No problem. I've already checked. The cameras are off. We can get the exchange done without anyone noticing."

The Technician felt woozy. He appeared to be lying on the floor. What were they talking about? He tried to say something, but his mouth wouldn't work.

"OK, get the old man on board."

The Technician felt himself being dragged towards the pod. Why were they doing this? He had done everything they had asked. Then it hit him. He hadn't done everything. He'd forgotten to switch the transiessence feeds. Both the clone and the original would be connected to the synthetic brain.

"What's it to be this time, sir?"

"The old man will be Re-Lifed with data from a few months back, just like last time. It's better this way; no body, no mess."

"And the clone?"

"Our faction will engineer for him to escape from the rehabilitation unit. That way they can play dumb when the rest of the organisation investigate what happened. Once we've picked up the original, it won't take long for the clone to be blamed for the girl's death."

The Technician felt himself carried towards the transporter. As he moved from under the hanger roof he saw that the night sky appeared to be glowing green.

"Do you see that?"

"Yeah. They said it would start tonight. I've always wanted to see the northern lights. Never thought it would happen here though."

His brain, for so long his strength, felt confused. What did they mean, that they would Re-Life him from memories of a few months ago? Then the realisation hit him. No! Don't do that. Please! It won't be me. It will be a copy of me. Re-Life only works if there is a constant link. His mind raged but nothing came out.

Then the second phrase hit home. It had happened before? Then what did that make him? His screams echoed around his skull as the doors to the transporter sealed.

Epilogue

The Investigator

The winter gone had been one of the coldest in years. Nico could still see patches of dirty snow hidden under branches or in shady corners of the park. Maria and Gino had loved the cold snap, almost as much as he loved seeing the children enjoy it. They had even tried to build a snowman, despite it being too cold and too dry for the snow to bind properly. He wondered where their desire came from. Was it genetic? As a child, all his winters had been wet, rain being the feature he remembered most. A few years back, when the first snows came, it was hailed as a sign that the environment was truly returning to normal. Now scientists argued that things had tipped too far, that the planet was in danger of entering a new ice age.

The park was empty, unusual for this time of day. The invitation had been clear. Come alone, speak to no-one.

The journey here was like every day since the riots. People stopped him to shake his hand. He was the hero, feted by everyone for bravely gathering the evidence that led to the capture of those responsible. Forced to endure the adulation, Nico felt sick every time, knowing full well that his account of that day had sent innocent people to stasis. His life was a sham, but a sham that was minutely monitored. The strain was unbearable. Now there was this. In a way, the invitation had come as a relief. Was this going to be the end of it, in whatever form that might take?

He turned a corner and saw a figure sitting on a bench, their coat glowing red despite being shaded by trees. Snowdrops grew by the foot of the bench, little spots of white against the muted background. Nico walked towards the figure and his fate. His lack of nerves surprised him, but then again, what more could they do?

The figure turned as he approached. No, he thought, that's not possible.

"Sit down, Investigator, or should I say *Chief* Investigator Tandelli. We've a lot of catching up to do."

His legs took him towards the bench but he couldn't take his eyes off her face. "You're meant to be dead."

"Whoever you think I was is no more. My name is Juliet now."

"I attended your funeral. There were hundreds there. People were distraught." Nico couldn't move. His understanding of the world had shifted once more, and he wasn't sure if it was for the better.

"Watching from afar didn't make it any less painful." She stared out into the park as she spoke, her voice hesitant, as if remembering a dream. Then she turned back to him, a smile on her face. "How are your wife and children? Are they OK? Enjoying the new house and garden?"

Nico stiffened. "They're fine."

Her smile broadened. "Good. It must have been tough, the last few months. It's unfair, really, what you've been put through. That's one of the reasons I asked to see you. There's no need for you to be scared any more. I'll be looking out for you from now on."

"How…? Why…?"

"I said to you a long time ago that you could trust me, and I meant it."

Nico closed his eyes. I should be happy, he thought, but the images were still there, images that kept him awake at night: that poor girl's naked legs, the baby with a hole where its stomach should have been; all those people, littered across the road. "You can't just let this go. The people who did those things, the ones who gave the orders... they need to be brought to justice."

"It's not as straightforward as that."

"If you won't say anything, I will. If what you say is true, there is nothing to stop me from going after them and—"

"You'll be crushed. My protection can only go so far. I can stop you from being monitored all the time, but if you're stupid enough to go public with all this—"

"So you'll let them get away with it then."

"No." Her expression hardened at his accusation. "I didn't say that. I just said it wasn't straightforward."

A blackbird swooped onto a branch above, its tail pointing skywards as it sang out a mating song. Nico watched the bird with envy. His world had been simple once too; there were good guys and bad guys. The good guy's job was to catch the bad guys and keep the public safe. He thought back to that night, like he had every day since. There was a question he needed to ask, a debt he had to pay.

"Were you the one who protected me, that night?"

"No."

Nico felt confused. As soon as he had seen her he had felt so sure. "Then who?"

"Chowdhury called in a lot of favours."

"Chowdhury? But why?"

"Who knows? Guilt perhaps, or maybe he wanted to protect an investment. Perhaps he didn't like what was happening or maybe he just did it for the hell of it. I haven't asked."

Nico gazed out into the park. Chowdhury had saved him? They'd hardly spoken since that night, despite his high profile and awards. Nico had been sure that Chowdhury knew something wasn't right and had ostracised him.

"So why are you getting involved? You're obviously one of them now?"

Juliet glanced at him sharply, then her face softened. "I spoke to somebody, not long ago. She told me a story about diverse group of people who put aside their petty squabbles to join together and beat something that seemed impossible. It was a good story. The first part was true, but since then their early ideals have been compromised. Some of them want to increase their control and innocent people are getting hurt. I want to stop that from happening."

"If you're talking about the Fabian case, you should know that I don't think Randall Jones killed her. I think he's an innocent man."

A shadow flickered across her face. All of a sudden, Juliet looked worn. Nico could see the dark patches under her eyes. "You may be right about the Fabian case, but you're wrong about Randall, at least now. He's not innocent, not any more. In fact he's not even the Randall I once knew. He's a copy, created to take the fall for the missing girl."

Nico felt dazed. If it had have come from anyone else he would have laughed. "And the real Randall?"

"Dead."

"So you're happy for this clone—"

"Not a clone, a copy. There's a big difference."

"Then you're happy for this copy to take the blame?"

"In public, yes. There are some things that the public need protecting from—"

"It's not just the public you're protecting. How can you let them get away with that poor girl's death?" Nico had seen the images. Jennica's face had been black, her tongue distended. Whoever had decided she needed to die had dumped her alone in an airless room to suffocate.

"Who said anything about protecting them? I promise you that the person who made *that* call is no longer with us. What I meant was that there are some things that it would be better the public didn't know about. Justice *has* been done. Going public with what happened would only cause more innocent people to get hurt. I've made sure that Jennica got justice for what happened."

Nico stood up. "I'm sorry, I don't get it. If you don't like the people who are doing these things, why have you become one yourself?"

"A friend of mine once told me that the best way to change something was from the inside. It took me a long time to understand what that meant, the sacrifices that are required. I joined because somebody had to make a stand. Somebody had to change what was going on. When people get hurt for the greater good, you have to ask the question—good for who? Confronting them head on would have been hopeless. This way, at least I have a chance."

"But why? Why you? Why not leave it to somebody else?"

"Who else is there?"

The anguish on Juliet's face stabbed into Nico. He was shamed by her bravery, for the sacrifice she had made to do this thing. She hadn't meekly agreed to do as she was told like he himself had done, but had decided to take back control and do something about what was happening. It was humbling.

Nico sat back beside Juliet and took her hand in his own, hoping she wouldn't feel how much it was shaking. "There's me."

"You know that if you become part of this there's no turning back."

"Turning back to what, the life I'm now leading? If you want me, I'm in."

A broad grin broke across her face and she leant forward, hugging him fiercely. "Thank you," she said. "I was hoping you were going to say that. Now before we go any further, I need to give you a history lesson…"

Printed in Great Britain
by Amazon.co.uk, Ltd.,
Marston Gate.